D1485544

Man-Eater

By the same author

DEATH MAY SURPRISE US
THE LEFT-HANDED SLEEPER
WOMAN IN A DRESSING GOWN AND OTHER PLAYS
WHATEVER HAPPENED TO TOM MIX? (Autobiography)

Other works by Ted Willis include:

Television Series:

Dixon of Dock Green
Sergeant Cork
Mrs. Thursday
Taxi
Hunter's Walk
Crime of Passion
The Four Seasons of Rosie Carr
Etc.

Stage Plays and Films:

Woman in a Dressing Gown
Hot Summer Night
Doctor in the House ⎫
Doctor at Sea   ⎬ adapted from the novels
No Trees in the Street
The Blue Lamp
Etc.

MAN-EATER

TED WILLIS

BOOK CLUB ASSOCIATES LONDON

© Ted Willis Limited 1976

All rights reserved. No part of this publication
may be reproduced or transmitted, in any form or
by any means, without permission.

This edition published 1977 by
Book Club Associates
by arrangement with Macmillan London Ltd

The characters in this novel and their actions are
imaginary. Their names and experiences have no
relation to those of actual people, living or dead,
except by coincidence.

Printed in Great Britain by
Richard Clay (The Chaucer Press), Ltd,
Bungay, Suffolk

To
Elaine Greene

CHAPTER ONE

1

Ranee, the tigress, was the first to stir. She stretched and sat up on her haunches, her ears pricked, conscious that the truck now seemed to be slowing down. She had been lying motionless but awake, her head resting on folded paws, her body swaying gently to the easy, rhythmic movement beneath her. But now she could feel a change; the engine-sound was louder and more strident, the truck was labouring forward, bumping and twisting from side to side.

She gave a low, deep-throated growl of irritation as a sudden jolt rocked her against the steel bars of the travelling cage. The tiger, Mohan, who had been sleeping, opened his eyes and looked at her, as though in mild reproof. He gave a huge, sighing yawn, stretching his jaw and pulling back his lips. The white, powerful teeth, the clear amber eyes gleamed in the semi-darkness.

Then he, too, became aware of the change in the motion of the truck. Like the tigress, he was familiar with the routine of travel, it had been part of their lives since they were cubs. He sensed that the journey was coming to an end. The hunger ached in his flanks, the hunger which was always there and which, in these days, was so seldom fully appeased. He felt the saliva rise and moisten his mouth, his tail twitched, lazily, and he growled in anticipation. When the movement stopped, there would be food.

2

The truck bumped over a last pot-hole, its springs complaining bitterly, and pulled to a halt. The man at the

7

wheel switched off the engine and peered through the windscreen into the darkness. Since leaving the road he had been driving with the headlamps off, and he did not want to risk using them now.

The steep, uneven track ended abruptly here, as though it had been swallowed by the earth. All around him stretched the moor, stirring slightly in the light, summer breeze like a dark, tranquil sea. It seemed to go on without end, except to the west where, in the distance, there was a darker blur which he judged to be the beginning of the forest.

This will have to do, he thought, I can go no further. He leaned over the steering-wheel for a moment, and closed his eyes. The weariness rose in his body like a tide and he sighed for sleep.

A movement of the animals, and a low, impatient, muffled roar from the tigress, roused him, and he sat up. The throbbing in his head began again and he was conscious of the familiar tightening in the pit of his stomach, the tension which seemed to lock into his limbs. That was how it had been for many months now, and it was getting worse, he knew it was getting worse. There were times when he wished he could release himself in a great cry of anger and protest, like the beasts in the cage behind him. After all, he was a prisoner too; bound as inescapably to them as they were to him. At times, he even shared the same cage, staring out through the bars at those rows and rows of blank, ignorant, human faces. It was those faces, those white, waiting faces, that he hated most of all.

He shook his head as though to free himself of these thoughts and dropped down to the ground. The heather was almost waist-high, just as it had been on his only previous visit, just as he had hoped it would be. Cover was essential, all-important. There was no light, no sign of any habitation, no sound except the gentle whispering of the moor.

He went round to the rear of the truck and, fumbling

8

with the key, unlocked the heavy, metal doors. There was an answering, deep-throated growl from the tigers as he swung the doors open and the tigress, always the bolder of the two, came towards the man, her teeth bared in a snarl. But she stopped short of the bars as she picked up his scent and waited uncertainly, her tail swishing.

'Back! Get back Ranee, you bitch!' said the man sharply. He took a torch from his pocket and played the beam on her face. She cowered away as though in pain, spitting angrily, turning her head from side to side to avoid the light. Eventually she crouched alongside the tiger and put her head down.

The man watched them for a moment. The thin, yellow light seemed to emphasise their scrawniness, the lack of sheen and colour in their coats. You poor bastards, he thought, you poor, poor bastards. The last of the bloody Mohicans, almost the last representatives of a doomed species. Man has done for you, my beauties. The strange thing is, you don't seem to realise it, you don't seem to know when you're licked. You go on surviving, even behind bars; you even have enough spirit left in you to hate.

He slid back the steel bolts which held the smaller of the two gates. It operated as a sort of hatch, and sliding it upwards, he locked it into the open position. The tigers growled again, their flanks heaving, but they made no move.

'There you are then,' said the man. 'It's all yours. Help yourselves. Live a little.' He began to laugh, but seemed somehow to lose control of his voice; it rose momentarily to a high-pitched cackle, then broke and died away. The man was aware of himself listening as though to another person, to a stranger.

He stood in silence by the open hatch for a moment, then went round to the front of the truck, and climbed up into the driving cabin. He glanced through the observation window at the interior of the cage. The tigers had not moved.

9

He adjusted the rear-view mirror so that he could see the open hatch at the rear of the truck, then he sat back and lit a cigarette. It was some time before he realised that the hammering inside his head had stopped.

3

Ranee stretched at full length facing the open hatch and waited, looking into the night. She was puzzled, she could not understand the break in the familiar routine. For years, she had associated the opening of the hatch, the appearance of the man, with the coming of food. She began to sniff, drawing the air noisily into her nostrils, hoping to catch the scent of meat, but there was nothing her senses could recognise.

What to the man had seemed like a deep silence was, to her, a medley of strange, unusual noises, sounds which were part of the strange world out there, in the whispering shadows beyond the open door of the cage. They were new to her, at once disturbing and exciting. A vixen howled in the far distance, a good mile away, but her sharp ears picked up the sound and she tensed herself, feeling some old, almost-forgotten instinct stir in her blood.

The tiger, too, had thrown off his lethargy and lay alongside the tigress tight and watchful. From time to time he glanced towards her, as though waiting for her to move, to make a decision. Once he muzzled against her nervously, but she snapped at him angrily, viciously, and he drew back.

Suddenly Ranee flattened out on the floor of the cage and began cautiously to edge towards the gate as though she were stalking some hidden prey. Inch by inch she slid forward, ears pricked, lips parted slightly in a silent snarl. Mohan watched her warily, but made no attempt to follow. At the opening the tigress paused, sniffing the air once more. Her great, ringed tail stiffened and rose behind her like a curved mast. Something moved on the moor, and she turned her head quickly, cold eyes staring into the darkness. She rose slowly to her feet, and as she did so, the breeze stirred the hair which fringed the white patches above her eyes.

She stood there almost motionless for a long time, and then, abruptly, she lifted her head and loosed her lungs in an immense, bellowing roar, as though she were issuing a challenge to whatever enemy lay waiting in the strange, velvet world beyond. Mohan was at her side in an instant, matching her roar for roar.

They stopped as suddenly as they had begun, as if at a signal, and stood in silence, every muscle tensed for action. Watching in the mirror the man saw the tigress turn her head and look back into the cage towards the observation window. She appeared to be searching for something, someone. Then she caught the gleam of the mirror and she stared into his face. Her eyes glowed in the darkness like jewels, and it seemed to him that they were icy with contempt and hatred. A chill seemed to penetrate the cabin and he shivered, his whole body shaking for a moment as though with ague.

And then she was gone, leaping into the night with the tiger close at her heels.

The man smiled slowly, lit another cigarette, and smoked it down to the stub, waiting. Then he switched on the torch and went round to the back, where he rebolted the gate, and swung the heavy doors back into place.

A few moments later he was driving back down the track towards the road. He heard someone whistling a tune that he knew well, and suddenly realised, with surprise and pleasure, that the sound was coming from his own lips.

4

The tigress moved cautiously at first, perplexed by the unusual surroundings and by the unaccustomed freedom.

11

Mohan stayed close to her, content to follow, and Ranee found a certain comfort in his presence. From time to time she paused, flattening herself into the earth, her lithe body coiled for action.

It was the space which worried her most of all. She had never known anything but the strict and limited confines of a cage, the stone floor, the metal bars: now, suddenly, there were no limits, the ground was soft and yielding to her tread, the air was full of pleasing scents and sounds. It was hard to understand, a world beyond her experience. At any moment she expected to hear the crack of the whip, to feel its sharp tongue bite into her flanks, to hear the harsh guttural voice of the man who wielded it.

But slowly, very slowly, she began to relax, to yield herself up to the pleasure and excitement of this new-found freedom. She remained alert, but moved more easily through the tall heather; once she stopped and allowed herself the luxury of a long, challenging deep-throated roar. Mohan, sensing her mood, jumped at her playfully, and within a moment they were rolling and fighting together like exuberant young cubs.

Intoxicated by the sense of liberty, they played together in this fashion for a long time, and when the game palled, they chased each other in widening circles across the moor. Even to run was a new experience; to stretch their limbs, to move without restraint was sheer delight. The heather bowed before their onslaught and then closed behind them in ripples, like the wake of a ship.

And then, in the fold between two slopes, they came to a small lake, and they halted, alert with suspicion. Water, to them, was something that lay in a small hard trough and was for drinking. Occasionally, very occasionally, in hot weather, the man had played a hose upon them and they had revelled in this pleasure, but that was all.

This water had a different scent, it lay before them placid and inviting. They watched it for a long time, their tails swishing gently. This time it was the tiger who made the first move; he approached the bank and experimented with a forepaw, feeling the water. Emboldened, he lowered his head and drank deeply, thirstily. The tiger's presence disturbed the nesting wild-fowl and they fluttered up into the night, clacking in alarm. The tiger made a vain snatch at one of them and then plunged into the water, swimming as vigorously and expertly as though he had been doing it all his life.

It was some time before Ranee could make up her mind to follow, but when she did, the lake seemed to act upon her like a stimulant, more potent even than the freedom she had found on the moor. The buoyancy of her body, the clean, soothing touch of the water on her skin, the frightened calling of the wild fowls, excited her, and for a few minutes she was almost hysterical with pleasure. It seemed as though the years of captivity were being washed away in that soft, green water.

Afterwards they settled down in the heather to rest, tired by both the unaccustomed and strenuous exercise, and their own exhilaration. But before long the tigress remembered that she was hungry, she could feel a great aching pit of emptiness in her stomach.

She rose, and as though by instinct, led the way towards the forest.

5

'Did you see that truck?' said Tom Pickford.

'Truck, darling?' The girl in the passenger seat leaned towards him and slid a soft hand along his thigh. Her mind was clearly on other things.

'It came out of that track leading to the moor. What the hell is anyone doing up there at this time of night?'

'The same as us, I expect.' She snuggled against him. 'Pull up along here, darling. Just off the road.'

'I ought to be getting back.'

13

'Oh, for Christ's sake!' said the girl, and added, more gently, 'I want you, Tom. It's the wine. Wine always turns me on, you know that. Don't you want me?'

'Of course I do,' he said uneasily. Her directness embarrassed him, it always had. It seemed to reduce their relationship to the level of a physical transaction. That's exactly what it was, of course, he had long realised that; but there was a part of his nature which wrestled against this blunt, matter-of-fact approach. He needed to colour the affair with a romantic veneer, to believe that it was something more than the lusting of two bodies each for the other. Only in this tortuous way could he justify it to himself.

'Pull up then.' She leaned over and kissed him on the neck.

'Careful, Penny!' he said sharply as the car swerved.

'I want you,' she said drunkenly. 'Come on, it'll be another week before we can be together again. I'll go crazy if I have to wait. Come on—I want to feel you inside me, darling.'

She resumed her pressure on his leg, and he felt a flicker of response stir in his limbs. He grinned, and brought the car to a halt at the edge of the forest; her lips found his almost before he had time to switch off the lights. There was no doubt or hesitation in him now, as his hands began to fumble desperately with her clothes.

'Gently, darling, gently,' she whispered.

'These bloody long skirts,' he muttered.

She opened the car door. 'Let's get into the back.'

'Let's go into the forest. It's cooler there.'

'No thank you,' she said. 'Not at night. It gives me the creeps.'

'We don't have to go far, Penny. There's a clearing—'

'No,' she interrupted firmly. 'In the back.'

'I'll bloody well rupture myself one day in the back of this car!' he grumbled.

They coupled quickly, fiercely, awkwardly, in the confined space. Afterwards the girl lay back against the cushions her eyes closed.

'You're marvellous,' she murmured, 'you're bloody marvellous, darling.'

But looking at her in the dim light, the lipstick smudged on her full mouth, her hair awry, her skirt still gathered up above her waist, Tom felt depressed and ashamed, filled with disgust not so much for her as for himself. How the hell had he got himself into this situation, why did he lack the courage to break with her?

It was hot and sticky in the car, and the air, heavy with her perfume, sickened him. He opened the door.

'Where are you going?' she asked languidly, her eyes still closed.

'To get a breath of air.'

'Do you know what?' she said. 'I could do it again, right now, I really could.'

6

The tigers were mystified and a little intimidated by the forest. The dark, brooding trees, the heavy, mossy scent which rose from the undergrowth, the frightened sounds and warning calls of the animals and birds who had been aroused by the presence of these invaders, stirred their blood and intensified the pangs of hunger; but, at the same time, they moved cautiously, uncertainly, like explorers in a new and hostile land.

They tried in vain to seize some of the smaller forest creatures which scuttled in panic before them. Tigers are, by nature, swift and deadly hunters, possessed of infinite patience in the approach, and immense speed, ferocity and efficiency in the kill; but Ranee and Mohan were creatures of captivity, their powers and reactions crippled and blunted by the unnatural circumstances in which they had lived their lives. The instincts were there, burning more fiercely as their hunger increased, but they lacked the skill and cunning to satisfy them. With each failure, they grew more desperate.

Then, at the edge of a tiny clearing, their sharp eyes picked up a clear view of a small dappled deer. It was standing with its head up, body taut and alert, for it had heard the warning calls, and knew that there was danger in the forest that night.

The tigers stopped on the instant and crouched, waiting, in the undergrowth. They had already learned that these other creatures were swift and cunning, and they had, moreover, the advantage of being on their home ground. Minutes passed. The hunters and the hunted remained motionless while around them the forest fell into an uneasy silence, waiting.

The tigress could feel the taste of meat on her teeth, her throat felt harsh as it tightened in anticipation. She fell into the stalking position and began to edge forward so delicately that hardly a crackle came from the undergrowth. The tiger fell into place alongside but just behind her, instinctively copying her movements.

The deer moved slightly, restlessly, still on the alert, but seemingly uncertain whether to leave the clearing or stay. The tigress stopped for a moment and waited, then she continued the same cautious, forward progress. She had learned quickly, and she restrained the urge to break cover and go in for the kill; this time she wanted to be sure.

The tigers reached almost to the edge of the clearing and now the scent of their quarry was strong in their nostrils. The tigress felt the hunger beat desperately at the walls of her stomach, and at the same time, the sense of exhilaration came back with a rush. She pulled her lips back over the long sabre-like canines and rose on all fours.

And then, suddenly, her ears picked up another sound, a crackling movement in the undergrowth on the other side of the clearing, and she hesitated. The deer heard it too; and in the instant, it raced away and was swallowed up by

16

the forest. The tiger released a great, brassy roar of anger and frustration and charged forward after the deer, but the tigress waited, her senses distracted by something else.

A man was standing on the opposite edge of the clearing. He stood there, looking in the direction from which that terrifying trumpet-roar had come. The tigress growled threateningly and moved slowly out of the undergrowth into the clearing to face him. A mere fifteen or twenty yards of open space separated them but the tigress, perfectly camouflaged, was almost invisible against the dark background of tree and shrub. It was the eyes Tom Pickford could see, greenish now in the filtered moonlight glittering with menace.

The tigress growled angrily, but she did not move. Old fears, the long-established habit of submission to man, made her uncertain. She crouched, waiting to hear the harsh, familiar word of command, to feel the sting of the whip on her flanks.

The man was uncertain too, apprehensive and then fearful as those great unwavering eyes challenged him from the darkness. The sweat oozed up through the pores and trickled stickily down his skin. He felt powerless to move or cry out, hemmed in by a silence so tense that it seemed to have taken on a physical presence. Around him the forest waited, scarcely stirring, as though it was holding its breath.

Slowly, very slowly, the tigress raised herself from her crouched position. She had caught, across the distance, the scent of this man's fear, and a strange thrill of excitement quickened her blood. She growled again, louder this time, and took a pace forward as though to test him.

As she rose and moved, Tom saw her clearly for a moment. A small, croaking sound came from his throat, and then panic surged through his body to explode in a high, piercing scream of terror. Slobbering with fear he turned and stumbled back towards the road, his hands tearing wildly at the thick undergrowth which seemed to have closed in to bar his path.

The girl, Penny, could not identify or understand the shattering animal roars which had risen from the forest; she only knew that they were more terrifying than anything she had ever heard. Sick with fright, she crouched down in the car, as though to hide herself from this hidden enemy.

Had she been dreaming? Had she dozed off, as she often did after love-making, and simply imagined it all? The roars which seemed to shake the trees, the scream, and then the clamour from the forest as though every living thing within its confines was raising its voice in fear and protest; had all this occurred only in a nightmare?

A slight smell of burning roused her, and looking down, she saw a lighted cigarette on the carpeted floor. As she picked it up she remembered. She had lit the cigarette a few moments before the forest had erupted with noise; she had not slept, what she had heard was no fantasy of her imagination.

She drew on the cigarette and this helped to steady her nerves a little. She told herself to be sensible, not to exaggerate her fears. After all, she knew the forest well, she had walked its trails a hundred times, she knew it to be a peaceful, friendly place, at least in the daytime. At night she was more hesitant, she had never liked the dark; but even so, she could not believe that any real danger lay in wait beneath those trees.

She opened the door of the car and stepped out. She could almost feel the silence now, a silence which, in its own way, was more frightening than what had gone before. Everything around her lay still, as if in shock. Even the air seemed sluggish and heavy; the slight breeze that had stirred the tree-tops only a few minutes before had died away. When she drew the back of her hand across her face, the skin felt hot and clammy.

A car came towards her, its headlights opening up the

darkness, and she stepped forward eagerly, driven by an impulse to wave it down, to see and speak to another human being. But then the thought of what this would mean took over. Suppose it was someone who knew her, or who knew Tom? She stepped back into the shadows and the car flashed by without checking its speed.

Calmer now, she took a torch from the glove compartment, and behind its comforting beam, moved across the verge on which the car was parked until she reached the trees. There was a narrow path through the undergrowth and she advanced along it for a few paces, calling his name.

'Tom? Tom? Tom—are you there?'

But her voice died away in a silence broken only by the faint humming of insects dancing in the light of the torch. She called again, louder this time, an edge of hysteria in her voice. Then something brushed against her face in the darkness, and her nerve broke. Dropping the torch she fled back to the car, wrenched open the door, and tumbled in.

She waited ten minutes, fifteen, a half-hour. She knew that she could never find the courage to go back into the forest, and she knew also, with a certainty that grew with every moment, that Tom would not be coming back. Beyond this, she was incapable of coherent thought.

At the end of the half-hour, she gave herself another five minutes, then started the car and drove away. She switched on the radio, tuned in to BBC Radio One, and turned up the volume, hoping that the familiar clamour of the pop songs would help to drown the sound of the scream which still reverberated in her head.

8

David Birk had been standing by the dry-stone wall which encircled the house for over an hour. He had learned the discipline of stillness a long time ago, so that it had become almost instinctive, a part of his nature.

From beyond the wall, where the land began to fall away, the beck chuckled happily as it hurried its clear waters towards the rock gorge sixty feet below, and, on all sides, the dark moor reached for the horizon, whispering gently. But David was listening for something else.

He had been sitting in the living-room of the old stone house, an oil-lamp burning at his side, when he heard the first call, so faint and far-away that it seemed like a trick of the mind. Yet, immediately, as out of long habit, his senses leaped to the alert. The call had come again, more prolonged, but a little fainter the second time as though it were moving away, and David had set down his book and gone out into the night.

Now, as he waited, he was remembering other nights in other, distant places, nights when that great, majestic, challenging roar had shattered the silence like glass, warning him that his friend the enemy was coming. He thought of the long duels, the many failures and, most of all, the bitter, self-defeating moments of victory.

He had decided long ago to put the past behind him, and disconcerted that it should have defied him, he strode back to the house. He trusted his senses more than did Penny, the girl in the car, but even he was beginning to doubt what he had heard, to reduce it to terms more capable of rational explanation. This was England, not India; he was in the heart of the English countryside and it was inconceivable that there should be tigers out there, calling to each other across the dark moor. He knew from experience that nature loved to mock man, and the sound might easily have been one of her little jokes at his expense. And if not that, then he must have pulled the incident out of some drawer in his memory; it had been no more than a kind of playback of something heard years before.

Yet, whatever the explanation, the call seemed to have breached those inner defences which he had so painfully built up over the recent months. Try as he might he could not stem the flow of half-buried memories which surged through his head, and at last, he gave up the effort to do so.

On an impulse he went to the spare room, to the big trunk which had stood unopened ever since he had come to the house. He took from it two long bundles, wrapped in sacking, and uncovered the contents with care. Under the sacking there were further coverings of oil-stained rags, and beneath these, the two rifles. Both were old. The first was a Winchester 270 which he had bought almost thirty years before, an accurate, reliable weapon which he had good cause to respect.

But it was the other, a D.B. 450/400, which he took up and turned in his hands, remembering, with the clarity of sunlight, that afternoon in 1947 when, as a young man just out of his teens, he had stood at the bedside of a man more than sixty years his senior. It had been hard for David to believe that this tiny, frail, old man with the putty-coloured skin stretched like parchment over his bones, and the thin, trembling hands, was Bill Mannering, the hero-hunter whose name had rung like a bell through the years of his childhood. His father had told him stories of Bill Mannering as other men tell their sons fairy-tales or read to them from books of adventure, and they had never palled.

The old man's china-blue eyes had brightened at the sight of his sturdy young visitor and he had looked at him for a very long time. When he spoke the voice crackled, like brittle ice breaking underfoot.

'Neil Birk's boy.'

'Yes, sir. That's right. David.'

Again, the long stare and then, without any preliminary: 'Got something for you. Under the bed, boy, under the bed.' The bony hand made a jerking, impatient movement towards the floor, and stooping down, David found the D.B. 450/400 wrapped in part of an old sheet.

21

'Yours,' said the old man. 'Want you to have it.'

David hadn't argued, it would have been graceless to do so. He'd stumbled his thanks, but as though a switch had been pulled inside his body, the old man seemed suddenly to lose interest. The eyes, duller now, closed and he lay back on the pillow.

The next morning David heard that he had died in the night. Slipped quietly away, the nurse told him.

He put the rifles away and went to the bedroom. As he hung up his clothes he saw, on the floor of the wardrobe, the locked wooden box in which he kept the third rifle, an almost new 66.SP Mauser. It was, to all intents and purposes, the standard sniper rifle which came on the market in 1974 but it had been carefully modified to suit David's tastes and needs. It was almost new because, apart from tests, he had fired it only once, almost a year ago.

He had not opened the box in all that time and he did not do so now. He felt a special, personal attachment to the other rifles, they were friends, they evoked rich, good memories of people and places, they did not jar his mind. For the Mauser he felt nothing, it was an inanimate object, an efficient tool, it reminded him of a time and a persona that he wanted to forget. He had told himself a dozen times to get rid of the thing, but it was still there and he couldn't quite understand why.

He heard a low, plaintive whining from beyond the door and when he opened it he saw the dog, Buster, crouched at his feet, looking up at him with anxious brown eyes. Buster was a mongrel, half-Alsatian and half-Labrador, a refugee from Battersea Dogs' Home, where David, in a rare impulsive moment, had bought him for £3 some months earlier.

The dog and the man suited each other exactly. Each, in his own way, was stubbornly independent; they lived together under the same roof, but to a great extent their lives were separate. The dog seemed content to withdraw into himself as did the man, to surround himself with the

22

same brooding silence, as though he, too, was working over the sweet and sour memories of other years. There were whole days when the dog would lie awake but silent, scarcely moving, only acknowledging David with a sad movement of the eyes. They rarely showed emotion or open affection, each seemed to understand that the bond between them needed no such emphasis.

It was strange, therefore, that the dog should be so restless, that he had sought out David in this way.

'What's the matter, old boy?' David stooped and stroked the dog's head, and he responded by muzzling the man's hand with his soft mouth; then he went into the bedroom and settled down by the side of the bed, his restless eyes following David as he moved around the room.

Later, half-way between sleep and waking, David heard again the long, far-away calling of the tigers, but this time he was sure that it really was just part of a dream, an echo from the past which had no existence outside his head, and he made no move.

The dog at his side heard the calls also, and he cocked his ears warily, his skin bristling with apprehension. In the past months he had grown accustomed to the sounds which drifted in from the moor, but this was something new again. He could not recognise these unfamiliar voices, but unlike the man, he knew that they were real, and he sensed that they carried both a threat and a challenge.

He found comfort and reassurance in David's stillness, in the sound of his deep, even breathing. He had learned to trust and respect this man, he felt safe with him. Slowly the tension of his body relaxed, and he settled down again.

CHAPTER TWO

1

May Pickford sat up in bed reading the book she had got from the Whitford library that afternoon. It was a biography of Christabel Pankhurst, the militant suffragette leader, which had been recommended to her, and she found it completely absorbing. Although May did not approve of what she regarded as the wilder shores of Womans Lib, she did hold firm views on the subject of woman's role in society and on the process of conditioning that gave them a status inferior to that of men. 'Equal but different' was the slogan she had advanced in a debate at the local Literary Society. She was proud that she had been one of the first women in the town to adopt the title Ms.

It was almost half-past midnight when she lifted her eyes from the book to glance at the bedside clock. She frowned slightly. Tom was late, he should have been home an hour ago. Thursday was his regular evening out, when he drove across the moors to visit George Leppard, an old friend with whom he shared a passion for chess, but he was usually back well before midnight. What if the car had broken down, and he was stuck miles from anywhere on one of those high, lonely moorland roads?

She shrugged off the thought and returned to her reading, but a part of her mind was listening for the sound of the car, and she could not concentrate as before. Eventually she laid the book aside and went down to the kitchen to make a cup of chocolate. While she was waiting for the milk to heat up she opened the front-door, and looked out. The little semi-circular close was in darkness, the only light showing in any of the eight modern, chalet-type bungalows was at No. 6 and this did not surprise her. Mr

Ayres lived there, and the whole of Mortimer Close knew that he spent his evenings and almost half his nights researching and writing a book on the 'History and Development of Radical Thought in Britain'. He'd been working at it for eight years now and when asked if he were nearing the end of his self-appointed task, Mr Ayres would only smile sadly and shake his head. Still, the residents of Mortimer Close were rather proud to have an author in their midst, he was a good talking-point.

May went to the gate and looked towards the entrance to the close, where it joined Mortimer Street, straining her ears for the sound of an approaching car. The air was still and heavy; she could feel the heat and humidity seeping through the thin cotton pyjamas she was wearing. It is cooler in the house, she told herself; and, in any case, it is stupid to wait here, it won't make him come any quicker.

She caught the milk just in time to prevent it boiling over and made up a small jug of chocolate. She poured some into a cup for herself, and put the rest into a flask for Tom. The chiming clock in the hall announced that it was now 1 a.m.; she thought of those narrow, winding moorland roads and of the thick mists which seem to come from nowhere to blot out all visibility in a matter of seconds. The last role she wanted to play was that of the anxious, little wife, but she had to do something. Suppose Tom was marooned up on the moors, or on one of those lonely forest roads and needed help?

2

George Leppard heard the telephone ringing in his sleep, and he climbed reluctantly back into consciousness. He waited, hoping the sound would stop, but the caller was persistent. Cursing aloud, he went downstairs.

'Yes?' he said rudely.

'George?' It was a woman's voice, and the tone was full

of apology. He did not immediately recognise it.

'Yes. Who is that?'

'May. May Pickford. George, I'm sorry to disturb you at this hour. I hope you weren't asleep.'

'No,' he lied. 'I was reading—having a night-cap. What can I do for you?' Warning lights were flashing in his head now. Be careful, George, he told himself, watch what you say.

'It's only that—I mean, I was just wondering about Tom.' She was trying to make it sound light, inconsequential almost. 'What time did he leave you?'

'Oh.' He thought desperately for a moment. 'Oh, he was a bit later than usual. We got locked into the last game and it took hours. It must have been half-eleven give or take a few minutes. Why, is anything wrong, May?'

'No, no,' she said. 'It's just—well, he isn't home yet and I was beginning to wonder—you know.'

'What time is it now?'

'Turned one o'clock.'

'Well, he definitely left here around half-eleven. Allow three-quarters of an hour, an hour at the most. He should have got back by now.' The lie came out easily, with no tell-tale hesitation. There was a moment or two of silence.

'What's it like up there?' she said.

'How do you mean?'

'Is it clear on the moors?'

'I don't know. Hold on.' He went to the window, drew the curtain and looked out. There was only a tiny crescent of moon, but he could clearly see the outline of the stand of young trees beyond his cottage fence. He went back to the telephone.

'It's clear enough here. But that's not really anything to go by. Up on the moors the weather has rules of its own. I could ring the weather people and find out.'

'Would you?' She was no longer trying to keep the anxiety out of her voice.

'Of course. Do it straight away and call you back.'

26

'I'm sorry to put you to this trouble, George.'

'No problem. Glad to do it. And May, listen.'

'Yes.'

'Don't worry. No, sorry, that's stupid. You're bound to, I know that. What I mean is—he is only—what?—a half-hour or so late. He could have had a bit of trouble with the car. Nothing he won't be able to fix, if I know Tom. He can work a small miracle with a bit of silver foil, a pen-knife and a rubber band. I know, I've seen him do it.'

'Yes. I know, I'm probably over-reacting.'

'Look, you go and pour yourself a large gin-and-tonic and try to relax. I'll call you back in a few minutes with any news I can pick up about the weather. O.K.?'

'Thank you, George. I am grateful.'

'Forget it. Now, don't forget. A big gin-and-tonic.'

As he put the phone down he remembered that she didn't drink alcohol and even disapproved of Tom doing so. She was a funny bitch all round, certainly a funny choice for Tom to have made. She'd been attractive enough a few years back, but of late she'd taken on a kind of stringy masculinity. There was no humour there to speak of, not much warmth, and not too much sexuality. On the other hand, he told himself, there were two sides to every coin. If she'd grown like that, there must be a reason. Old Tom was a good bloke, but you couldn't say he was the strongest or brightest person in the world.

He looked up the night-service number of the Auto-mobile Association in the telephone book. They were engaged when he tried to call them, so he went through to the little sitting-room and poured himself a stiff scotch. With this in hand, he went back to the telephone. The response was immediate this time and he was told that there was no mist on the moors, that visibility was good and clear.

So what had happened to Tom? Where was he? Was he still rolling on the moor with his little bit of spare? It was all beginning to add up to one hell of a mess!

He phoned May Pickford and gave her the news. She

27

had obviously been waiting by the phone for his call and there was now no mistaking the strain in her voice. He felt a twinge of pity for her, and of guilt too because of the part he was playing in the deception.

'Give him another half-hour,' he told her gently, 'and if he's not home by then, I'll go out and look for him.'

But as he put down the phone and sipped his whisky, he was thinking—where? Where the hell would I start looking?

3

Eight miles away from George Leppard's cottage, in a small farmhouse, a man named Toby Waites lay awake in a big double-bed waiting for his niece to come home. For a long time there was no sound except the night-noises from the farmland beyond the open window and the steady, even breathing of his wife as she slept beside him. He was wearing only a pair of short underpants and had thrown back the bedclothes, but he still felt stifled by the heat in the little room.

At last he heard what he had been waiting for—a light, careful footfall on the gravel path outside the cottage—and his blood quickened. Still he waited. A minute or two went by, and then he heard the slow creaking of the stairs, the tinkle of a latch, and the slight snap as a door nearby opened and closed. He felt his breathing quicken, the anticipation tingle in his blood.

He glanced down at his wife and began to ease his big body out of the bed. The springs murmured and he held his breath momentarily, but she did not move. His heavy working trousers were hanging over a chair and with painstaking care he reached into the pocket and drew out a small fold of pound notes. Beads of sweat bubbled on his skin, and began to trickle down his face and neck as he edged his way out of the door.

He paused on the narrow landing, taking a moment to gather himself, then moved along to the other door, his hand trembled as he lowered the latch.

Penny was lying on the bed, still dressed in the blue top and long skirt in which she had gone out earlier that evening. He had watched from the window as she left the cottage and a trick of light had silhouetted her body beneath the thin skirt; his eyes had marked the dark blue outline of her brief pants, followed every tantalising movement of those long legs. He had dwelt on this moment all the evening, his hunger for her growing as the long hours passed.

She was not aware of him at first, for she was holding a pillow around her down-turned face and against her ears, as though to keep out some hostile sound.

'Penny.' He spoke in a hoarse, anxious whisper.

'Go away!' she said, without turning, her voice half-muffled by the pillow.

He sat down on the bed but she edged quickly, impatiently away from him, pressing herself against the wall.

'Penny!' he pleaded. He dropped a hand on her thigh, and she turned wearily. He saw that she had been weeping; her eyes were red and smudged with mascara.

'Please, leave me alone,' she said, 'please.'

'What's the matter?'

'Nothing. I'm just not in the mood, that's all.'

He took her hand and pressed the notes into it. 'There's £20 there. Like I promised. For that dress and shoes you want.'

'I told you, I'm not in the mood!' she said savagely and flung the money to the floor, at his feet. He gripped her wrist angrily and pulled her towards him.

'Don't play games with me, lass!'

He pressed his hot face down upon her. She could smell the stale sweat on his body, and she turned her head from side to side, resisting him; but he was too strong for her, as always, and too weary to fight she said flatly: 'All right, all right. But be quick.'

29

It was not the first time he had taken her in this way and over the years she had learned, when he lay with her, to let him use her body as though it were a thing apart from the rest of her being. She had taken nothing from Tom, or the other men she had known, nor had the idea entered her head. But with her uncle it was different. She behaved like a whore with him because he treated her as one and because she despised him. He was no more to her than a client, to be forgotten the moment the transaction was over.

So, when he went from the room he went from her mind also and the thoughts he had interrupted came flooding back. She rose painfully from the bed and went to the window. She threw it open wide and gulped the night air into her lungs. In spite of the heat, she felt a chill in her body and hugged her shoulders to stop herself shivering.

She tried to put the memory of those frightening roars, the scream of human agony out of her mind; in the familiar surroundings of the room they seemed unreal, creatures of her imagination, too incredible for belief. There had to be a reasonable explanation for what had happened. Tom must have lost his way in the forest, it was as simple as that. She should have waited longer for him, she shouldn't have panicked, but it was too late to remedy that now. He would get out eventually and make his way home, the car would be found in the morning in the lane where she had left it, and Tom would explain the whole thing away somehow. When they met again he would be angry with her for a little while; but afterwards they would have a good laugh together about it all. And make love, real love, the kind she ached for and to which she could give herself wholly, without reservation, for its own sake.

She clung on to these thoughts as if they were a talisman against the fears which still lurked at the back of her mind and, calmer now, she moved back to the bed. She remembered the money and saw that it had gone. Her uncle must have picked it up as he left. Next time he'll pay double, she thought bitterly, I'll really put the screws on the fat, old bastard.

As she undressed, she wondered vaguely about her pants. She was not wearing any; nor could she find them on the bed or in the drawer where she kept her underclothes. She was almost certain that she had put on the new, black pair before going out, but she couldn't be sure. As often as not, when she wore jeans or a long dress, she just didn't bother. Anyway, her brain was too tired to think about it any more. She realised that she felt both hungry and thirsty and went down to the kitchen.

Toby Waites heard as she creaked down the stairs and thought of her with loathing. He hated the way she allowed him to take her, without concern or passion, as if he were not a man with feelings but a thing. But most of all, he hated his recurring need of her, the uncontrollable fever that changed him into another person and robbed him of reason and self-respect. It would have to stop, he would have to send her away, put himself beyond the reach of temptation. He had told himself the same thing a hundred times before, but this time he meant to hold to his resolution.

He whispered a prayer, asking for forgiveness and strength; as always, he felt better for it, purged and clean, and he settled down to sleep.

At his side his wife lay still, her hands crossed over her thin breasts, fully awake although her eyes were closed. When her husband moved and inadvertently touched her, she edged away; the slightest physical contact with his flesh sickened her, as it had done almost from the beginning. She was thinking that she would like to pray also, but she was a sternly religious woman and she knew that there were some requests you could not direct to the Almighty because, by their very nature, they were sinful. So the prayer remained unspoken, though it had lain on her heart like a hot stone for seven years.

It was quite a short prayer, striking in its simplicity: it

31

asked merely that she might be free of this man. Each night she prayed (but only to herself, not to God) that death would come in the darkness and relieve him of his shame. Sometimes she asked that she might be the one to die. She didn't really care either way, she was past caring about life; the important thing was that one or the other should happen, and happen soon, before her reason snapped.

Later, in her sleep, she dreamed that, suitably clad in her new black dress, she stood up in chapel and, in ringing tones, proclaimed her husband's mortal sin to a shocked and crowded congregation.

4

It was 2 a.m. and May Pickford was on the phone to George Leppard again.

'George, do you think I ought to ring the police?'

'No, no! Don't do that!' He realised that he had spoken much too sharply, and added: 'It's only a couple of hours, May. They'd only tell you to wait a bit longer.'

'There could have been an accident, that's what I meant.'

'You'd have heard. You'd have heard by now. No, look, leave it with me. I'll get out the car and scout round a bit. Say I ring you in an hour, how's that?'

'Would you, George? I know it's asking a lot but I don't know who else—' Her voice stopped abruptly, as though she could not trust herself to go on without breaking down.

'Leave it with me,' he said, consolingly. 'We're probably getting worked up about nothing. I'll either ring you or pop in. Play it by ear.' Tom, you bastard, he thought savagely, for God's sake get home, get home quickly.

He felt his face redden with guilt when she thanked him. He poured himself another drink and sat down to think the thing through. He was as concerned as May now.

32

He knew that Tom wouldn't have the guts to spend the night out with the girl, not the whole night. The car? Tom was an excellent amateur mechanic, but he might have had a breakdown too serious even for his skill to mend. He might have run out of petrol, though that was unlike him. What about the girl? He had never asked about her, he didn't even know her name, feeling that the less he knew the better, so there was no help there. No, it seemed the only possible answer was that Tom had been involved in an accident, and there was one simple way to check on that. He rang Whitford police, and was informed that no road accidents had been reported that evening.

Well, he thought, as he hung up, that's closed one door. Tom must still be out with the girl somewhere, he's obviously had a sudden rush of blood to the head. It wasn't like him, he was a cautious man as a rule, but perhaps, after all, the affair was more serious than he had imagined. One thing was certain. He was not going to spend the rest of the night chasing round the moors in search of him, and he was certainly not going over to Whitford to sit and hold May Pickford's hand! He had done quite enough, he had his own problems to contend with.

He went into the kitchen and made himself a bacon sandwich and a cup of instant coffee. He was a fastidious, tidy man who could not bear the idea of coming down in the morning to an array of soiled pans and dishes, and when he had finished he washed up and tidied around. Well over an hour had passed since he last spoke to May and he judged that it was time to ring her again.

'May? Any news?'

'No, no. He isn't back. George, where are you?'

'Back home.' The lies tumbled out easily now. 'May, I've had no luck, I'm afraid. I drove almost into Whitford along Tom's usual route and then back on the lower road. No sign of him.'

'Oh God—' He could hear the sharp intake of her breath.

33

'Listen, May. I've also been in touch with the police.'

'What did they say?'

'He hasn't been in an accident. That's some consolation.'

'George—what could have happened?'

'I don't know. I'm as baffled as you. But I'm sure there's some reasonable explanation. He'll come bowling in, large as life, any minute, you'll see.' He tried hard, but the words came out without conviction. There was a long pause and then she spoke again, her voice firmer now; clearly she was making an effort to pull herself together.

'Yes, George, I'm sorry. I'm being very selfish. It's not fair of me to lay my troubles at your door. I'm grateful, I really am, for all you've done. Now I mustn't keep you from your bed any longer.'

With a sense of relief, he promised to ring her in the morning, murmured what he hoped were a few cheering words, and hung up. He went upstairs and climbed wearily but thankfully into bed.

The first hint of dawn was showing behind the drawn curtains when the telephone aroused him for the second time that night. It was May again, this time to tell him that police had found Tom's car parked in a lane a mile or so from the tiny village of Cullington. What had aroused the interest of the patrol-car policeman who made the discovery was that the front door on the driver's side had been left open, the radio switched on, and although he had kept it under observation for some time, no driver had appeared to claim the car.

5

Two other men had their rest disturbed that morning. The first was Chief-Inspector Charles Gosford of the County police, the officer in command at Whitford. He received a telephone call at 5.30 a.m. from the sergeant on duty at the station.

It might well have come a half-hour sooner, for the sergeant, a newly-promoted young man named Sanders, had found himself in something of a dilemma and delayed the call. He was under strict instructions to ring Gosford at any hour if anything of real importance came up. But how important was important, he asked himself? Clearly, a murder or a bank hold-up would qualify—though there hadn't been a murder in Whitford for 62 years, and the only serious bank-robbery, back in 1948, had been an inside job, when the manager had departed in some style, taking with him his secretary and the cash contents of the safe.

Sanders, anxious not to get on the wrong side of his superior, chewed the problem over anxiously for some time. Was the disappearance of one Thomas Pickford, an established if not well-known local citizen, and the discovery of his abandoned car of sufficient importance to justify the ruin of the Chief-Inspector's sleep?

When he did finally make up his mind to take the plunge, he was relieved to find that Gosford, after a gruff beginning, confirmed that he had done the right thing.

He ordered Sanders to place a guard on the car, which was not to be moved or touched until he got there. Two men were to make a preliminary search for Tom Pickford in the immediate area. The sergeant was to telephone Mr George Leppard, who seemed to have been the last person to see Pickford, and ask him if he would be so kind as to present himself at Whitford police station as soon as possible.

Jill Gosford, who was half-awake, watched her husband put down the phone and move to the bathroom. She waited until she heard the shower running and then followed him.

'Did I hear you say Tom Pickford?'

'Yes.'

'The name rings a bell.'

'He's a member of the Golf Club.'

35

'Ah. Yes. I've got him now. What's he done?'

'Disappeared.'

'How do you mean?'

'Just that. He went over to Ravensdale last night to see a friend, left there at half-past eleven, and hasn't been seen since.'

'Oh.' She sounded disappointed. 'The way you sounded on the phone I thought you'd got a murder on your hands at least. He's probably shacked up with a girl-friend for the night.'

'Tom Pickford?' He considered the idea for a moment, and then rejected it. 'I doubt it.'

'Why? There's a lot of it about, Charlie. It must be the air up here, or the sheer boredom of living in Whitford—I don't know which. Probably a bit of both.' A strand of hair strayed across her eyes and she pushed it away. 'If you could lift the roof off this town, you'd find half its worthy citizens in some very strange beds and even stranger positions.'

'Half is an exaggeration,' he said smiling. 'And it's none of my business. I'm a custodian of the law, not of morals.'

'Well, well!' she said, smiling at him.

'As for Tom Pickford, I don't say he wouldn't like a bit of extra now and again. But I doubt if he'd have the courage.'

'Is that what it takes—courage?'

'If you're married to Mrs Pickford—yes.' He turned off the shower, wrapped himself in a towelling robe, and prepared to shave. She sat down on the bathroom stool, and began to run a comb through her long, fair hair. They both found great pleasure in these moments; Jill often told her friends that all the vital Gosford family decisions were made in the bathroom.

'Time for coffee if I make some, Charlie?'

'No. I'll get something at the station.'

'The bald bit. It's getting bigger.'

36

He examined his head in the mirror and nodded: 'Must be all the worry.'

'Suppose when you get to the station you find that Mr Pickford has turned up at home, safe and sound. What will you do?'

'Tear a strip off a couple of constables, just to appease my temper. But it won't happen.'

'How can you be so sure? And don't tell me it's a gut feeling!'

'Gut? What gut?' He grinned and patted his lean muscled stomach. The little gesture of vanity amused her, and smiling she moved forward to kiss his lathered cheek. 'I love you very much, Charlie,' she said.

'That's understandable,' he said with mock complacency. 'I mean, a tall, handsome, intelligent, dynamic, sexually-attractive—'

'Conceited,' she said, 'don't forget that.' She rubbed her lips against his shoulder, wiping away the white smear of soap.

'Tell you what,' he said. 'If when I get to the station I find that this Tom Pickford business has sorted itself out, I'll turn round and come home for breakfast.'

'Breakfast?' she asked innocently.

'Or anything else that might be going,' he said.

6

The second man to be disturbed was David Birk, whose sleep was troubled by strange and uncomfortable dreams, from the last of which he woke abruptly, his hand reaching for a rifle that wasn't there.

The incident that had aroused him the previous evening was still strong in his mind, and driven by an impulse which he could not have explained, least of all to himself, he dressed and set out across the moor, heading in the direction from which he thought he had heard the call.

A slight, freshening breeze had moved in from the south, but it seemed to be too weak to stir the heavy, oppressive air or penetrate the blanket of heat which lay on the land.

But, strangely, the heat and the humidity pleased Birk, even exhilarated him. It reminded him of another place which he still thought of as home.

CHAPTER THREE

1

The hours of darkness brought little satisfaction to the tiger. The deer had escaped his clumsy pursuit, and he found no other source of food except a dead brown rat which only served to whet his appetite. The entire population of the forest seemed to have disappeared, to have fled before him. As the hot night slipped away the hunger mounted, hammering insistently at his stomach like the rising beat of a drum, and his desperation grew.

Once he ventured beyond the cover of the trees to find himself faced with a narrow ribbon of road but the sound and headlights of a passing car drove him back in fear. From time to time he called to the tigress, lifting his voice in a high-pitched, half-plaintive moaning sound, but she made no reply. The sheer joy of freedom which had lifted his spirits to such heights of intoxication only a few hours before was gone now. The disdainful trees surrounded him like the bars of a new and unfamiliar cage; the forest mocked him with its brooding silence, the undergrowth maddened his senses with a score of subtle, animal scents.

Then, in the first hour of dawn, his luck changed. Forcing his way in desperation through a thicket of harsh, entangled bushes, he reached a point where the land fell away abruptly on either side of a long, deep crevice, as though it had been furrowed by some gigantic plough. Here the trees huddled together even more closely, their dark foliage forming a roof which blotted out the sky as if in a conspiracy to hide this place from the world, and the moist, yielding earth sloped downwards into a lank brown marsh.

Above the dank smell which rose like a mist from the

soggy ground, the tiger caught another, sharper scent which fired his blood. He had already learned something from his hours in the forest and he dropped silently into the crouch position, staring into the grey, artificial twilight. Almost immediately his keen eyes picked up a dark shape standing on the fringe of the marsh; then something moved nearby and he saw another, smaller figure.

It was a hind and her calf. Earlier that night they had fled before the frightening roars of the tigers, and in her blind panic and concern for her fawn, the normally sure-footed deer had stumbled and lamed herself so badly that for a time she was unable to move. Fear had driven her on at last, and slowly, her senses prickling with pain, she had brought the calf to this secluded, sheltered spot. But unwittingly, she had moved into a trap.

She heard the tiger and scented his approach long before he saw her, but though the urge to take flight screamed within her, she had exhausted her strength and was unable to respond. The little, frightened calf also sensed the presence of the unseen enemy, and he moved closer to his mother, muzzling her flanks as though puzzled by her immobility.

The tiger edged nearer, inch by cautious inch. He had never learned the tricks of the hunt, but some sixth-sense warned him that the deer had scented him, and he moved along the slope so as to make the final approach from another direction. But the deer seemed to know this, and turned her head, shifting her ground slightly.

Instinct told the tiger to wait, to move in closer, but the desperation of hunger proved stronger. He arched his great body, stretching every muscle, paused for one long, silent moment, and then, with a roar which seemed to blare out from the depths of his being, he charged forward.

The terrified deer made a last, frantic effort to run, but it was useless. Great shock-waves of pain shuddered through her body as she tried to move her crippled limb. She stumbled, righted herself, and as she braced and

40

twisted round to place herself in front of the calf, the tiger was on her. She screamed in agony as the claws tore into her flesh, and even as she fell the powerful canine teeth locked on her throat and neck, crushing the wind-pipe and almost severing her head from her body.

The calf stood for a moment as though paralysed, then with little bleating cries of terror scampered away, dragging its spindly legs through the clinging marsh. But the vegetation was too thick to allow any real freedom of movement, and time and time again he was forced back. Leaving the dead mother momentarily, the tiger leaped at the calf and brought him down with a single, contemptuous blow from his forepaw, crushing his skull as a steamhammer might pulp an apple.

A brassy roar of triumph shook the forest, to be answered briefly by the frightened calling of the jays in the unseen sky above the tree-tops.

And then, there was silence.

2

Faithful to Gosford's instructions, Tom Pickford's car had remained untouched. It stood in the lonely, narrow lane in the same condition as it had been found, the door swinging open, the radio switched on. The only difference was that since 6 a.m., when the BBC transmissions began, the faint, irritable buzz of the radio had been replaced by a mixed programme of popular music, and by 7.15 when Gosford arrived, this had given way to the more strident and well-defined pop style of Radio One.

Edmonds, the portly, middle-aged constable who had been placed on guard noticed the frown that furrowed the Inspector's brow, and said quickly: 'Sorry about that racket, sir, but I was told not to touch anything.'

'That's all right, Fred,' said Gosford. 'Where are the others?'

'Still having a punt round to see what they can find, sir,' said Edmonds.

'Nothing so far then? No sign of Pickford?'

'No, sir. Apart from our two lads I haven't clapped eyes on a living soul since I got here.'

'What's the nearest bit of civilisation from here?'

Edmonds walked a yard or so to the point where the lane met a slightly wider, secondary road. 'Take the right hand here, sir, and about two miles up you come to Cullington village. Just before then, about a half-mile this side is Toby Waites' place. Take the left fork here and—well, you know that, sir, for you've just come that way. It takes you to Barton, and then the main road to Whitford.'

'And what about up there?' Gosford turned his back to the junction and pointed up the lane.

'Nowhere, sir. Used to lead to Camdale Farm, but that's long since gone. About there it becomes no more than a track, and that doesn't last. Beyond that is the high moor. Only one up there is Mr Birk.'

'A car couldn't get up as far as that, could it?'

'Very much doubt it, sir. There is another approach from the West—'

'Yes.' Gosford interrupted the constable, who was inclined to go on a bit. The music blaring from the car was beginning to get on his nerves and he turned towards it.

'Radio One, sir,' said Edmonds. 'Couldn't be anything else, could it? I get it from the kids every morning, and if I'm lucky enough to be on duty and miss it, I catch it in the evening.'

Gosford dropped a knee on the driver's seat and peered round the interior of the car, taking care not to touch anything with his hands. After a moment or two he leaned over and holding the tip of the grooved switch with his handkerchief, turned off the radio. 'Sorry,' he said amiably to the unseen disc-jockey, 'but we have to think of the sheep.'

He swivelled his body to look into the rear of the car,

42

where something lying on the floor caught his attention. He studied it for a moment. 'Get me a stick, will you, Fred?' he asked over his shoulder.

'What sort of stick, sir?'

'Any sort. A longish stick—I want to get at something in the back.' He tried hard to keep the impatience out of his voice. Edmonds was a solid, reliable man, but a slow mover and a slower thinker. He came back at last with a branch plucked from a young sapling. Gosford leaned over the seat and after one or two experimental prods, managed to get the tip of the stick under the article on the floor and lift it up.

He found it difficult not to smile as he eased himself back from the car and held his catch up for Edmonds to see.

'What do you make to this, then, Fred?' he asked.

'Knickers, I'd say, sir,' he replied, without visible emotion. 'Or pants, as my girl would call them. A pair of black nylon pants. Must belong to some kid. Wouldn't see a grown woman wearing the likes of them, would you, sir?'

'Why not?'

'I mean, a grown respectable, married woman, sir.'

Gosford did not press the point. Instead, he asked: 'Do you know Tom Pickford's wife, Fred?'

'Only to say good morning to, sir.'

'Would she wear this sort of thing, do you suppose?'

'No, sir. I don't see her in those, do you, sir?' He spoke seriously, offering a considered opinion. If he saw any humour in the conversation, there was no hint of it on his broad, brick-red face. 'And if she does wear them, I don't see her taking them off in the car, do you sir?' he added.

'No,' said Gosford reflectively, as though he were mentally stripping the lady down to her underwear. 'No, Fred, I don't.'

3

Gosford was not a particularly squeamish man, but when it came to the point, he found himself unable to question Mrs Pickford in any real depth. Face to face in his office with this plain, undecorated, eminently sensible woman, he saw not only the absurdity of such questioning but the needless cruelty involved in such a course of action. Despite her adopted status as an emancipated woman, he sensed that respectability and pride in her social position still loomed larger in her life, and that she would shrivel up with shame if he posed the questions which were on his mind. Towards the end of the interview he moved as closely as he could to the subject.

'Mrs Pickford, there is something I have to ask you.'

'I think I know what it is,' she said.

'Yes?'

'You want to know—well—if everything is all right between Tom and myself, isn't that so?'

'I'm sorry,' he said diffidently, 'but it is the sort of question—'

'There's no need to apologise,' she interrupted, 'I quite understand. I expected you to ask. Naturally, I've thought about it and I think I can say, in all honesty, that Tom and I are very happy. Content is perhaps the better word. We're neither of us young, but then we're not old either. We enjoy each other's company, we have mutual interests like the theatre and music and so forth, we rarely quarrel. Yes, it's very good really—not exciting or anything—but good.'

She means it too, thought Gosford, that's exactly how she sees it. There was a sort of earnest complacency in her manner which he found distasteful. He suspected that she laid down the domestic ground rules and her husband meekly followed them. For the first time he felt a twinge of pity for the absent Tom.

Aloud he asked: 'Why didn't you go with him tonight?'

'It was his chess evening,' she answered in a tone of surprise. 'That's partly what I meant, don't you see? He has his chess, I have my Luncheon Club and Literary Society meetings. We both agreed some time ago that it would be a good thing if we had the odd evening off from each other, so to speak. It does us both good.'

'Does he always go to George Leppard's house for these chess evenings?'

'Usually. I think they both prefer it.' She smiled. 'For one thing, we don't drink at home, don't keep it in the house. It's a decision we reached some years ago. I don't drink, and we both agreed that it would be unfair to spend what, after all, is our joint income on something which only one of us could enjoy.'

'Your husband drinks when he is with Mr Leppard?'

'Oh, yes, but not excessively. He's far too sensible for that. If you think he may have had too much to drink last night—'

'It could be a possible explanation,' said Gosford. 'He might have decided he'd taken more than was good for him, and got out of the car to walk it off.'

'No,' she said firmly, 'that wouldn't be Tom. He knows how I feel about that sort of self-indulgence. No.' She shook her head vigorously. 'You can put that thought right out of your mind, Chief-Inspector.' Again, the note of smugness in her tone jarred his mind and irritated him.

There was a knock, and the Station Sergeant put his head round the door. 'Mr Leppard is here, sir.'

'Ask him to come through,' said Gosford, and added quickly, rising from the desk: 'No, wait. I'll come out myself. Excuse me for one moment, Mrs Pickford.'

George Leppard was waiting in the station office, and when Gosford appeared he turned an anxious face towards him. 'Is there any news, Chief-Inspector?'

'I'm afraid not. Please come through to my office. Mrs Pickford is with me.'

45

'How is she?'

'She seems to be bearing up.' As they moved out, Gosford turned, and as though it were an afterthought said. 'Sergeant. Has anybody reported a missing girl this morning?'

'No, sir,' said the sergeant, his eyebrows raised in query.

But Gosford was not looking at the sergeant. He had turned back just in time to catch the sudden, nervous gleam in the other man's eyes which was all the confirmation he needed.

4

The old track which led to the summit of the high moor was steep and narrow, its line almost obscured by the invading bracken and heather, but David Birk hardly checked his steady, even strides as he thrust his way upwards. As the gradient eased, the heather slowly released its hold to be replaced by Wavy Hair Grass, clumps of tall, bay willow-herb and fox-gloves.

Above him loomed the Kestle Stones, huge columns of dark rock which seemed to twist out of the earth like the dead trunks of giant trees. At the foot of the three main stones, like fallen fruit, there was a scattering of loose boulders, and as David moved upwards, an adder brushed his foot hissing in fear, and slid swiftly through the grass to the refuge of the heaped stones.

David paused in the shadow of the rocks and looked around. From here, the light seemed to have a clearer, crystalline quality, and the cooler air rippled with the incessant hum of bees. A snipe, disturbed by his approach, fluttered away on its curious zig-zag course; a pair of wary curlews circled overhead, and above them a skylark flashed and wheeled in the sunlight, bursting its breast in song.

Below him, he could just discern the shadowed outline of the old stone house which was his home, but this apart, there was no other sign of human habitation. On three sides the moor bellowed towards the horizon, its surface scored by the rocky outcrops which marked hidden valleys and gorges; only to the east, where it met the forest, was its progress challenged.

It was a land in which past, present and future seemed to have merged into timelessness, and, as always it matched his mood. This, he thought, is why I came, nothing can touch me here. This was the land he had known as a child, and he had come back to it, seeking something of the peace and pleasure and, above all, the security of those boyhood years. The image of a woman named Sarah formed in his mind, and for the first time in many months, he made no effort to push it aside. He remembered, in calmness, an evening almost a year before, in the little apartment behind Baker Street, when she had said that she was leaving him, that the long affair was over. She had spoken directly, with the kind of quivering honesty which he'd always admired in her.

He had laughed at first, in sheer disbelief, but she had silenced him angrily.

'Don't laugh, David! I don't find it funny.'

'You can't mean it!'

'Every word! Haven't you seen it coming? Haven't you felt it?'

'Oh, come on, Sarah—' He tried to take her in his arms, but she turned angrily away.

'No!' she said, 'no! Listen, for heaven's sake, listen! It's over, kaput, finished. Once and for all.'

'Why?' He looked bewildered, as though still unable to believe what she was saying.

'Why?' She laughed harshly. 'The man wants to know why. All right, all right! I'll tell you. Because there's a limit, there has to be a limit. With you, I feel like an interlude. A drink and a quick bit of the other between the acts. You go away for weeks, even months. If I'm very lucky, I get a postcard. Then, just as I'm settling into some

47

semblance of a normal life, you come charging back in and —bingo!—it's off to the races again. When we're not in bed, you're filling yourself up with scotch. But we never talk, we never really talk. We're like two people caught in a revolving door, going round and round. We make signs to each other, but we don't communicate. Well, I've had it. It's as simple as that. I'm not getting any younger, I need some certainty in my life. Does that answer your question?'

He fumbled in a pocket for his pipe and began to twist it in his fingers. 'Is there someone else?' he asked, hating the distasteful sound of the cliché almost as he spoke it.

'Yes,' she said calmly, 'as a matter of fact, there is.'

He nodded slowly. 'Who is it?'

'Nobody you know. Anyway, what does it matter? I'd made up my mind when you went off last time, before I met him.'

He looked down at the empty pipe for a moment, and nodded again. He was overwhelmed by a sense of loss, and when he raised his head to look at her she must have seen something of it in his eyes, for she continued, more gently: 'I'm sorry, David, I'm truly sorry. The truth is, I suppose, that I'm not the kind of person who can settle for half. Do you know what I liked about you when we first met? It was your honesty. I thought, thank God, here at last is a man who says what he feels. Heaven knows, I'd had my share of pseudos and shams. But it was an illusion. Tell the truth, you've never been wholly honest with me, have you?'

He began to go through the motions of filling the pipe, unable to answer her with a lie. 'Go on,' he said, 'I'm listening.'

'This job of yours, for instance. I still don't know what it is. You gave me the impression that you were some top-level international salesman jetting round the world in search of orders, but you never actually told me.'

'It's all pretty boring,' he said.

'But I would have been interested. Didn't that occur to

you? I loved you, and I wanted to know all about you. But you only told me so much, you only showed me what you wanted me to see. It's as if there is another man inside you, looking out—a stranger. It's puzzling, frightening. Take the drink. You don't drink like other men, I don't even think you enjoy it. And no matter what you put down, you never seem to get drunk. Why? Why do you need it so badly? What are you trying to drown? After three years I ought to have some idea of who you are, what you do, what goes on inside you, but I haven't. I loved you, I wanted to help you—' She stopped suddenly, as though it was useless to continue, and then added quietly, with an air of finality, 'Do you know what I feel, I honestly feel? I think you're incapable of giving yourself wholly to a normal, human relationship. You're a solitary, David, you should live alone.'

He had longed to tell her then, but the habit of restraint was too strong; and what was the use anyway, he thought bitterly. He had lost her, and to tell her the whole, complicated story would only make that loss the more certain and the more painful. How do you explain that while other men earn their bread as lawyers, journalists, politicians, Civil Servants, bus-drivers, mechanics, miners and so forth, you are gainfully employed as an assassin, a kind of licensed murderer? Set the table, darling, light the candles, serve the supper, open the wine, and then, over the coffee and brandy, if you're a good girl and promise not to interrupt, David will tell you all about his last trip and how jolly interesting and successful it all was, especially the part where he actually killed this man, this complete stranger, plugging him through the heart with a single bullet from the Mauser at a range of almost 800 yards.

'I love you, Sarah,' he said quietly, and this was the truth. He had loved only two women in his life; the first was dead, and Sarah was the other.

'It's too late,' she answered. 'Too late, I'm afraid.'

He had left her calmly, without argument; his eyes no

longer hinted at the desperation which churned within him. He could see that she was hurt by his control, she longed for him to rage at her, to plead, to break in some way, and in a curious, perverse way, this little victory pleased him. Why, after all, should he be the only one to suffer?

'Don't come back. I shan't be here if you do. I've sold the apartment,' she said coldly. 'I'm getting married.'

'Thank you for telling me. I must send you something— a gift.'

'If you do, I shall give it to Ox-Fam.'

It had all been scratchy and childish, two people trying desperately to draw blood. Going out, he had passed a tall, well-built man, and their eyes had met for a moment in a flicker of mutual curiosity. The man's face was tanned, his skin glowed with health, he exuded an air of well-being and self-confidence, and David hated him on sight.

He had waited on the landing below. The man reached the door of Sarah's apartment and rang the bell. A moment later he heard Sarah's voice.

'Oh, darling, I'm glad you came.'

A pause, and he knew that they were embracing. Then the man's voice.

'Was that him—just leaving?'

'Yes.'

'How was it? How did he take it?'

'Don't let's talk about it. It's all over. That's what counts. It's all over.'

And the sharp, final click as the door closed.

The longing for Sarah was still with him after all these months, but the bitterness had gone. He was even grateful to her, for by her honesty, she had illuminated his own problem, faced him with the need for action.

The day after his encounter with Sarah, he had gone to the Department and told them that he wanted to quit. He had expected an argument, but McCallum, the head of the Section was all sweet reason and understanding, it was almost as though he had been expecting David's request. To leave, just like that, might be difficult, there were cetain problems. But a year's sabbatical, that could certainly be arranged. David had earned it, he'd had a long spell in the field, and it was natural that he should want a rest.

'I'll never make another strike,' David had said.

'Fine, fine. If that's how you feel. Take your leave. Make up your mind what you'd like to do next. No hurry. Put your feet up, enjoy yourself and when it's over, we can talk.'

David had wanted to resist, to makc the break complete, but in the end he hadn't argued. At the time he had even found comfort in the thought that there was still a place for him somewhere. In a way, he had become institutionalised, there was a part of him which longed for the security of routine, the discipline of an ordered framework to his daily life.

And so he had come back to this place, back to the countryside of his childhood, embracing the isolation and solitude like a monk. Slowly, under the healing touch of the moor, the tension eased, the quivering nerves relaxed, and the man within retreated into the shadows of his mind. He had put the past behind him, as an act of will, but he saw now that this had been a mistake. Since last night it had returned in full flood and he was relieved that he could think of it with reasonable dispassion, and certainly without pain. Perhaps this, more than anything else, was a sign of recovery.

He moved into the sunlight and as he did so, he heard the call again, faint and far-away, but unmistakable. He waited, holding his breath, and then, fainter still, he heard a response, coming from the direction of the forest. The long, musical cry sounded again, slightly louder now, as though in joy and recognition, and once more, the distant voice answered.

David felt his whole body respond, he felt as though he

wanted to lift his own voice in reply. It was incredible, beyond belief, but it was no dream. Those jungle voices were as real as the curlews that complained above him. He scrambled down from the little plateau, and forcing his way through the heather and bracken, set off towards his home.

5

The tigress waited on the moor for Mohan to come. From time to time he called and she answered, guiding him to the hollow near the beck where she lay hidden. It was cool here, protected from the strong sunlight which she disliked, and the ground was soft and damp beneath her. She felt the cubs stir within her belly and purred with pleasure.

Mohan came at last, relieved to find his mate, but he approached her warily, knowing her moods. His eyes were bright and already, in a few short hours of freedom, his coat was beginning to lose its dullness, to assume its natural gloss. She allowed him to muzzle her flanks for a moment or two and then drew back, spitting and hissing.

Eventually he stretched out beside her and slept. But Ranee was more cautious, she was still not certain of this strange, new environment. She licked her paws and cleaned herself, her ears alert for any intruder. Once, when she heard a sound, she rose, her tail twitching, and peered through the heather. In the distance she saw a man, thrusting his way forward. She watched him for a long time, but he was moving away from her, and when he disappeared from sight she settled down again.

She glanced at Mohan, who hadn't moved. And then, fatigue getting the better of caution, she closed her eyes.

CHAPTER FOUR

1

'Can we just go over it again, Mr Leppard?' said Gosford. He leaned back in his chair, smiling easily, tapping a pencil against the palm of his left hand.

May Pickford had been sent home, but George Leppard had been asked to stay on for a few minutes. He'd been relieved to see her go, he felt uneasy and guilty in her presence; the constant repetition of the lie about her husband, and the embroidery he was forced to add to make it convincing, worried and frightened him. But he was committed, he had embellished the lie in the presence of the police, and he felt that there was no other course open to him but to flounder on. And in any case he had another commitment to Tom Pickford and if he broke that, the consequences might be more disastrous for him than any action the police might take.

'Do we have to, Chief-Inspector?' he asked, mustering what he hoped was a friendly, understanding smile. 'I've got rather a lot of work on hand.'

'Busy, are you?' asked Gosford affably.

'You could say that. Secretary on holiday for a start. Always happens at the wrong moment. And it's nearly impossible to get a temporary at this time of the year. They're all snapped up by the holiday resorts on the coast.'

'I imagined that with all these cuts in public expenditure, architects like yourself would be feeling the pinch.'

'I've been lucky. I've kept the practice small, the overheads down. I survive. It isn't easy.'

'It can't be,' said Gosford sympathetically. 'What do you specialise in?' He ran an exploratory hand through his untidy, sand-coloured hair until he reached the small bald

53

patch at the crown. Jill was exaggerating he thought, it hardly shows. But he pushed the hair over it nevertheless, and brought his mind back to the interview. 'I don't specialise,' Leppard was saying. 'I do what comes along.'

'Much local government work?'

Leppard tightened warily. He didn't like the trend of the questioning, but Gosford's manner was affable, there was nothing in it to suggest any motive deeper than polite interest. 'Some,' he said. 'It's a hell of a job to compete with the big boys, but I've been lucky, as I said.'

'This new school they're talking about building. Are you in for that?'

'I shall be, if they don't cancel it.'

'Oh, I understand that it's definitely going ahead. They could hardly put it off again. The old place is a hundred years old, a disgrace.'

'I shall have a go for it, of course. But there'll be a lot of competition.' Leppard looked casually at his watch. 'Sorry, Chief-Inspector, but—'

'Of course. You must excuse me. I've only been in Whitford a few months, and I'm still in the process of finding out. Right—I'll cut it short. Is there anything else that you can tell me about Tom Pickford's movements last night?'

Leppard tried to look as if he were giving the question serious thought. 'No. No. I don't think so, Chief-Inspector,' he said.

'How well do you know him?'

'We were at school together. We lost touch for a while after that. Then we met up again when he came back here and took up his present job.'

'Deputy Borough Treasurer—is that the correct title?'

'Yes.'

'Of course, you'd run across him in your local government work.'

'Sometimes. But, of course, we have no direct professional connection. I work to a different department.' Leppard's voice lifted a note and the words came out too insistently. He wondered uneasily if the other man had noticed it, but there was no change in the smooth, affable manner.

'At any rate, you resumed your old friendship?'

'In a way.' Leppard hesitated. He wanted to keep a distance between himself and Tom Pickford, not to give the impression that they were too close. And this, in a sense, was no more than the truth. 'The fact is, we don't have a greal deal in common. The one thing really is chess. Apart from that—there isn't much.' He smiled at Gosford as from one man of the world to another. 'One of the problems, to be honest, is his wife. I'm afraid she doesn't like me. She accepts our evenings of chess—tolerates would be a better word—but that's about all.'

'What have you done to offend the lady?'

'Nothing.' Leppard scraped a fingernail over a small spot on the sleeve of his new corduroy jacket. 'It's just one of those things. She's the possessive type, I suppose—doesn't want anyone else to get too close to her husband.'

'I thought she was a great one for Woman's Lib.'

'She is. In a genteel, suburban way.'

'But liberation doesn't extend to her husband?'

'I doubt it. But don't let me give you the wrong impression. As couples go, they get on very well, I believe. May tends to rule the roost, but it doesn't seem to bother Tom. He's a placid, easy-going chap, he's quite happy to have other people take the decisions.'

'Was he having an affair, Mr Leppard?' The question, sharp and direct, seemed to tighten the atmosphere in the little room, replacing the casual friendliness of the interview with a touch of menace.

'An affair?' Although Leppard had been expecting the question, and had steeled himself to meet it, the words came out in a sort of uncomprehending stammer, betraying his nervousness. He tried to bring his voice under control. 'I hardly think so, Chief Inspector.'

'Why?'

'Well, knowing Tom. It takes some courage to have an affair, there's an element of risk. And he is a pretty cautious type. Besides, this isn't a big place. He'd be known to a lot of people, by sight anyway. It wouldn't help him in his job if he was seen with another woman.' It was sounding better now, the arguments coming out just as he had rehearsed them in his mind.

'He was with another woman last night, Mr Leppard.'

'That's impossible. He was with me.'

'Until 11.30 p.m.?'

'Yes. Give or take a few minutes. I've already explained——'

'You know where we found his car?'

'Yes.'

'Way off the route he would have taken if he was driving straight home from your place.'

'Yes. He could have decided to go another way.'

'Even though he was late leaving you and in a hurry to get back?'

'Look, Chief-Inspector, I wasn't there. I can't possibly know what was in his mind.'

'I think I do, Mr Leppard.'

'Then I wish you'd tell me!'

'Some time last night Mr Pickford met a girl. She was in the car with him, her fingerprints are all over the steering-wheel, the back-seat, the doors and so forth. They could belong to his wife, of course, but I very much doubt it. There is other evidence to suggest that they had sexual intercourse in the car—or got damn near it!'

Leppard stared at Gosford in silence. The temptation to tell everything was strong in his mind, but fear proved the stronger.

'You look surprised,' said Gosford mildly.

'That's hardly the word. Frankly, I'm flabbergasted, Chief-Inspector. I don't know what to say. I suppose it goes to prove that you can never really know anybody, the people close to you least of all. I'd have laid bets on Tom.

The notion of him having an affair, running off with another woman—' He shook his head in disbelief.

'I didn't say he'd run off with her.'

'But if he's disappeared—'

'If he did intend to go off with the girl, it's hardly likely that he would leave his car behind, is it? And leave it suddenly, with the door open and the radio switched on. No. It looks as if he intended to go back to the car, as if he left it only for a moment or so. In which case, why didn't he go back? What happened to stop him?'

'Are you asking me?'

'There's no-one else here, Mr Leppard.' A sharp edge of impatience was on Gosford's tongue now. The other man was covering up, he knew that, he'd been around long enough to read the signs. He understood his reluctance to speak in front of Pickford's wife, which was why he had sent her away, but he was annoyed that Leppard had refused the opportunity to talk freely, to tell him the real facts. It was nothing unusual and certainly no great crime for a man to provide an alibi for a friend's infidelity, and anyway, as he had told Jill only a few hours before, he was not a custodian of morals. But the relationship between George Leppard and Tom Pickford nagged at a part of his mind. Was it simply loyalty to a friend that made this man stick so stubbornly to his story, or was there something more to it?

He was tempted for a moment to challenge Leppard directly, but instinct told him to hold off. A man who lies and goes on lying will often reveal more of himself than if he speaks the truth—this was a lesson he'd learned a long time ago.

'I can't help you, Chief-Inspector, I wish I could,' Leppard said. He tried to look Gosford in the eye, to impress him with a display of frankness, but his glance wavered and he ended by looking down at the worn hair-cord carpet. Then he rose from the chair with a gesture of apology. 'If Tom should turn up—'

'We'll let you know.'

At the door, as they shook hands, Gosford said: 'We have one consolation. Whether the girl was a chance pickup or a regular date, it's pretty certain that she's local. As you say, this is a small place. It shouldn't be difficult to find her. Then we'll learn the truth one way or another. About a lot of things.'

He was amused to see, for the second time, the gleam of unease glisten in the other man's eyes.

2

This was the oldest part of the forest, where Scots and American Lodgepole pine fought with Japanese larch for possession of the crowded soil. The earth beneath David's feet was peaty and moist, and as the downward slope gathered pace, the undergrowth thickened, barring his path. The four 130-gramme bullets chinked together in the side pocket of his short-sleeved bush jacket as his foot caught against a half-buried root. He steadied himself and wiped the sweat from his forehead and neck.

And then, ahead of him, he heard the furious barking of the dog. He slipped one of the cartridges into the Winchester 270, and eased himself forward, silently cursing the sucking squelch which rose with every footfall, the noisy protests of the entangling bushes. His approach was too obvious, he knew that, but he had little choice.

The dog barked again; he waited for an answering roar but nothing came. And then he saw in the soft earth the prints of the tiger, unmistakable pug marks leading down the slope. As far as he could judge in the gloom, the tracks were some hours old; he followed them for a few yards and came to the broken undergrowth through which the tiger had forced a passage.

He broke a way through, heedless of the noise, and found himself on the edge of the crevice, the dank earth sliding sharply downwards to the brown marsh. The dog greeted him with a renewed burst of barking, but slipping up the safety-catch of the rifle, he paused again, his body tensed, every sense alert. And now the dog fell silent, as though he too were listening.

It was a full two minutes before David moved, two minutes in which he seemed to merge with the forest and match its stillness. Only then did he go forward, slithering swiftly down the incline until he reached the dog.

'Good boy,' he murmured, 'good boy,' and motioned him to silence. He waited again, the heel of the rifle pressing lightly against his shoulder, finger hovering on the trigger, his body turning in a slow circle as his eyes scoured the forest.

The dog had found the remains of the deer, and these lay at David's feet. He knew that it was not unusual for a tiger to lie up near a kill, guarding it from other predators until he is ready for his next meal. The sloping, thickly-wooded ground around the low-lying marsh provided exactly the sort of natural, dense cover from which a tiger prefers to launch its attack, and with its immense speed over short distances the great cat could be upon him in seconds. Experience told him that such an attack was unlikely for the tiger is usually wary of man, and contrary to popular legend, the man-eater is a rarity. But he knew also that with this animal even experience could be a treacherous guide; it was wiser to leave nothing to chance.

There had been a time, many years before, when as a young man and inexperienced hunter, he had faced just such an ambush. On that occasion the tiger came so close that the blast of its bellowing roar struck his face like a sudden wind and one great paw ripped into his shoulder. He was in luck that night, for as the tiger swept across him he managed, before he fell, to put in his shot. The tiger screamed as the heavy bullet tore upwards at an angle which took it through the underbelly and into the heart. The momentum of the leap carried it onwards a good three or four yards, then, pulling itself upright, it turned back and faced David. The animal paused, as though gathering its strength, opened its mouth in a half-choked roar of defiance and anger, and lurched drunkenly towards the man. David was on his feet now, and the second bullet took the tiger under the left eye. It staggered on for another yard before it stopped, then, with a shake of its great, striped head, toppled over. The flanks quivered, the thick tail thrashed the air, and then it lay still, as if crouched in sleep.

He remembered the incident now, and wondered at the strange irony which had brought him to the heart of this English forest. Was he, after all, simply reliving an old memory? But this was no trick of the mind. The heavy pug-marks were there in the soft earth at the edge of the marsh, along with the pathetic remains of the deer. It was incredible perhaps, but it was real.

True to its old instincts, the tiger had removed the intestines and stomach of its victim and set these aside. It had clearly been ravenous, for there was little flesh on the crunched bones. Some of the meat had been carried away, for David could now make out the dark stains which ran almost parallel to the pug-marks, and which disappeared as the dense undergrowth took over. Nearby, almost untouched, lay the dead body of the fawn.

The dog whined, as if to say that he wanted to leave this strange place and get back to the sunlight and certainty of the moor. David was tempted for a moment to follow the tracks further, but as the dog whined again, he turned away. He had gone into the forest for proof, and he had found it. That was enough for the moment. The tigers could be anywhere in this vast expanse of moor and forest. The first and most important task was to alert the authorities.

On the edge of the forest he saw a group of workmen thinning a dense stand of pine, cutting out some of the older trees. The sight of these men emphasised the urgency of the situation. And, at the same time he thought wryly, there was an element of absurdity in it also! There they were, surrounded by friendly trees, enfolded by familiar hills, in a countryside where danger was almost an unknown word. How could he approach them and tell them to beware tigers? They would stare at him in their steady, quiet way, nod politely, and privately put him down as an amiable eccentric!

He avoided them and made his way back to the point where he had parked his land-rover. There was, he judged, little threat to the men at this moment. The tigers would be lying up after their night of activity, it was unlikely that they would move during the day; and even if they did, they would almost certainly keep away from human beings. There were, after all, enough deer in the forest to satisfy their appetites.

But as he drove down the valley he saw a summer camp on one of the open hillsides and a group of children chasing a ball in an improvised game of football; and nearby, sitting by their cars near the beck, families were setting out picnics, relaxing in the warm sunshine. Lower down, he saw groups of walkers, weighted down with packs, setting out on the more arduous forest walks.

The sense of urgency came back, prickling his skin, and when he reached the main road, he turned towards Whitford, his foot hard down on the accelerator.

3

A detailed and thorough search of the area around the abandoned car, out to a radius of about a mile, had yielded no clue to the whereabouts of Tom Pickford, and Gosford decided to call it off.

'If anything happened to him, it would have happened near the car,' he told Sergeant Sanders. 'He wasn't intending to go far, that's obvious.'

'What's the next move then, sir?' The young sergeant tried to sound as though he were eager for more action, but he could not disguise his weariness, and Gosford was quick to notice it.

'Your next move is to go home and get your head down,' he said. 'You've got another night shift ahead of you.'

'Oh, I'm all right, sir.'

'Home!' said Gosford. 'Tout suite.' He walked to the centre of the T-junction, where the lane met the road. 'Cullington village—how far is it from here?'

'A couple of miles, sir.'

'And Barton is about three miles the other way, towards Whitford?'

'Yes, sir.'

'I'll try Cullington,' said Gosford. He got into a Ford Escort which was parked in the bright sunshine and winced as his body came into contact with the upholstery, 'Christ! It's like a furnace in here.'

'Yes,' said Sanders. 'I was thinking of that this morning. If this weather keeps up we could have fire-trouble on the moor.'

'Thank you for the kind thought,' said Gosford, 'that's all I need.' He started the engine, and added: 'Get a couple of men to run Pickford's car back to the station. The rest can go back to their regular duties.'

He followed the narrow, winding road to Cullington, a cluster of old stone houses and a few modern red-brick bungalows, and pulled up outside the 'Star of India', the local public-house. It had started life as a small country-inn, but successive landlords, in the name of progress and enterprise, had adapted and added to the old building, and it now boasted a cocktail bar and an expensive restaurant. It was a favourite evening and weekend haunt of well-to-do county folk and of professional people from Whitford and beyond. Gosford had taken Jill there for dinner once, soon after their arrival in the area, and he had hated its chrome pretentiousness.

'A good pub ruined,' he had remarked to Jill. 'Like taking an honest woman and painting her up like a tart.' And he added savagely, when he saw the bill: 'Christ. They charge bloody brothel prices too!'

Cars were already beginning to pull into the car-park, business men from Whitford, Scarby, and other towns bringing friends, clients, even an occasional wife out to the country for an expense-account lunch.

Gosford entered the smaller of the two bars and ordered a pint of draught ale from the cheerful, pretty girl on duty. As he paid, he asked: 'Is Mr Crane around? Or Mrs Crane? Either will do.'

'I will see,' said the girl. 'Who shall I tell them is asking?' She spoke with an accent, which he judged to be Swedish.

At that moment Mira Crane entered the bar, a brisk, handsome woman, dark-haired and strongly-perfumed; her bright, fixed smile topped by cold, watchful, dark-brown eyes.

'This gentleman was asking—' began the girl, but Mrs Crane interrupted her. Part of her success as a publican rested on the fact that she seldom forgot a name or a face, and she quickened the smile as she turned towards Gosford.

'Why, Chief-Inspector! How nice to see you here again. We thought you'd abandoned us!'

He murmured something about lack of time, and added: 'I was wondering if you could spare me a minute or two, Mrs Crane.'

'Well,' she said hesitating, 'we are coming up to lunch-time.'

'Just a couple of minutes,' he said.

'This is an official visit?' she asked, and he could almost hear the questions tumbling through her mind.

'Yes, it is. Where can we talk?'

She lifted a flap on the bar and showed him through to a small room at the back, half-office and half-storeroom.

'Well, what can I do for you, Chief-Inspector?' she asked pleasantly. Her tights gave a faint electric crackle as she crossed her legs and smoothed down her dress. The legs and thighs, he noted, were strong and shapely. The manner, like the smile, was part of her stock-in-trade. She dispensed a sort of sterilised sex which hinted of delicious but forbidden pleasures, like a geisha girl who is trained to stimulate but not to satisfy. And, thought Gosford, she is very good at it, if you like that sort of thing.

'Do you know a man called Pickford, Thomas Pickford?' he asked.

'Yes,' she replied immediately, 'he comes in occasionally. Usually at week-ends. He works for the Whitford Borough Council. Quite a big wheel there, I understand.'

'Does he come alone?'

'Sometimes. Usually he is with his wife, or with a friend, an architect named George Leppard.' She seemed to accept his questions without wanting a reason for them. She lit a cigarette and waited calmly for him to speak again. He sipped his beer, studying her over the rim of the glass.

'You've never seen him with anyone else?'

'A girl-friend, you mean?' Her lips parted in amusement, revealing white, even teeth. He guessed they were dentures, and for a moment his imagination played with the vision of this attractive woman lying in bed, her hair in a net, the teeth gleaming in a glass of water on the bedside table.

Mrs Crane shook her head, answering her own question. 'No. I've never seen Mr Pickford with anyone like that. It would be stupid anyway, wouldn't it? I mean, he's known here, people talk. It would be stupid.'

'But you wouldn't put it past him?'

'To have a girl-friend?' Her eyes widened. 'Mr Gosford, I wouldn't put it past any man under a hundred.'

The door opened suddenly, and a girl in the brown uniform of a waitress came in. When she saw them, she pulled back.

'Oh, sorry, Mrs Crane! I didn't know—'

'What is it, Penny?' Mrs Crane said sharply, moment-arily abandoning the smile.

'I wanted to fill the ice-bucket, Mrs Crane,' said the girl.

'Well, go ahead. Excuse us a moment, Chief-Inspector.'

The girl directed a sudden frightened glance at Gosford, and he saw how, under the make-up, her face was white and strained. Her hands trembled as she opened the ice-machine, and when she filled a scoop of ice, some of the pieces fell to the floor.

'Careful!' said Mrs Crane. She crossed to help the girl. 'What's the matter with you today? You're all thumbs!' She filled the bucket, closed the machine, and urged the girl towards the door. 'Find Mr Crane. Tell him I shall be held up for a few minutes, and ask him to check things in the kitchen.'

The girl caught Gosford's eye over the woman's shoulder, looked away quickly, and went out. The smile re-appeared as if on cue, as Mrs Crane sat down again.

'That's your problem, Chief-Inspector. When you're running a place like this, I mean. Staff. That's your main problem,' she said.

'Must be.' He was still thinking of the girl, of the startled look she had given him. 'Where do you get them from?'

'Locally—in the main. Cullington, Barton, the farms. A few from abroad, who live in. The girls are the real trouble. You train them, pay them good money, and then they up and leave you.' She patted the skirt over her thighs. 'Is there anything else I can do to help you?'

'I'm not sure,' he said.

'Has anything happened to Mr Pickford?' she asked tentatively.

'He has disappeared.'

'Oh!' She lifted an eyebrow. 'And you think he may have run off with some—some other woman?'

'No,' he said. He drank the last of his ale. 'I'm just

checking every possibility. All we know for sure is that he hasn't been seen since half-past eleven last night. His car was found abandoned in Watts Lane, a mile or so up the road.'

'Near here?' she said.

'Yes,' he said, watching her face.

'He didn't come in last night,' she said warily.

'I know that.'

'Why should he leave his car in Watts Lane?'

'I don't know.'

He waited. The smile had gone now, she was chewing her bottom lip thoughtfully, her dark eyes frowning at a faded stocklist pinned on the wall, as though she were studying it. She seemed on the point of speaking, but as the silence continued, he decided to prompt her.

'It's a very worrying business, Mrs Crane. A respectable man just doesn't disappear. We can't rule out the possibility of foul play.'

There was a touch of anxiety in her eyes as they left the stocklist and came back to him. 'Of course,' she said carefully, 'in this job you see all sorts of things. Or rather, you learn not to see them, to keep your mouth shut, if you know what I mean.'

'Yes, I imagine that would be so, Mrs Crane.'

'Mr Pickford does have an eye for the girls, I can tell you that much. I'm not saying there was any harm in it, a lot of men like to flirt. Flatters their ego, you know, you must have seen it.'

'What sort of girls did he like?'

'Young girls. Kids really. Loved to chat them up and all that. I can't say it went any further—I'm pretty sure it didn't in fact.'

'Any one girl in particular that you can recall?'

She hesitated again. 'This is very difficult for me, Mr Gosford. I have my trade to think of. If my customers got the idea that I was in the habit of talking about them— well, you see my position, don't you?'

'Whatever you tell me, Mrs Crane, will be regarded as confidential. I shan't reveal the source of my information, if it can be avoided.'

'Yes.' She considered this for a moment. 'Well, let me see—how shall I put it? I want to be fair, you understand.'

'Quite so,' he said, nodding his head gravely, playing up to her.

'Well,' she said again, lowering her voice and leaning towards him. 'I really don't know if there is anything in this or not.' He caught a gleam of malice in her eyes, and realised that she was beginning to enjoy herself. 'That girl who came in a moment ago. Penny. Penny Waites. Some weeks ago, I had occasion to reprimand her. Not for the first time, I might add. She has a tendency to be over-familiar with some of the customers. In this business, a certain amount of that sort of thing is inevitable, but I felt she was taking it too far.'

'What happened on the last occasion?'

'I went up to my bedroom for some reason. It overlooks the car-park. I looked down and saw Penny talking with one of the customers.'

'Who?'

'Mr Pickford. It was really no more than that. I mean, nothing happened. It was just—just the way of it. I couldn't hear what they were saying, but it looked—what's the word?—conspiratorial. Do you know what I mean? After a moment, she came back inside and he drove off.'

'You tackled her about it?'

'Oh, yes. I told her that she was paid to wait at table, not carry on with customers in the car-park.'

'What did she say?'

'She laughed in my face. She can be a cheeky hussy when she's a mind. If it wasn't for the fact that we just can't get the staff, I'd have sacked her long ago. And I'll say this, she's a good worker, willing, never complains about over-time. Anyway, she just laughed, said that Mr Pickford was not her type and that she didn't go in for old men.'

'You didn't say anything to Mr Pickford?'

'Oh, no. I couldn't. Come to think of it, I don't believe he's been in since that night. No, he hasn't! That's odd isn't it?'

'Does she live in?'

'Oh, no. She lives just outside the village with her aunt and uncle. They have a small farm. I blame them to some degree, especially the uncle. He's a narrow man, a rigid Methodist or some such thing—and he was too strict with her. I mean, really strict—quite Victorian in his attitude. Well, it doesn't do, does it? She was bound to break out. And in the last year or so, that's exactly what she has done. He kicked up a row when she came to work here, but she defied him, and he gave in. But he still doesn't approve. He's a strange man, very strange.'

'Do you think she could be having an affair with Tom Pickford?'

'I really don't know. She has plenty of young admirers so there's no real need for her to get tangled up with a married man twice her age. On the other hand—'

'Yes?'

'Well, I suppose it is possible. She could have been flattered by his attention—an important local man, with a bit of sophistication—and money. But I honestly don't know, it could have been no more than a flirtation.'

'Was she on duty last night?'

'Last night? No, she wasn't. It was her evening off.'

Gosford rose to his feet. 'I think, if you don't mind, I'll have a word with the young lady. Could you ask her to step in here?'

'You won't tell her that I—'

'I'll be very tactful, Mrs Crane,' he said.

She came back a minute later with a frown on her face. 'Funny,' she said, 'funny. She's gone. Made some excuse about having a headache and just cleared off! And I'm already one girl short! Really, it's too much, it really is too much!'

Penny was quite certain now that something terrible had happened to Tom and that the police would blame her for it, perhaps even arrest her and send her to prison. The presence of the policeman in Mrs Crane's office, the way he had looked at her, had frightened her, thrown her into a panic. Her one thought was to run away, to get out of the district and hide until it all blew over.

She cycled furiously to the farm and, relieved to find that her aunt and uncle were both out, she went to her room, changed into a pair of jeans and a T-shirt, and packed a few things. She took the money she had saved from its hiding place, and as she did so a thought occurred to her.

She went down to the scullery and selected a crowbar from the large wooden box in which her uncle kept his tools. Then she went back upstairs, to the main bedroom, where he slept, and from under the sagging bed she pulled out a heavy metal trunk. Breathing heavily she attacked its padlock with the crowbar. It proved to be more difficult than she'd expected and after a minute or two, with the sweat rising on her skin, she gave up.

She went to the window and looked down at the front gate and the track beyond. There was no sign of anyone coming, and with renewed determination she went back to the padlock.

This time it cracked under the leverage of the crowbar; her hand slipped as the pressure was suddenly released, and she tore her knuckles on the sharp rim of the box. Irritation and pain brought tears to her eyes and she sat back on her haunches for a moment, overcome with self-pity. The blood was bubbling up through the broken skin at the back of her hand; she licked it away and wrapped a handkerchief around the wound. The chime of the wall-clock downstairs reminded her that she had no time to waste, and she turned her attention to the trunk.

Tears, of frustration and anger this time rose to her eyes as she saw what it contained. She had expected to find a store of money, but all she could see was a collection of girlie magazines and books, with garish covers and odd ruttish titles, most of which seemed to be concerned with the theme of corporal punishment. Tucked inside one of the magazines she found a brown manilla envelope containing a number of photographs, each of which featured a young girl—she was little more than a child—in a variety of sexual positions with one and sometimes two men. In some she was wearing a school-tunic, in others she was in the nude, revealing her immature, boyish body.

Penny did not know the girl, but her uncle's heavy-jawed face seemed to leap up at her from the photographs; and she had a vague feeling that she had seen the other man also.

'You sod! You filthy old bugger!' she said, aloud and viciously. In an excess of anger she took up a handful of the magazines and threw them at the walls. She began to laugh, and seizing some more magazines and the photographs she crossed to the window, opened it, and scattered her find in all directions. The magazines dropped to the strip of garden below, leaves fluttering, to be caught up in the rose-bushes or lie on the dry, almost brown patch of lawn and the narrow gravel path. One fell into the branches of a cherry tree near the gate, where it hung like some strange fruit.

The photographs slipped and eddied in the heavy air like paper darts, and dropping slowly, landed in the garden or on the track outside the gate.

Her breasts heaving, shaking with laughter, Penny sank down on the bed. As the hysteria subsided, her eye fell on the open trunk, and she saw the money. It had been stacked under the magazines in neat bundles of £5 and £1 notes. She fell on her knees, her hands scrambled feverishly at her prize. It seemed as if there was a fortune there, hundreds of pounds, perhaps even a thousand!

Calming herself, she collected the duffle-bag from her room, and packed the money. She had to dispense with a pair of shoes and some jeans, but she tossed these aside without concern, telling herself that with her new-found wealth she could buy all the clothes she desired, new, smart clothes from the finest stores.

She strapped the bag on to the carrier of her cycle and rode away, smiling to herself as she saw the litter of magazines and photographs that lay all around. She half-wished that she could stay and see the look on her uncle's face when he saw what she had done!

When she reached the lane at the end of the track, she turned, at first, towards Whitford, but then had other thoughts. The police might be looking for her there, they would expect her to head for the station. She swung round, dismounted, and heaved the bicycle over the low dry-stone wall which fringed a field of young cabbages. Panting from this exertion, she wheeled the bicycle along the edge of the field.

A difficult walk of over a mile lay ahead of her, but she would then emerge on to the Scarby road. An eight mile ride and she would be in Scarby itself and there she could lose herself in the holiday crowds, buy some clothes, and take her choice of a dozen different destinations—London, Birmingham, perhaps even Scotland. And after that, with the fortune in the duffle-bag, there was scarcely a limit to her movements. America, she had always liked the idea of America, of Hollywood especially—and now it was within her grasp!

She played with these dreams, glowing with pleasure, as she pushed the bicycle over the dry, rutted, brown earth.

As Penny left the cabbage field behind, Gosford arrived at the farmhouse. He stared in amazement at the scene—an amazement which increased as he stooped and picked up a photograph which lay on the track at his feet.

He collected a couple of the magazines from the path, and shaking his head, tried the front door. There was no answer to his heavy knocking, and after a short wait, he walked round the back. But here again, he could get no reply.

He went back to the car and switched on the short-wave radio. The sergeant on duty, a man called Miller, answered his call.

'Sergeant, I'm out at a place called Little Chase Farm, about a mile and a half on the Whitford side of Cullington. I want you to get a man here right away.'

'Will do, sir,' answered Miller.

'And I want to talk to a girl who lives here. Her name is Penny Waites. About 18 or 19, long fair hair, about five foot three, possibly wearing a brown dress, possibly riding a bicycle. She may be heading for Whitford, for the station. Issue a description—she's to be brought in for questioning.'

'I know young Penny, sir. What's she been up to now?'

'Never mind. I want to talk to her.'

'Right, sir. I'll send Parker out to you, sir, in Panda Two. Will you be coming in yourself, sir?'

'As soon as Parker gets here.'

'Only there's a fellow waiting to see you. Been here the last half-hour. Name of Birk.'

'What does he want?'

'Something about tigers, sir.'

'Tigers?' asked Gosford, incredulously.

'That's right, sir.' From his tone, the phlegmatic Miller might have been talking about a lost dog. He showed no surprise. 'I couldn't make head or tail of it. So he said he'd wait and talk to the top man.'

'Well, tell him that while I'm away, you're the top man. And if he still won't explain, he'll just have to go on waiting.'

While he waited for P.C. Parker to arrive, Gosford collected up all the magazines, books and photographs he could find, then he sat in the car and browsed through them. Once, for a short period, he had been a member of the Vice Squad in Sunderland, and this was familiar territory to him. He had no taste for pornography himself and his feelings veered between pity for the people who seemed to need its mechanical stimulus, and dislike of the people who peddled the dreary merchandise.

Nevertheless, as he heard the police car pull up behind him, he closed the magazine in his hands, and hid it, with the others, under a blanket on the back seat; and when young Parker thrust his bearded, smiling face in the car window to greet him, Gosford was annoyed to feel a guilty blush glowing in his cheeks. To cover his irritation at this stupidity, he spoke curtly to the constable, unjustly berating him for taking so long to get to the farmhouse.

On his way back to Whitford, Gosford decided to call in at his home for a sandwich.

'You need more than that,' Jill said. 'You had no breakfast.'

'No time, lovey. There's a fellow waiting to see me.'

'Then he'll have to wait a bit longer. I'll do you an omelette,' she said firmly.

She watched him while he ate, her face cradled in her hands. 'Did you find Tom Pickford?'

'No. Not yet.'

'Something's happened. I can tell by your look.'

He pushed the plate away, stood up, and gave a deep sigh. 'Everything's happened! It's been quite a morning.'

'Well, you're always complaining that things are too quiet.'

73

'I know. But this is ridiculous!' He told her about Penny, and his discovery of the magazines and photographs. 'I think the whole place has gone crazy!' he added. 'Stark, staring mad! First, Tom Pickford disappears into thin air. Then the girl. Then someone decides to decorate their front-garden with a load of porn. And finally some nut turns up at the nick and says he wants to talk to me about tigers!'

'Tigers? You-have-to-be-joking!' she said, emphasising each word.

'Tigers,' he said solemnly.

CHAPTER FIVE

1

When Gosford arrived back at his office, David Birk had been gone for over an hour.

'Said he couldn't wait any longer, sir,' said Sergeant Miller. 'But he left this note for you.' He handed a folded sheet of paper across the counter. By this time, Gosford's mood was one of resignation to events; he had decided that this was one of those days on which the extraordinary happens with such frequency that it becomes almost commonplace. He read the note with no visible sign of emotion.

'To Chief-Inspector Gosford. I am going from here to the District Office of the Forestry Commission to warn them of a discovery I made this morning. You can contact me there, or later at my house, Stowcroft, off the Upper Moor Road. I hope you will be less sceptical than your sergeant. I have good reason to believe that two tigers have escaped into Whitford forest. They are probably from some zoo or circus and I suggest that you contact the owner or keeper immediately. The animals would not be adapted to conditions in the forest and might well respond to someone with whom they are familiar. I doubt if they present any immediate danger to humans, but clearly, every precaution ought to be taken. Visitors should be warned to stay clear of the forest, the nearby roads, and the higher moors, and local farmers should likewise be alerted.

David Birk

The handwriting was clear and strong, underlining the rather peremptory tone of the note itself. Gosford had seen many letters from cranks, but this was unlike any of them, it had a different feel to it. He glanced at the sergeant.

'Did you read this?'

'Yes, sir.'

'Did you treat him like a nut-case?'

'No, sir. I was very polite. I pointed out that you didn't get two tigers escaping every day. They'd be missed, the alarm bells would be ringing in all directions. But we'd heard nothing, not a whisper. Nor had the press, because they'd have come out with headlines a mile high. I checked with the zoo at Scarby and they nearly blew the phone laughing. They've got one tiger, and he's safely locked up. I checked with that small safari park out beyond Kingsby— they've never even owned a tiger. We've had one circus visit the area in the last month—again, no tigers.'

'There's a man called Aspinall who keeps tigers on his estate near Canterbury. Anyone like that up here?'

'No, sir.'

'You're certain?'

'Dead certain.'

Gosford tapped the note with his finger. 'This fellow seems to know what he's talking about. Doesn't sound like a crank. What's he like?'

'Doesn't look like a crank either, sir. On the short side, actually, but rugged, nose a bit squashed as if it had been broken some time. Very sharp bright blue eyes—first thing you notice about him almost. Knocked around a bit, I'd say. Odd manner, too. Sort of detached. As though he was telling us all this as a favour, wanted nothing to do with it himself.'

'How old?'

'Between 40 and 45, I'd guess.'

'How long has he lived in the area?'

'I believe he came from here originally. There was a Birk family lived up beyond Costwicke years ago. He took the house on Upper Moor about a year back.'

'What does he do for a living?'

76

'No idea, sir. Must have private means of some sort.'

'Has he got any friends—local people?'

'Not that I've heard. Keeps himself to himself.'

At that moment the telephone rang. It was Peter Street, the District Officer of the Forestry Commission, a quiet, capable composed Devonian, not given to shows of temperament. But there was an agitated note in his soft voice as he told Gosford of his encounter with David Birk.

'He just walked into my office. Said there were a couple of bloody tigers loose in my forest! He said he'd—'

Gosford cut him short. 'Is he there with you?'

'No. Not now.'

'Where the hell is he?'

'He just walked out. Delivered the message and went. Is he crazy?'

'I don't know,' said Gosford carefully.

'Have any tigers got out?'

'Not that we know of.'

'Then the fellow must be crazy. What do you want me to do?'

'Have you been up in the forest today?'

'Not today. But I've had men working up there—they've reported nothing. Oh, come on, Charlie—you don't believe this cock-and-bull story?'

'I don't think I believe it, Peter. But I can't ignore it either.' Gosford considered the situation for a moment, turning Birk's note in his hand. 'Could you get a few of your men to do a reccy in the forest?'

'Jesus!' said Street, 'do you realise what you're asking? There's sixty thousand acres of forest, not to mention another twenty thousand acres of private woodlands. It would take days to cover! And what do I tell my chaps anyhow? I want you to come tiger-hunting with me? Can you see their faces? And suppose the tigers are there and we find them? What do we do? Stroke them until they purr, call them Pretty Puss, Pretty Kitty? Bring 'em back alive?'

'Sorry,' said Gosford.

'Tell you what,' Street said, more reasonably. 'Birk said he'd found tracks up at the N.E. corner in the older part of the forest—and he said he'd seen the remains of a deer they'd pulled down. I'll go up there and check.'

'No!' Gosford was surprised by the sharpness of his own response. He had suddenly thought of Tom Pickford. 'Look, Peter,' he continued, 'I don't think we should panic, but we can't take chances either. I'll put on a thorough check this end. While I'm doing that, can you quietly close the forest trails?'

'There's a lot of people who are already out there. Too late to stop them.'

'Get them out if you can. But the main thing is to stop fresh walkers going in!'

'What the devil shall I tell them?'

'Post notices saying the trails are closed because of the fire-risk. That's reasonable with the weather we've been having.'

'That'll still leave a hell of a lot of people. At this time of the year they come in hundreds—park their cars on the edge of the forest and bring out the picnics.'

'I'll get a police car up there on patrol.'

'You'll need more than one.'

'I'll send more than one then! It's probably a false alarm, Peter, but better safe than sorry. As soon as I can give you the all-clear, I will. And for Christ's sake, keep this to yourself. We don't want a bloody panic on our hands!'

As Gosford hung up, he caught Miller's questioning eye, and as much because of his own uncertainty as for anything else, he reacted angrily. 'All right, man!' he snapped, 'you heard me. I want two patrol cars sent up to the forest roads. They're to keep the cars moving, keep picnickers out of the forest. And then I want you to check all the zoos and all the circuses, not just around here, but within a hundred miles. I want to know if any tigers were in transit through this area yesterday. Right?'

'Right, sir,' said Miller promptly.

'Tell the men in the cars that we're doing this because of the danger of fire. If this gets out, if the press or anyone else gets to know of it and I find you're responsible, I'll have your guts for garters. Clear?'

As Miller went out, Gosford reached out for the telephone and asked the girl on the switchboard to connect him to County headquarters in Scarby, to the Deputy Chief Constable, Gordon Hale. But as he spoke he changed his mind, told her not to bother, and dropped the receiver down on its cradle. Hale was a man he tried to avoid if at all possible. He virtually ran the County force—the Chief Constable was little more than a figurehead—and with him there was never any debate, no way of talking over a problem. He issued the orders, took the decisions, and expected them to be followed to the letter. Behind his back the men referred to Hale as the Fuehrer; he knew of this and, oddly enough, drew a certain satisfaction from the description.

How the hell, thought Gosford, can I tell Hale that we're chasing a couple of tigers that may not even exist? He could hear the man's icy reaction: 'Facts, man, facts. When you've got the facts, I'll listen!' And Gosford knew that he wouldn't argue. He was just like all the others, he had no respect for the man but he played up to him, laughed at the right moments, said all the right things, swallowed his pride. He rationalised his attitude, but in his heart he knew he was weakly following the path of expediency, and it made him bitter, ashamed, resentful.

He sat at the desk, tapping a pencil against his hand. How was it possible that two tigers could escape into the English countryside and not be missed? Someone, somewhere, would surely have reported the matter to the police, raised the alarm? It was this point, more than any other, that worried him. God, he thought, if it is a hoax, I'll be the laughing-stock of the county.

He shifted uneasily in his chair. The windows were open, but it was stifling in the little office, the air seemed to be without life or movement. A pearl of sweat splashed from his forehead on to the desk; he wiped it away, and swabbed at the moisture on his face and neck with a couple of tissues.

The atmosphere depressed his spirits still further, and he had to force his thoughts back to Tom Pickford. If only they could lay their hands on that damned waitress! She was probably the only one who could tell the truth about what had happened last night, give him some clue to Pickford's whereabouts. This, in turn, reminded him of his talk with George Leppard. He drew a pad from a drawer and put the words *Follow Up* at the top of a blank sheet. Beneath this he wrote: *George Leppard. Business connection with T. Pickford. Borough Council contracts? Check.*

He put the pad back in the drawer, and locked it. That is something for another day, he told himself. I shan't forget you, Mr Leppard. Feeling a little better for this, he pushed back his chair and went through to the outer office.

'Where's Sergeant Miller?' he asked the policeman on duty.

The policeman motioned towards a door behind him. 'In the charge-room, sir. On the telephone. Shall I get him?'

'No,' said Gosford. 'When he's finished, tell him that I'm going up to Stowcroft to see Mr Birk. Tell him to contact me there if anything comes up.' He turned back at the door. 'Oh—and ring my wife. I was taking her out for a Chinese meal tonight. Tell her something's come up, I doubt if I'll be able to make it. Then hang up before she blows your ear off!'

'I'll do that, sir,' said the policeman with a grin.

There was no relief in the air outside. Gosford felt as though a hot, damp hand lay on his body; his whole skin seemed to be sticky with moisture. Above him, the sun gleamed sullenly, struggling with banks of cloud which had drifted in from the west. Black-edged with the threat of storm, gathering strength with every moment, they hung over the town, sapping it of life and vitality.

2

Towards the middle of the afternoon Ranee, the tigress, stirred and woke. She too could feel the change, the heaviness, in the atmosphere; under the striped fur her flesh seemed to be baking in the heat.

She rose and stretched herself, then padded down to the beck and plunged her paws into the clear water. Jays and wood-pigeons flew up at her approach, protesting at the intrusion, and she lifted her head to spit back a reply. She felt the weight of the cubs within her, and lay down in the stream with her head resting in the water, sucking its coolness up into her body.

A few moments later, the tiger came in search of her. He was still unsure of this place, and of himself; the freedom was exhilarating but somehow disturbing also, there was too much that was unknown and strange. He sensed the greater confidence and resourcefulness of the tigress and had come to rely upon it.

Ranee growled as Mohan appeared, warning him off, and he gave a low resentful growl in reply. But he did not dare challenge her, nor did he approach too close, for he knew that she was near her time and that her only concern was to protect the unborn cubs. He eyed her warily for a moment before splashing into the beck to quench his thirst. The touch of the cool liquid on his tongue and throat seemed to wash away his resentment and turning over on his back, he splashed and rolled around in the water; the freshness, the gentle pressure of the under-water stones on his body filled him with sensual pleasure. Ranee turned her head towards him and watched as he frolicked in the water, but she made no attempt to join in.

She tensed suddenly and uttered a low, throaty growl of warning. Mohan rose upright and shook himself, scattering drops of water in all directions, but he stiffened as Ranee growled again, and stood listening. The tigress was looking across the stream towards a fold in the hilly moorland beyond. She could see no movement, but her keen ear had picked up a strange sound. Followed by the tiger, she padded across to the other side of the stream and slid silently into the cover of the bracken, her head turned towards the slope.

They heard the sound again, closer this time, a low, drawn-out baa-baa, and then two black-faced sheep emerged on to the summit of the slope. Peering mournfully down, as if bewildered by the unfamiliar animal sounds coming from below, they stood silhouetted against the darkened sky like the advance scouts of an army, bleating uneasily.

The tigress had no experience of such animals, but she knew that she need have no fear of them. She felt no urge to attack, she had no desperate longing for food, she simply wanted to rest and enjoy the cool water. What concerned her was a possible invasion of what she considered to be her territory; as long as these creatures kept their distance she was content to leave them.

But the tiger had other ideas. He was in the mood for sport, and, stronger than this, he felt the need to demonstrate his masculine strength and cunning not only to these intruders but to the tigress also.

Under cover of the bracken and ling he moved silently towards the sheep, which by now had been joined by a half-dozen others. They huddled together fearfully, as if they sensed a threat but were uncertain of its real meaning. All they could see was a faint quivering of the top-most fronds of the bracken, a movement on the surface of the moor which seemed to be coming towards them in a slow, straight, silent line.

'Go-back! Go-back! Go-back!'

The silence was shattered as a brace of Red Grouse, disturbed by the advancing tiger, rose on frightened wings, uttering their strangely-apt call. The air quivered as dozens of other birds—Golden Plover, Lapwing, Curlews, Meadow Pipits—fluttered up from their secret places on the moor. The startled sheep turned and disappeared over the slope, moving off in a clumsy gallop.

Mohan abandoned his concealment and lifting his head towards the circling birds, emptied his lungs in a threatening roar. He repeated it three times, and with each ritual call, he felt the blood quicken in his veins, the urge to kill quiver in his throat. An enormous sense of power and strength surged through his body and he bounded forward.

Beyond the rise the ground levelled out, and here the bracken and heather had given way to a small clearing lightly-covered with Mat-grass and patches of the darker green Bog-rush. Here and there, tiny yellow and white flowers lifted their heads, standing out against the green background like stars.

The sheep, terrified by those stupendous roars, were running in all directions, turning this way and that, as if they were hemmed in by an invisible fence which blocked their escape. Mohan brought down an ewe almost casually, in passing; the great paw smashed downwards, crushing the skull to a bloody pulp.

The tiger hardly paused. Excited by the scent of blood, revelling in his own power, he attacked the other sheep in turn, in an orgy of wanton destruction. The last one, an old ram, made a desperate effort to reach the cover of the bracken beyond the clearing, but Mohan headed him off. The ram turned and began to gallop off in the other direction, but Mohan headed him again. It was as though he was deliberately postponing the moment of execution, enjoying the helpless terror of his victim.

The ram twisted and circled, only to be confronted at each point by the savage, striped face of his enemy; and then, quite suddenly, he halted. Flanks heaving, he braced himself, horns thrust forward, his mild, frightened eyes watching the tiger.

Mohan circled his quarry for a few moments as though amused by this pathetic show of defiance; then he stopped a yard or so in front of the ram, staring into the black grey-muzzled face with a look of arrogant contempt. With a sound that seemed almost like a sigh, the ram lowered his head and charged, butting the astonished tiger full in the face with all the force he could muster. Mohan fell back a half-pace, shook his great head in surprise, and then he sprang. The ram went down beneath the crushing weight, and as it fell the tiger clapped a paw to either side of the head, and sank his teeth into the soft throat.

Ranee was lying in the stream when Mohan came back from the scene of carnage, carrying the dead ram in his mouth like a trophy. As he crossed, a trickle of blood reddened the water. He paused momentarily, as if expecting her to challenge him for his prize, but she did not even lift her head.

3

Toby Waites and his wife had been into Whitford to see a member of the chapel, an old lady who was confined to her cottage with arthritis. Toby was a leading figure in the Church of the True Gospel, a sect which had been founded at the end of the 19th century by a fiery local evangelist whose teachings were based on the formula that every word in the Bible was literal truth which had to be accepted and followed without question. In recent years the sect had declined; only about thirty elderly members now attended the little tin-roofed chapel on the outskirts of Whitford. It was largely the single-minded dedication of Toby and his wife, Edith, that kept the organisation going.

They had taken the sick member, a Mrs Jarvis, some

eggs and a bunch of flowers, and prayed at her bedside. The old lady thanked them with tears in her eyes. 'May the good Lord bless you for your kindness,' she said.

'You are one of the flock, Sister Jarvis,' replied Toby simply. He felt a real affection and concern for the members of his little Church, the visit was an act of genuine thoughtfulness. Both Toby and his wife drew a deep satisfaction from their association with the True Gospellers, as they were called; they had developed the ability to switch off their private lives when involved in Church affairs, they became different, kindly dedicated people who gave the impression of being happily united in the pursuit of God's work.

But now they were clothed in their private rather than public personalities, and sat in silence as Toby drove homewards in the old Triumph-Herald. She was thinking of the previous night, of all the other times, of the awful weight of sin that lay on the house. Apart from the True Gospellers, it was the only thing she had thought about for years.

She had first come upon Toby and her niece years ago, when Penny was still a schoolgirl, seen them thrashing around together in the long grass of the Old Meadow, and watched in shock and disbelief, wondering why the cries of horror were frozen in her throat. She had turned and stumbled away, and as she did so, the vomit rose in her mouth and spewed down her dress.

She had never spoken to either of them about that incident or the others, and this added to the weight of guilt. She lived in terror that others might learn the secret, that the affair would become a matter of public gossip. Just the thought of the shame that would follow turned her blood to ice. How could she face the pity of her neighbours, of the congregation at the Chapel?

Once, timidly, she had suggested that the girl should be sent away but her husband opposed it so fiercely that she had retreated instantly. She was afraid of him, that was the bitter truth; afraid of his physical strength, of the violent, sexual side to his nature which had remained concealed during their two years of courtship and which he had released, like some animal, on their wedding night, and so many times afterwards.

Sometimes, as she saw his kindness to members of the Church of the True Gospel, or heard him preach from the little wooden pulpit with such eloquence and sincerity, she could hardly believe that he was the same man. It seemed that her husband was possessed both by God and the Devil, that in his thick body good and evil were forever locked in their timeless struggle; and there were times when she rebuked herself for hating him, telling herself that she should have found the strength to bring him back to God, to free him of sin.

It was too late for that now. The hate had taken hold like a malignant inner growth and could not be checked. Worst of all, there was no one she could talk to about it, not even God, especially not God.

If anyone had told Toby that his wife hated him, he would have laughed in disbelief. To him, this grey-faced, shapeless, melancholy woman was a complete negative, as incapable of generating the fire necessary to sustain an emotion as powerful as hate, as she was of physical passion. Over the years his attitude to her had declined from indifference to contempt. She was the daughter of a dale shepherd, and he had once told her that she had been so long around sheep that she had grown like one.

He was thinking of Penny, feeling the need of her again. He had forgotten his resolve to send her away, forgotten the prickings of conscience. His one thought now was to plan some way in which he could spend time with the girl, perhaps take her off somewhere for a day or so. He was tired and dissatisfied with these quick, night-time swoops on her room, he wanted time to savour her, there was so much he longed to do to that lithe young body, so many games to play, so many humiliations to be avenged. He would pay her well, he had the money, and he knew that it spoke a language she seemed to understand.

He was surprised to see the police-car outside the farmhouse and a bearded police-constable lounging on the grass in the shade of the cherry-tree. The constable rose languidly to his feet as the Triumph-Herald drew up, tapped his pipe out against the bole of the tree, brushed spikes of dead grass from his uniform.

'Good afternoon, sir,' he said as the couple approached.

'Afternoon, constable, anything wrong?' Toby cocked his head to one side, the broad, red face creased in a smile of greeting, the deep voice easy, affable, but slightly patronising. Edith hovered in the background, an indistinct figure in the thick shadow of her husband.

'Mr Waites?' asked Parker.

'Yes, yes.' Toby allowed a tiny note of irritation to edge into his voice; he was a well-known local figure, he expected to be recognised even by this bearded young man.

'Police-Constable Parker, sir, from Whitford. Sorry to trouble you, but have you any idea where we might find your niece, Miss Penny Waites?'

A tiny thrill of apprehension trembled in Toby's mind, like the touch of an icy finger. Edith began to speak, but he cut her off quickly, his tone still smooth with affability. 'Edith, my dear, why don't you go in to the house? I'd like a cup of tea and I'm sure the constable won't say no to one.' He smiled and patted her arm.

She went off immediately, head slightly down, walking with small, quick steps. As she put the key into the lock she turned briefly to glance back at Parker, and then she went inside, leaving the front-door ajar.

'Now, constable, what do you want with my niece?' asked Toby. He folded his arms and gave Miller a half-stern, half-condescending look, the genial patriarch indicating that he was prepared to spare this bearded youth a little of his precious time.

'Chief-Inspector Gosford is anxious to speak to her, Mr

Waites. Have you any idea where she is?'

'Don't you think you'd better tell me what this is about? I'm the girl's guardian. I think I have the right to know why your Chief-Inspector should wish to speak with her. She is still a child, under my roof and my care.'

'You had better speak to Mr Gosford about that, sir. He would like to see you, in any case.'

'I shall be delighted to meet the Chief-Inspector at any time,' said Toby, in a tone which suggested that such an arrangement would be more in keeping with his status in the community than this discussion with a young man just out of the egg. 'As for Penny, she is at her employment, I should hope.'

'No, sir. Apparently she left suddenly, without warning. Chief-Inspector Gosford was there at the time—around 12.30—he wanted to talk with her. But she can't be found.' Parker was pleased to see an uncertain, puzzled look appear in Waites' dark eyes. That's knocked a bit of the pomposity out of you, he thought, with a certain relish.

'I don't understand.'

'Any idea where she might be, sir?'

'None.' Toby glanced towards the house. 'Perhaps she came home for some reason.'

'I've been here almost an hour—I've seen no sign of her.'

The finger-tip touch of apprehension had now become a cold hand. Why should Penny have run off? Where did the police come into it? Why were they so anxious to see her and why did they want to see him? Where had the girl gone? The questions pounded through his head, all he could do was stare blankly at the policeman, his mouth half-open, the thick lips moist. Parker was surprised by the change in the big man, even a little sorry for him now.

'I shouldn't worry, sir,' he said. 'She won't have gone far, I'm sure.'

'Yes, yes.' Toby relaxed as the spasm of terror passed. There could be a dozen reasonable explanations of what had happened, it was ridiculous to panic. His wife came out of the house, a thoughtful look on her face, and he said: 'How's that tea coming along, my dear?'

She ignored the question. 'Penny's gone,' she said, and Parker could have sworn that there was a touch of something like triumph or pleasure in the way she spoke.

'What do you mean?' said Toby roughly.

'I just looked into her room. She's taken a bag and some of her best clothes.'

'Did she leave a note?' asked Parker.

'Nothing,' said Edith, still watching her husband's face. There was an odd tension between them which puzzled Parker.

'Well, sir,' he said, 'I'll be getting back. If she should show up, would you let us know. I expect the Chief-Inspector will call you before the day is out.'

Neither of them seemed to be listening. He shrugged, walked back to the car, and started the engine. As he reversed, he saw the man hurry into the house.

Toby pounded up the narrow, creaking stairs and flung open the door to Penny's bedroom with a force that sent it crashing back against the wall, bringing a shower of flakes down from the faded distemper of the ceiling. The brown, waitress uniform lay on the floor with a jumble of other things, the top-drawer of the dressing-table was open and empty, the row of creams and make-up had gone.

'I think you should take a look in our bedroom too.' Edith's voice was flat and expressionless. Toby stumbled over a pair of Penny's long suede boots as he turned quickly and pushed past his wife.

His first reaction when he saw the open trunk was of disbelief. He crouched beside it and scrabbled through the few magazines which Penny had left inside, his breath forcing its way through his teeth in short, desperate bursts.

He sat back on his haunches, and Edith was surprised to see tears glinting in his deep-set eyes. When he spoke it was in an anguished, almost inaudible whisper: '£2,000! Almost £2,000! She's taken it, she's taken every penny!'

He picked up the crowbar and pulled himself to his feet. He stood for a moment, his head rolling from side to side on the thick neck, his red cheeks twitching, and then with a cry of anger he brought the crowbar down on the bed's wooden headrest, splintering it to pieces. He staggered around the room like a madman, hitting out at any object in his path. Plaster ornaments, framed texts, the clock, the old mahogany-framed mirror, the shelf filled with religious books—all went down under his fury, to lie shattered on the floor. Each blow was underlined by a roar of fury.

Whirling round, he hurled the crowbar through the window, and as the glass crashed to the garden below, he sank exhausted on the bed.

Edith had not moved from the doorway. In a low voice she said, 'I didn't know we had that amount of money.'

'We?' he muttered without looking up. 'We? It's mine, I sweated for it!'

'I mean, you didn't tell me about it!'

'I don't tell you everything!'

Two thousand pounds, she thought bitterly. It was a sum her mind could hardly comprehend. She thought of the shabby curtains, the worn clothes which she struggled to repair and keep neat for chapel meetings, the dozen and one things she needed, the long years of drudgery and meanness. Whenever she had summoned the courage to ask him for a little extra money he had preached at her, extolling the virtues of thrift, warning her of the sin of extravagance. And all the time he had this money—this fortune!—hidden away.

Aloud, she said, 'Leave her go, Toby. It don't matter, it's for the best. Leave her go.'

'Leave her go! You're out of your mind! She's a thief! We took her in, gave her a home, looked after her—'

'It was our Christian duty.'

'Aye. And she repays it by robbing me!' He stood up. 'I'm going after her. She won't be far. I'll find her before the police get her, and drag her back by the hair of her head!' He crossed to the door. 'You clear this mess up.'

'What about the—books?' She hesitated over the word.

'Burn 'em,' he said savagely. 'That ought to please you.'

'I couldn't,' she said, with a shudder, 'I couldn't touch them.'

'All right!' he shouted. 'All right! And don't stand there looking at me like a lame cow! They're not mine, you don't think they're mine, do you? I've been collecting them—evidence—for our campaign. I was going to give them to the police, demand that they take action against the people who peddle this filth. There are bookshops in Whitford and Scarby—'

His voice was beginning to take on the rolling, pulpit-note of censure which she knew so well, but there was something in her manner which checked and frightened him. In a softer, placatory voice he continued: 'That money. Maybe I should have told you. But I was saving it for us, for the future. It's been hard for you, Edith, don't think I haven't realised that. Perhaps I—well, never mind. I'll find Penny, I'll get the money back, and then I'll send her packing. She was born in sin and wickedness, and it's there still, deep in her soul. We've done all we can do. We'll have no further part of her.'

She shrank away as he put a hand on her shoulder, the disgust rising in her throat. As he spoke she could see one of the magazines on the bed, its lurid cover mocking her.

'Everything will work out,' he said, 'you'll see.'

She followed him downstairs and watched from the doorway as he drove off. For the first time in years, he even lifted a hand in farewell and smiled at her! She was a slow-thinking woman, she had still not quite understood what had happened or its full significance, and she stood in the shadowed porch for a long time, trying to make some order of the thoughts which churned through her mind. A black-and-white kitten, whom Toby would not allow into the house, rubbed itself against her legs, mewing plaintively;

she picked it up and held it against her thin breast, finding an obscure comfort in the purring warmth of the little creature.

She sensed, if only vaguely, that what had happened in the past hour or so held some deep significance for her life, that it was not something which would pass and be forgotten; and, slowly, a single thought began to emerge from the whirling mass in her head, and take on a stronger shape. The one thing she had left, the only thing of any value, was her respectability. It was to preserve this that she had suffered for so many years, bearing in silence the weight of her husband's sin. But if the girl were to leave, and leave for good, that suffering would not have been in vain. The secret could be buried, if not forgotten, the threat of exposure, and the shame which must follow, would vanish. Her husband would not change, she knew that, but the basic temptation would be removed, at least; she could continue to put on her public face in Chapel or in the village shop. That had become second nature, it would be no hardship.

She went through to the kitchen, opened a small tin of salmon and put it down for the kitten. It was an extravagance which would have enraged Toby, but as the kitten gulped hungrily at the fish she found herself smiling, wishing her husband were there to witness this tiny gesture of defiance. And wistfully, as she watched, she envied the kitten its evident happiness. Its needs were so simple, it knew nothing of the burdens that lay upon the human soul!

A frown darkened her face. There was a danger that she had not considered—suppose Toby found the girl and simply brought her back to the house? He was like wax in her hands, she might simply give him back the money and persuade him to say nothing about the theft. Well, she thought grimly, there is one way to stop that!

She went to the telephone and called the Whitford police station. In a low, shocked voice she reported that a large sum of money had been stolen from the house and—though she could not be completely certain—it seemed probable that the culprit was her niece, Penny. She added, for good measure, that the thief had also done considerable damage to the bedroom. She felt rather proud of this last touch. People would be that much more horrified by the girl's ingratitude towards an aunt and uncle who had given her nothing but kindness!

The police told her that a C.I.D. officer would come out as soon as possible, and that in the meantime, nothing in the room should be touched; but in spite of this injunction and her own distaste, she went to the bedroom and gathered up the books and magazines. Even the feel of the paper seemed to burn her skin and it was with relief that she carried the stuff to an outhouse and covered it from view under a mound of hay.

It was not until this task was completed that she began to have doubts. She was not a clever or quick-witted woman, the police had ways of finding out the truth. If they came to the house to investigate the theft, what more would they discover?

She knelt by the settee in the living-room and asked God for guidance and forgiveness. The kitten came to her again, and she held it close, her eyes closed, her lips moving, and its rhythmic purring seemed to accompany her, like a harmony. But, strangely, although she prayed for quite a long time, it brought her little comfort.

4

At about the time that Edith Waites was down on her knees, a certain Mrs Kershaw was tapping gently at the door of an upstairs room in her neat house on the outskirts of Wetherstone. During the summer months, Mrs Kershaw earned herself a little much-needed extra money by taking in the occasional paying-guest, usually on a bed-and-breakfast basis. She had never experienced any difficulty with her visitors, mainly because she was careful in her selection of them; if anyone came to the door of whom she was the least bit doubtful, she always made an excuse about the rooms being full and sent them politely on their way. She was quite sure that it was her care in this respect that had given her such a good name.

Unfortunately, while she had been out shopping that morning, her husband had let a room to a man called Davin. It was unusual for a casual guest to book in so early—normally people arrived in the late afternoon or early morning—but this man had told Mr Kershaw that he'd been travelling all night, and although he only wanted the room for a few hours he was quite prepared to pay the full rate. This apart he had said very little, simply retired to the room where, presumably, he had gone to sleep.

Mrs Kershaw was curious and a little puzzled about him. There had been a time when her husband had very nearly let the best front room to a pair of hippy characters, a boy and a girl, so identical in appearance that it was hard to tell which was which. Moreover, although they wished to share a room, the girl wore no wedding-ring and Mrs Kershaw was certain that they were not man and wife. Only her providential arrival on the doorstep at the crucial moment had prevented her husband from taking them in. 'I've nothing against them,' she had told him afterwards, 'nothing at all. If they want to go around like that, that's their affair. But I don't want them in my house.' Ever since this incident she had mistrusted her husband's judgment.

It was for this reason that she was knocking upon the door of Mr Davin's room. She intended, under the guise of asking if he would like a cup of tea, to take a good look at the man. If necessary, she was quite prepared to tell him that her husband had made a mistake and that the room was required for other guests.

94

There was no response to her initial knocking, and she repeated it, more firmly this time, and called his name. It was then that she caught the first faint whiff of gas. She frowned and shook the handle of the door: 'Mr Davin! Mr Davin! Are you there?'

She called her husband to bring the spare key and he came at last, with his usual, exasperating slowness, trudging up the stairs as though nothing were amiss. Seizing the key, she turned it in the lock, but the door was blocked on the inside and would not open.

'Gas!' she said. 'Gas! Can't you smell it?'

He bent down and sniffed by the keyhole, then looked at her in alarm, his lethargy gone. He was a big man, a former farm-worker, and pushing her aside he put his shoulder to the door. There was a slight tearing sound as it gave way and he saw that it had been sealed along the edges, and wedged with a chest-of-drawers. At the same time a wave of gas, acrid and sickening, surged through the opening.

Mrs Kershaw was seldom lost for words but she stood in horrified silence by the banister-rail as her husband hurried to the bathroom. He came back with one of her best, new, candy-striped towels, and as he squeezed it between his hands, streams of water poured on to the fitted carpet.

'Keep back, mother!' he said sharply and pushed her further away, to the top of the stairs. He tied the towel around his nose and mouth and applied himself once more to the problem of the door. It gave way gradually as the obstruction behind it was forced back and eventually he was able to squeeze through.

The gas was hissing angrily from the fitted heater in the fireplace, the air so sharp and harsh that it burned his eyes. A glance showed him that the windows were sealed with Scotch-tape; he seized a chair and smashed at the glass, then coughing under the cover of the towel, he turned off the gas-tap.

Mr Davin was lying on his back on the floor, his head on a pillow near the heater. Beside him there was an album of some sort, open at a page filled with photographs and press-cuttings. Mr Kershaw kicked this aside and picked up the unconscious man, just as he'd been taught in 1943 as a young auxiliary in the war-time Fire Brigade. The towel slipped from his face as he staggered, spluttering and choking, from the room.

He carried Davin downstairs and laid him on the settee in the living-room. His wife watched in horror, still silent.

'Open all the windows!' he shouted. 'And the front-door. Hurry, mother, hurry!' It occurred to her later that it was only the second time in their 34 years of marriage that her husband had raised his voice to her, but later she was to tell her friends of it with pleasure, proud of the way he had taken command, of his calm and courage.

Neighbours, aroused by the noise of the broken windows, were already converging on the house. An ambulance was summoned by telephone but Kershaw had seen three dead men in his lifetime and he knew that it was too late, a view that was confirmed by the ambulance-driver.

Later, when the air had cleared, the police went in to check the dead man's room. It did not take long. A canvas hold-all containing a couple of shirts, some underclothes, and a small toilet bag stood by the bed; an empty half-bottle of Bell's whisky lay in the waste-bin; three £1 notes, the cost of the room, had been placed under an ashtray. There were no personal papers or documents, either on Davin or among his effects. The album was the one thing which gave the police an indication of the man's identity and background.

It was a record going back over twenty years, page after page of yellowing clippings, programmes, faded photographs, and letters. The first photograph in the book showed Davin, as a much younger man; wearing a flamboyant, military-style outfit, and smiling at the camera, he was standing in a cage with his back turned towards two snarling tigers.

Underneath the photograph, in bold type, was the caption: THE GREAT DAVINO AND HIS ROYAL BENGAL TIGERS.

CHAPTER SIX

1

Penny Waites reached Scarby shortly after 3.30 p.m., free-wheeling with relief down the long, slow gradient which led from the moors to the narrow, coastal plain. The long haul over the fields and the painful climb up the steep hills had exhausted her; her legs throbbed with fatigue, the T-shirt she wore was soaked with sweat and clung to her flesh like a damp, second skin. But, most of all, she was frightened. On the long journey, with time to think, the realisation of what she had done grew heavier with each revolution of the pedals, overwhelming her former sense of confidence. At each bend she expected to find a police-car waiting, in every village she passed she imagined curious eyes at the windows, recording and reporting her movements.

She abandoned the bicycle at the back of Sainsbury's supermarket, in one of the racks provided for shoppers, and shouldering her duffle-bag, made her way along the busy High Street to the railway station. She felt easier now; a freshening breeze was blowing in from the sea, and the crowds of holiday-makers provided her with a cover beneath which she could move safely, anonymously.

A train, which would connect with the London service at Leeds, was due to leave in just over an hour; she bought a through-ticket, one-way, and went to the buffet to get a drink and some sandwiches.

Penny had never had much luck in her life and that unpredictable lady did not favour her now. Had she stayed in the buffet, she would probably have caught her train safely and got clear away to London, where the possibility of finding her would have been remote. But as she stood sipping her tea at one of the narrow, Formica-topped bars, she became aware of a trickling warmth between her thighs and realised, with horror, that her monthly period had begun. It was two or three days early, she was sure of that, and she was certainly not prepared.

Moving with great care, she left the station and went in search of a chemist's shop. With each step she could feel the blood soaking into her underwear, but she dare not hurry for fear of making the flow worse. At last she found what she was looking for—a Boots store, on the opposite side of the road—but the traffic was flowing too heavily for her to cross and she was forced to go twenty yards further down to a pedestrian crossing.

It was a double misfortune for Penny that a certain Woman Police-Constable, Iris Crampton, happened to be on duty in Scarby High Street that afternoon. W.P.C. Crampton had just been into local police headquarters to report on some routine matter, and while there she learned that the Whitford police were anxious to find and inter-view a Miss Penny Waites. She had no need to study the official description for although she was three or four years older than Penny, they had more or less grown up to-gether, and attended the same village school in Cullington as young girls. They had gone in different directions and to different schools after that, but she often visited old friends in the village and had seen Penny at her work in *The Star of India*.

As W.P.C. Crampton moved along the pavement at the steady, regulation pace, she found herself thinking of Penny, wondering what she had done to make herself the target of police enquiries. And then, as though the subject of her thoughts had suddenly jumped out of her head and assumed a tangible form, she saw her, a few yards ahead, crossing the pavement, pushing her way into Boots! Iris hurried into the shop and looked around, half-expecting to find that she had imagined it all, but there was Penny at one of the counters, speaking to one of the woman assist-ants.

Penny turned a moment later and saw the W.P.C. coming towards her. She made a half-hearted attempt to get away, but her movements were hampered by her condition, and Iris took her arm in a firm but friendly grip.

Thirty minutes later they were seated together in the back of a police-car on the way to Whitford. Penny had been allowed to complete the necessary purchases at the chemists, and to change into fresh underwear at the police-station, with the result that she was considerably more comfortable. She spent the first part of the journey chatting amiably of old times to W.P.C. Crampton who was herself in a cheerful mood, not only because she had been commended by her immediate superior for her initiative and observation, but because a car drive through the country was an unexpected bonus, far better than walking the Scarby streets on a sultry, summer day.

However, as they drew nearer to Whitford, Penny became silent, withdrawing into herself. She had almost forgotten about Tom Pickford, her mind was full of her own problems. The police at Scarby had told her nothing, but she was certain that her uncle must have discovered the loss of the money by now and named her as the thief. But what about all those dirty books, and those photographs? Ten to one the cunning old sod had collected them all up and burned them before calling in the police. Well, he wouldn't get away with it, she'd see to that! She'd remembered the identity of the other man in the photographs, she'd stir it up for both of them, make it really hot!

As in an action-replay, she saw herself at the bedroom window, scattering magazines and photographs to the four winds, saw them fluttering down like dead leaves to rest accusingly in the garden. Some had reached the track beyond the gate and she prayed that someone might have passed that way before her uncle's return; she pictured one of the local women stooping to pick up a photograph, imagined the look on her face changing from curiosity to outright horror! As the car drew up at the station, W.P.C. Crampton was astonished to see that her prisoner was smiling, as though at some private joke.

2

Gosford parked at the end of the brief track which led down to David Birk's house and looked around. As always, the stillness of the high moor, its space and the utter serenity of its summit, laid hold of him. Whenever he came here, the moor seemed to touch some spring in his spirit and when he left he took a little of the stillness back with him.

The threatening clouds had passed over now, sailing southwards, and the sky was a deep, uninterrupted blue. Below and around the house, the moor dipped and soared, patterned by sunlight and shadow, humming with hidden life. Behind it, the Kestle Stones looked down unmoved, as they had once looked down on the hunters of the Stone Age, on Ancient Britons, on Celts, Picts, Danes, Vikings, Saxons, Romans, and Normans, on the long, shuffling parade of serfs, farmers, shepherds, monks, ironstone workers, wood-carvers, roadbuilders, foresters, blacksmiths, pyrite miners, on all the men and women who, across a hundred centuries, had walked this wild land, changed it a little with their labour, and now lay somewhere beneath it.

Gosford walked up to the house just as David emerged, carrying tea to a white table in the neat front-garden. He went through the gate in the dry-stone wall, and David turned to him.

'I've been expecting you,' said David. 'I saw your dust rising on the road. Tea?'

'Thank you,' said Gosford stiffly. 'I'm afraid I haven't very much time.' It was all too casual, he hadn't driven all this way to take tea and make pleasant conversation!

'Birk. David Birk.' David held out a hand, and Gosford took it, looking directly into the sharp, blue eyes which Sergeant Miller had described with such accuracy, liking the firm certainty of the handshake, liking the man in spite of himself.

'Chief-Inspector Gosford,' he said, relaxing a little. 'I got your note.'

'Ah,' said David, and, after a pause, 'How do you like your tea?'

'As it comes.' Gosford mopped his brow and dropped into one of the garden chairs, watching David as he hovered over the tea-tray. He could see what Miller meant about this man's detachment; there was a curious air of completeness about him, as of a man able to stand alone, without need of the social crutches on which other men prop up their lives. There was a calmness there too—no, thought Gosford, correcting himself—it was a sort of *stillness*, a poised, brooding stillness, like the moor, as if he were waiting, listening . . .

'You're not on the phone up here, are you?' he asked.

'No,' said David. 'Part of the charm.'

They relapsed into silence sipping the strong, hot tea, and Gosford found himself smiling inwardly, amused by the incongruity of the situation. An unhurried afternoon tea in an English garden, scones and strawberry jam, a tiny, isolated world, separated by dry-stone walls, by the moor, by those dark escarpments, from that other world below, the world which obtruded its guilt and anguish into his life every day of every week. Which was the more real? And then, because he was essentially a practical man, he smiled inwardly, thinking—yes, it's fine now, it's beautiful because it's summer, but in winter it will be hell up here, sheer bloody hell!

'Your note—' he began tentatively.

'Yes?'

'Gave me a bit of a shock.' Gosford reddened under the other man's steady look, conscious that his words were ill-chosen, feeble. He tried again: 'Are you certain?'

'There are two tigers at large on the moor, Mr Gosford. I heard them last night, and I heard them again this morning.' He spoke quietly, but with absolute conviction.

'Heard them?'

'I heard them calling. I went down to the forest and picked up the tracks of one of them. He'd made a kill—a hind and its calf. I saw the remains. I explained all this to the Forestry Officer and to your sergeant.'

'You couldn't be mistaken?'

'In what way?'

'Well, the moor can be responsible for some strange sounds, especially at night. And the hind—couldn't it have been brought down by some other animal? A maverick dog, something like that?'

'It could have been. But it wasn't.'

'But tigers?' Gosford spread his hands. 'Where could they have come from? A circus, a zoo? Where else? If two tigers had broken out, we'd be the first to hear about it! God, it would be panic-stations all round, the newspapers would be screaming their heads off. There'd be no way we wouldn't know, no way.'

'You know about it now,' said David.

'Are you an expert, Mr Birk?' Gosford's voice was sharp, he felt the irritation beginning to flow back, he longed to crack the other man's quiet, unshakeable confidence.

'I know about tigers, Mr Gosford.'

Gosford plucked at his crumpled trousers where they clung stickily to his flesh. 'Good. I'm glad to hear it. Would it be an intrusion of privacy if I asked how you got to know about them?'

'I was brought up in India. My father was quite a well-known hunter. And I did a bit myself until I left there in 1948.'

'You hunted for sport, you mean?'

'Not exactly.' David's eyes held the glint of a smile. 'No. I'm not in favour of killing wild animals for sport. The tigers I shot were man-eaters.' The words had a touch of selfrighteousness about them but they didn't come out that way.

'Yes, I see.' Gosford was a little disconcerted. It was impossible to doubt this man, it was the situation itself that was unbelievable—that he should be sitting talking of killing man-eating tigers as another man might speak of delivering milk. 'What have you been doing with your life since 1948, if it's not a rude question,' he asked, trying to make it sound casual.

'This and that,' said David, in the same casual manner. He showed no inclination to go beyond that.

'Well,' Gosford said, after a pause, 'to get back to the business in hand. Did you actually see these tigers?'

'No.'

'Then how can you be certain that they are there?'

'I've told you,' David said patiently. 'I saw the pugmarks in the forest.'

'And as far as you're concerned, Mr Birk, what you saw is sufficient proof?'

'Yes.'

'Would you be willing to take me into the forest and show me what you found?'

'When?'

'Now.' As David hesitated, he added sharply, 'Mr Birk, I'm a policeman. In the course of any one year I am told some pretty incredible stories. Nine out of ten, ninety-nine out of a hundred turn out to be phoney, the work of cranks.' David opened his mouth to speak but Gosford overrode him: 'No—let me finish. I am not saying that you are a crank, I am not doubting your expert knowledge. I wouldn't still be sitting here if that were so. But as a policeman, I have to be sure, you must see that. No tigers have been reported missing, nobody—including yourself—has actually seen tigers in the forest or anywhere else. I've already taken certain measures as suggested in your note. Before I can go any further, I must have some hard evidence.' He paused and added drily: 'And if they really are there, I may well need your help.'

David sighed and pushed back his chair. He took a pipe from his pocket and stood looking down at it for a moment, twisting it in his fingers as though trying to decide whether to fill and light it or not. Gosford watched him curiously.

'Amber,' said David, as though to himself.

'Amber?'

David indicated the polished, yellow stem of the pipe. 'My father once told me that amber is the frozen heart of the tiger.' He stood in silence, touching the stem with a finger, deep in thought, and then, turned to Gosford abruptly: 'All right, Chief-Inspector. Give me a couple of minutes and I'll go back down with you.' He strolled casually towards the house and went inside.

3

Police-Sergeant Miller had seldom experienced a more exasperating afternoon. He had telephoned a dozen County forces to enquire about zoos and circuses in their areas, asking them to run a check on the tigers, and the reactions at the other end had run the whole gamut, from incredulity to outright mockery. Out of sheer frustration he had paused at one point to ring his girl-friend, Shirley, an attractive and willing red-head, who worked as a clerk in the office of the Ministry of Social Security in Whitford.

'Hey, Shirley,' he said, 'look out of the window, will you, and tell me what you see.'

'Are you serious?' she asked.

'Look out of the window,' he demanded.

There was a pause, and then she came back to him.

'Nothing, there's nothing. Just people.'

'You're quite sure you didn't see a tiger?'

'Norman—what's the matter?'

'I'm fine. Couldn't be better. I mean—I'm serving the

community, darling. Defending the nation.'

'Will you please tell me what you are on about?'

'You won't believe it.'

'Try me.'

'Some nut came into the nick a couple of hours back and said that a couple of tigers were loose on the moors.'

'What?'

'Tigers.'

'Tigers! Ooh!'

'So what happens? Mr bleeding Gosford tells me to check. Darling, I've been on the phone for the last hour, having the piss taken out of me right, left and centre. And there ain't no tigers. They're all safe and sound, tucked up in their little cages. You can tell everybody not to worry. Nobody's going to get eaten by a tiger today, I give you my solemn word.'

'If I do see one shall I arrest it?' A giggle trembled on the line.

'You do that.' Sergeant Miller paused, and added softly, 'Listen. What colour are you wearing?'

'What colour what?'

'You know.'

'I'm not sure.' A pause. 'Black. The black ones.'

'Christ,' he breathed, 'I wish you were here now. At this minute.'

'What would you do?' she teased. 'Tell me.'

'I'll do better than that,' he said. 'I'll show you. Tonight. Seven o'clock, the usual place. We'll take a nice drive up to the moors.'

'With all those tigers on the prowl?'

'You won't have time to think about them, my darling.'

'What about eating?' she asked plaintively.

'Afterwards. Anywhere you like.'

'That's what you always say,' she said. 'Afterwards. I bet we end up in the bloody Wimpy bar, noshing hamburger and chips.'

'Stop complaining. You know you like it.'

'I never said I liked hamburgers.'

'Not them. The other.'

'Yes,' she admitted sadly, 'that's the trouble.'

'See you then,' he said cheerfully, and with Gosford's caution in mind, he added: 'And listen. Don't go talking to anyone about the tigers.'

'Why? You just said they're all locked up.'

'I know, I know. So they are. But it's official police business still. Keep it between you and me, eh?'

Shirley worked in an office with five other people. They were impressed by her close association with the police, and always listened with great respect to any items of information which she could be persuaded to divulge. For her part, Shirley felt her responsibility keenly; there were some subjects on which her lips were absolutely sealed, and she did not hesitate to say so. But occasionally, where she felt the subject was not of vital national importance, she would unbend and throw her colleagues the odd tit-bit of inside news, taking care, of course, to indicate that she was speaking in the strictest confidence, between these four walls, and that not one word should be relayed to the outside world, not even to a wife, a husband, or the most trusted friend. Her colleagues, of course, gave her the most implicit assurances in this respect; hand over heart, they pledged themselves to the most solemn secrecy.

4

Thus it was that within five minutes of Sergeant Miller's telephone call, the message began to spread through Whitford. By the nature of things, the words lost some of their preciseness as they passed along, and rumours of man-eating lions and tigers, of savage wolves, of panthers escaped from the Scarby Zoo, began to circulate. It wasn't long before the rumours reached the bar of 'The Wool-pack', a small private drinking-club, and the ears of the

News Editor and Chief Reporter of the *Whitford Gazette*, a plump, untidy man named James W. Topping. He received the information with all the natural scepticism of someone who has spent thirty years in journalism, twelve of them in Fleet Street. Nevertheless, he was an efficient, thorough man, experienced enough to know that even the most luxurious rumour must have some root. The idea of wild animals loose in and around Whitford intrigued him, and when he arrived back at the office, he telephoned the local police personally, to check the stories.

Sergeant Miller took the call in the absence of Chief-Inspector Gosford and he assured Topping that the rumours had no foundation, absolutely no foundation whatsoever. He was almost too fulsome in his denials, and Jim Topping began to wonder why. He sat at his desk after the call, squeezing his broad nose between thumb and forefinger, turning the conversation over in his mind.

The business with the nose was subconscious, but significant. It meant, as his colleagues well knew, that he wasn't satisfied, that he had caught the scent of a story. They weren't fond of Topping; he could be mean and aggressive when he had a pint of bitter inside him, and he was over-fond of recounting his Fleet Street experiences, but they had to admit, albeit reluctantly, that he was a good newspaperman, that his instinct for news was seldom wrong.

Later, after attending to some routine matters, he ran his eye over the tapes from the Press Association, and his attention focused on a minor item which reported the death of the Great Davino, a former circus performer. Topping remembered seeing the man perform with his tiger act in Scarby, some years before. The P.A. report went on to say that Davino's last appearance had been with the Circus Romero at Birmingham, two days prior to his tragic death. Topping made three more telephone calls. From the first, he learned that the Circus Romero had moved on to Shipley; the second call told him where he could locate the manager of the circus; and with the third, after some difficulty, he managed to speak with Victor Romero, the proprietor, in person.

Mr Romero, despite his name, turned out to be an East-end Cockney with an accent as broad as the Whitechapel Road. He was a blunt, down-to-earth character who made it plain that he was very busy. No, he had not heard of the death of the Great Davino, but his tone implied that he was neither surprised nor stricken with grief by the news.

'He left your employment after the show last Saturday?' asked Topping.

'I sacked him,' said Mr Romero bluntly, 'I slung him his cards.'

'What about the tigers?'

'Oh, my gawd. Not another one! I've already had the bloody police on, asking if I'd lost any bloody tigers! It must be the weather, driving everyone round the bend!'

'You've still got them then. You're still doing a tiger act?' Topping tried to keep the excitement out of his voice, to make it sound like a casual enquiry.

'Do me a favour!' said Mr Romero. 'Tigers I don't need. Tigers are more trouble than they're worth. Tigers I can do without.'

'So what happened to them?'

'He took 'em with him, didn't he? They belonged to him. Listen, excuse me, will you? I got a business to contend with.' Topping blew a gentle raspberry down the phone as the other man hung up, then lit a Burmah cheroot and sat back to consider the situation. Where were those bloody tigers? What had the Great Davino done with them? You can't take two damned great tigers along to the Cats' Home and ask that they should be taken in, or put quietly to sleep; nor could you deliver them to a cattle market and offer them up for auction. The only possibility was that Davino had disposed of them to a zoo or a safari park. It had to be checked, though he doubted if that were the answer; he knew very little about tigers, but he guessed that circus-trained animals might present special problems.

But he was on to something, that was certain, there was more to this than mere rumours.

'Lucy! Lucy!' His reedy voice carried over the glass partitions which separated his office from the newsroom and within moments the newest recruit to the reporting-staff was at his side. As a general rule he hated juniors, but he had a soft spot for young Lucy; tall, long-legged, eager to please, she exuded a subtle sexuality which more than compensated for her somewhat scrappy shorthand.

'Lucy, love, listen: I want you to get a list of all the zoos and safari parks in the area. Say, within a hundred miles of the town. That'll do for starters. Then I want you to ring them up, one by one, and find out if they've bought any tigers in the past 48 hours. Got that?'

'Yes, Mr Topping.' She showed no surprise, which was one of the things he liked about her. 'I was supposed to go up to Burnwick Farm to see Mr Haynes. Do you want me to leave that?'

'What's it about?'

'He rang about a half-hour ago, while you were out, and spoke to Mr Dailey.'

'Oh?' Topping stiffened with irritation, scenting battle. Mr Dailey was the Chairman and Managing Editor of the paper and they had clashed time and time again because of Dailey's habit of going over the head of his news-editor, issuing orders to the reporters without even consulting or informing Topping. 'Listen, love,' he said, 'you work for me, remember that. If Mr Dailey or anyone else asks you to do a job, I want to know about it. Clear?'

'Yes. I'm sorry, Mr Topping.'

'It's all right. Not your fault. Now, what's this about Burnwick Farm?'

'It's about the sheep. Mr Haynes, the farmer, went up to Gridley Moor to check on some of his sheep. He found eight or nine of them, all dead. He thinks they must have been savaged by a mad dog. They'd been torn to pieces. He went back there with his son and a truck and collected the bodies. Mr Dailey thought we ought to get a photograph.'

'Sounds more like a pack of wolves to me—' He stopped suddenly, and banged the desk with his fist, his eyes bright with excitement.

'What is it, Mr Topping?'

'Hmph?' He looked at her as though he hadn't heard, then patted her arm. 'I'll go up to Burnwick Farm, love. You get on with that other little job. Start with the local zoos and work outwards. As soon as you find anyone who has acquired a couple of tigers in the last day or so, you can stop. And let me know. Right?'

'Yes, Mr Topping.'

'You're a good girl, Lucy.'

'Yes, Mr Topping,' she said again, allowing herself a small smile. She left a faint drift of perfume behind her; it lingered for a moment and then succumbed to the more pungent odour of the cherrot. Topping watched her out of long habit, admiring the legs, the well-rounded bottom under the floral skirt, until she disappeared from view, but his mind was elsewhere, racing with ideas.

He wasn't too concerned about the *Whitford Gazette* which was published only once a week, on Friday: he had a couple of days in hand there. But if his hunch was right, the story would be too big to wait that long, too big and far too hot. It was something that, with his connections, he could easily sell to one of the nationals for a good price. The important thing was not to jump the gun, to check and double-check, and above all, to tie up as many of the angles as possible, to build up the exclusive features of the story before others got to hear of it.

He rang up Tony Phelps, a free-lance photographer who often worked for the paper, and whose discretion could be trusted, and arranged to pick him up on the way out of town. He said very little about the purpose of the visit to Burnwick Farm; he could explain that in the car, get Phelps on his side, cut him in on any sale to a national paper. He stubbed out his cheroot, brushed the grey ash from his tie and jacket, and went down the backstairs to the car-park at the rear, clattering down the iron steps two at a time.

5

It had been the intention that David Birk should take the Chief-Inspector to that part of the forest where he had found the remains of the tiger's kill and seen its tracks, but the plan was changed once Gosford's car got within radio range of the Control at Whitford and he learned that Penny Waites was in custody, waiting to be interviewed. He pulled up and asked David, who was following in the land-rover, if he would agree to delay the visit to the forest for an hour while he talked to the girl.

'It may have some bearing on this business,' he explained.

'In what way?' asked David.

'A man disappeared last night. We found his car abandoned in a back lane near Cullington. I have an idea that he was out with this girl—that she could have been the last person to see him.'

'Cullington? That's what—ten, fifteen miles from the forest?'

'Nearer fifteen, I'd say.'

'And pretty open country, too.'

'Yes. These tigers of yours—'

'They're not mine, Chief-Inspector,' interrupted David.

'All right. Could they travel that sort of distance in a few hours—from Cullington up to the forest?'

'A tiger can travel upwards of twenty miles in a night, Chief-Inspector, and often does.'

Gosford leaned against the land-rover and sighed. He felt as though a stone was pressing down on his skull, he had to struggle to bring some coherence to his thoughts.

'In the note you left me, you said—you said that there was no danger to human beings.'

'I said—if I remember rightly—that I doubted if the tigers presented an immediate danger to humans.'

'But you could be wrong?'

'Wouldn't be the first time. What I meant was that, as a general rule, the tiger will avoid contact with man. He becomes a man-eater because he is wounded or old and an unarmed man presents an easier target than most other animals—we're slower, less capable of flight, more vulnerable. Or a tiger may turn on man because his normal source of food has been destroyed or driven away. The situation has a certain irony, as you can see. We kill off the tiger's supply of meat, and then condemn him because he turns man-eater.'

'Perhaps we could have the general lecture another time, if you wouldn't mind? At the moment, I'm only interested in these particular tigers, Mr Birk, the ones you say you heard,' Gosford said impatiently.

David smiled for the first time since they'd met, a slow, boyish smile that seemed to spread across his face, making him appear immediately less aloof and cold. Welcome to the human race, thought Gosford wryly.

'Sorry,' said David, 'but I don't know. I don't know enough about them. They've probably lived most of their lives in captivity. Their natural instincts will have become blunted. I wouldn't like to predict their behaviour without more knowledge.'

You're a great help, thought Gosford. Aloud, he said: 'O.K. Give me a half-hour with the girl, just to see what she can tell us. Then you can take me up to the forest.'

'Have you always been the same—hard to convince?'

'Look,' said Gosford, 'I'm just a copper, trying to do a job. At the moment I feel as though I'm swimming through a pool of treacle. Tigers aren't in the book, Mr Birk, they don't mention them at the police training colleges. I've got to work it out in my own way and at my own pace. O.K.?'

The two men looked at each other for a moment and David, seeing the lines of concern on Gosford's face, forgot his own impatience and nodded sympathetically. 'O.K.,' he said.

Gosford walked slowly, wearily, back to his car. The engine failed to start at first and he closed his eyes in despair. This, he thought, is all I need! But after three or more turns on the ignition key, the car shuddered falteringly to life, and gathered strength. He learned one other piece of information over the short-wave radio which did nothing for his morale. Sergeant Miller told him that a farmer named Haynes had reported the death on Gridley Moor of eight or nine head of sheep and that it was the farmer's view that they had been attacked and savaged by dogs. The knot of apprehension in the pit of Gosford's stomach tightened, the word *tiger* buzzed in his head like an alarm signal.

The sheer magnitude of the problem dismayed him. If tigers were at large in the forest, how could they be tracked down and killed? Sixty thousand acres of forest, plus twenty thousand acres of private woodlands, that's what Peter Street, the District Forestry Officer had said. God in heaven, he thought, it would take an army to surround that lot! Maybe that is what it would come to—the army would have to be called in! But that was almost the simplest part of the problem; roads would have to be blocked off, tourists turned away, campers cleared from the areas they were now occupying, the people living in the Forestry Commission village—or at least their children—would probably have to be evacuated. And all this only took account of the forest! What about the miles of moorland, some of it almost inaccessible, which could provide cover for the tigers? If they took refuge up there, it would take a half-dozen armies to flush them out!

He turned on the ordinary car-radio as much to give

himself some relief from this tidal-wave of depressing thoughts as for any other reason and was just in time to hear the 5 p.m. new bulletin on the BBC. The news-reader ran smoothly through the events of the day—uproar in Parliament, crisis at the United Nations, sterling recovering, tragic fire in a Glasgow tenement, the Queen back from a state visit to W. Germany, England's team for the next Test Match; but nowhere in the entire catalogue was there any mention of tigers.

Once again, Gosford's mood began to veer round. Tigers simply do not materialise out of thin air, he told himself, for the hundredth time; if two of the damned animals were loose in the forest, they must have escaped from somewhere, and that escape would not only have been reported, it would have made headlines.

The truth was that he had no proof of their existence, nothing except the word of the man in the land-rover behind. He liked him, he was impressed by him, but he needed something more than one man's opinion. Even experts can be wrong, he told himself, especially experts! He was on the outskirts of Whitford now, back on familiar, everyday ground, and his spirits were beginning to rise.

6

It was still only 5.30 p.m. on the first day, the tigers had known freedom for less than twenty-four hours. The clouds had passed over, taking with them the threatened storm, leaving the atmosphere as heavy and listless as before. The westering sun still burned down, though with less intensity, and the shadows of the trees on the fringe of the forest were longer now.

The tigress lay with Mohan in the shelter of the hollow. She had slept, but only in short, fitful bursts, for earlier in the afternoon her rest had been disturbed by human voices and the noise of a machine, and the incident had made her uneasy. The tiger heard the sounds also, and they went together to investigate: in the clearing, beyond the slope, they saw two men moving about among the dead sheep and calling to each other. Their fear of men was still strong, stronger than their hatred, but what most held their attention was the machine. It frightened Ranee, reminding her of the cage that moved, the box with bars which roared and made strange, rattling noises. Neither she nor Mohan dared to go near it.

They watched from the cover of the bracken, until the men climbed into the machine and drove away. After this, the tigress was unable fully to relax, and eventually she gave up the attempt. Instinct told her that they had remained too long in this place, it was time to move on.

She drank deeply at the stream, and then turned her head towards the forest. Hunger stirred her flanks, she began to feel the need for food, and changing direction she padded cautiously towards the clearing. There was no sign of the animals that Mohan had killed, only the strong scent of blood on the ground. She sniffed around angrily, but all she could find was part of a sheep's head which she crunched down in a single gulp.

Turning once more, she moved towards the forest, and after a moment or two, Mohan came bounding after her. Soon they reached the long, cool shadows and disappeared among the whispering trees.

CHAPTER SEVEN

1

'Well, Penny, you're in trouble, aren't you?'

The girl did not answer. She sat stiff-backed in the hard chair, her eyes big and fearful as she watched Gosford. A third person was in the room, a thin, solemn-faced man in a grey suit, who from time to time peered at Penny through square-shaped spectacles, and occasionally jotted something down in a small notebook. The little room seemed to be pulsating with heat; Gosford had taken off his jacket and was patting at his face and neck with some folded tissues. He tossed these into a waste-bin and tapped the piles of banknotes which were stacked neatly beside her duffle-bag on the desk.

'One thousand, nine hundred and forty-two pounds,' he said slowly, emphasising the figures. 'Not to mention this.' He laid a finger on a paperweight which held down another, smaller wad of notes. 'Seventy-two pounds. Wrapped up separately, in this.' He held up a creased brown-paper bag.

'That's mine!' she said quickly, 'my own money!'

'Ah,' he said, and indicated the larger sum. 'And this isn't? Is that what you're saying?'

'I borrowed it,' she said defensively.

'From your uncle?'

'Yes. I was going to pay it back.'

'Did you ask his permission?' She fell back on silence once more, and he went on: 'Do you know what they call borrowing without permission, Penny? They call it stealing. You stole this money, didn't you?'

She shifted uneasily, but again made no reply. 'Well,' said Gosford, 'let's leave that for a moment.' He saw the relief in her eyes and added quickly: 'But only for the moment.' He nodded towards the other man. 'This is Detective-Sergeant Bawden from the C.I.D. He'll have a lot of questions to ask you when I've finished. About the money—and about these.'

He watched her white face as he opened a drawer and took out some photographs. 'I found them on the ground just outside your uncle's house, shortly after you'd left. Are they yours?'

'No, they are not!' she said sharply.

'Whose are they?'

'His!'

'His? Your uncle, you mean?'

'I found them in the trunk under his bed. With a load of dirty magazines. So I slung them out—I mean, look at them! Enough to turn your stomach!'

She twisted her full moist lips in a sneer, sat back in the chair with her legs crossed, and gave Gosford a look which suggested that she, for one, knew all about men and their carnal appetites; for a moment, she took on the appearance of a cynical, experienced woman. There was an element of the grotesque in the girl's expression. She reminded Gosford of an immature *femme fatale* in a silent film; amused and saddened, he smiled wryly to himself.

He passed the photographs across to Bawden, whose long face assumed an even more solemn expression as he looked first at the pictures and then at the girl. He allowed himself a small sigh by way of comment and then laid the photographs face downwards on the table beside him.

'Mr Bawden will want to talk to you about those as well,' Gosford said. 'I've got something else on my mind.' She took a small, grubby handkerchief from her jeans and dabbed at her nose, watching him warily, as he continued: 'Where were you last night, Penny?'

'At work.'

'You were not, and you know it!' There was a sharper edge to his tone now. 'It was your evening off.'

'I forgot,' she said, defiantly.

'Well, don't forget again. I want the truth. And I haven't very much time. Where were you last night and who were you with?'

'I went out.'

'Who with?'

'A friend.'

'A boy-friend?'

'Yes.'

'By the name of Tom Pickford?'

Her body seemed to quiver, the fear came back to her eyes, and she began to pluck at her mouth with nervous fingers.

'Tom Pickford?' he repeated, puzzled by this new change of attitude, by the extent of her nervousness, and when she still didn't answer, he took a plastic bag from one of the drawers and, with his thumb and forefinger, removed its contents. He stood up, walked round the desk, and dropped the brief panties into her lap.

'Your knickers!' he said. 'You left them behind—in Tom Pickford's car.' He walked to the open window and leaned out briefly, but the air outside was no cooler, it brought no relief. When he turned back, he was surprised to see the tears glitter in her eyes and splash down the pale cheeks.

He felt a sudden twinge of compassion. She wasn't a woman, she was a child, and not a very bright one at that. She had little to offer except a good fluent body; she was the type who would be used by men and delude herself that she was using them. Until it was too late. But he had learned, by long experience, that too much sympathy, too soon, could distort the vision. He had to deal with people as they were, not as he would like them to be. And at this moment he had to keep the pressure on.

'What time did you meet him, Penny?' He spat the words out viciously, and she looked up, startled.

'Half-past seven,' she said, her voice little more than a

whisper. Gosford remembered George Leppard and made a mental note: one day soon, very soon, he would get that bastard into the office, call him a liar to his face, frighten the life out of his mincing little body!

'You spent the whole evening together?' he asked aloud.

'Yes.'

'What time did he leave you?' She looked at him in anguish, her lips moving soundlessly. 'Penny,' he continued, more gently, 'Tom Pickford is missing. He hasn't been heard of since last night. We think he may have met with an accident or worse. You were probably the last one to see him. What happened?' She shook her head, and a tiny, incoherent sound rattled in her throat, as she remembered the darkness, the great brassy roars which seemed to rock the trees, the scream, the clamour from the forest, and then the long silence and the waiting. Because it was beyond comprehension she had forced it to the back of her mind, but now, sitting in this office, facing this man and his questions, it came back to her with the force of a delayed shock. She knew now that Tom had not come out of the forest, that something terrible, inexplicable, had happened to him.

Gosford knew it too, knew it from her look. He knew that David Birk was right, he needed no further proof, and he closed his eyes, momentarily overwhelmed by the strangeness, the enormity of it all. And then it passed; his mind cleared and, perhaps because there was no longer any doubt, he was himself again, calm and deliberate, knowing now what he had to do.

He put a hand on her shoulder and she looked up at him with brimming, haunted eyes. 'Tell me, Penny. I have to know. There isn't much time. Tell me,' he said urgently.

And then it came pouring forth like a spring flood, a torrent of speech spewed on the air, each word pressing on the heels of the one before as though desperate to escape, until there was nothing left to say and empty, exhausted, she lowered her head to her knees.

Gosford waited for a full minute, and then he lifted her head, and looked into her dull, lifeless eyes. 'Penny. I want your help. I want you to take me to that place in the forest, where Tom left you. Now. Will you do that?'

She nodded, and rose slowly from the chair. Bawden opened the door for them and they went out.

2

An hour later, Gosford and David Birk, with two uniformed constables, entered the forest, leaving Penny in one of the cars with a W.P.C. Within a few minutes they found a torch lying half-hidden in the undergrowth. Moving in further, they came to a small clearing, where David paused, his rifle cocked, searching the area with his eyes. The undergrowth which fringed the far side, was crushed and broken in places and from a spike of bramble there hung, like a flag of surrender, a strip of white cloth, part of the sleeve of a shirt. Nearby, beyond the clearing, there were clear signs of a struggle; small clots of dried blood marked the soft earth.

David motioned the others to keep behind him and moved forward, deeper into the forest, treading carefully but confidently, as though he were following a trail. Unobtrusively, as though by right, he had assumed command, and Gosford was content that it should be so. This man seemed to be able to read the forest, to interpret its signs, and at moments, especially when he paused to look and to listen, he appeared to merge with the background, to become a part of it. They went on for about five hundred yards, and then David checked again, crouching down to examine a large, dark, irregular stain on the ground at his feet.

'More blood,' he murmured. 'Not quite dried out. Been there less than twenty-four hours.' He looked up at Gosford. 'This is it. The tiger attacked back there and carried his kill to this spot. Somewhere near here we should find—' He stood up without finishing the sentence, forced his way through a tangle of bushes, and stopped again. As Gosford came up alongside, he felt his stomach churn and heave, the bile rise in his throat.

At the foot of two trees, a swarm of flies hovered over the torn and mangled remains of a man, bits of naked white flesh, intestine and bone; and to one side, caught obscenely in a thicket, there was part of a human leg.

One of the constables, a sturdy, middle-aged countryman, turned away, retching and coughing. The other, a younger man, stood as though frozen, colourless as a waxen image, his eyes dark with horror.

David was the first to move. Stooping down, he picked up a black, plastic wallet, ripped and stained with blood. He unfolded it, and from one of the compartments he drew out a small oblong-shaped card. It was coloured blue on white, and under the words MIDLAND BANK, it bore the name and signature of Thomas Adrian Pickford.

3

At about this time, a young lady named Maud Ethel Pickering, aged eleven years and four months, was sitting by the window of her bedroom, looking out over the forest, and planning what she considered to be the most important step in her life.

Maud was an imaginative girl of sturdy character, and in consequence she often clashed with her parents, whose ideas on how a girl of almost twelve should behave were, in her view, totally unreasonable and old-fashioned. Their attitude to her given names illustrated the point to perfection. In the past year she had grown to dislike being called Maud, or Maudie; she felt that, whatever you did with it, the name was squat, ugly, unglamorous, suggesting by its very sound that she herself was also squat, ugly, and unglamorous. Nor could she fall back on her second name, for she believed that Ethel was, if anything, even worse than Maud.

She had suffered under this burden for some time, in silent envy of her close friends, who enjoyed the luxury of such modern-sounding and musical names as Cilla, Lesley, Angela, Jill, Lyn, and Jennifer, and then, in a moment of inspiration, had decided to do something about it. Why should she not change her name to something more suitable? Once this momentous decision had been taken, there followed an agonising period, during which she drew up a secret list, divided into possibles and probables. For weeks she deliberated, unable to make up her mind, torn in the final analysis, between Petula or Elaine, until one Sunday afternoon, when she saw the opening episode of a serial on television. Based on the book, *Anne of Green Gables*, it starred, in the role of Anne, an absolutely stunning, auburn-haired young lady by the name of Kim Braden.

The situation that Anne faced in the serial had so many parallels with Maud's own life (or so she felt) that she became an ardent, admiring fan from that moment, identifying herself both with the actress and the character. Maud was not an orphan, of course, she had not been adopted, but otherwise the serial seemed in her view, to mirror her own situation with uncanny accuracy. For a start, her hair, if not exactly auburn, was a rich, glossy chestnut, which at times, if the light was right, certainly looked a kind of auburn; and again, like Anne, Maud loved to read, to make up stories, to imagine herself in all sorts of interesting and romantic situations—though romance, in this instance, was not to be interpreted in the conventional sense. Boys, for the most part, did not feature in her imaginings, she regarded them as rather silly, juvenile creatures. Her conception of the romantic was to see herself as the heroine of adventures which found her on an island in the South Seas, on jet planes travelling the continents, as a film or television star (she had already played in four school plays and been highly complimented by Mrs Waring, the English teacher, on her ability) a famous writer, a missionary, or a Prime Minister; and, whatever her position in the world, she was always a lone figure, brave, upright, tragic, often misunderstood, sacrificing herself to help the less fortunate.

Maud's home, in the tiny village of Lyndholme, was almost entirely surrounded by the forest in which her father worked as an employee of the Forestry Commission, and from the beginning, she had made the trees her friends. Alone, among them, she could indulge her fantasies without fear of reproof, of being told to 'stop daydreaming'. And when at last, she decided to change her name to Kim, after the actress in the serial, she confided her secret to the forest first of all. The trees received the information, as always, with a kindly silence, which, from experience, she knew to be a sign of approval.

Not so her family. When, at high-tea one evening, Maud announced that in the future she wished to be addressed as Kim, the statement was received with ribald laughter by her three older brothers and a look of disgust from her father, while her mother asked fatuously:

'Kim? Kim? What put that in your head, girl? What's wrong with your own name?'

'Maud! It's horrible!'

'It was your grannie's name. It's the name you were christened with. You were named Maud, and Maud you'll stay! It's a good, plain name, you be satisfied with it!'

She had argued, but in the end, as he always did, her father ended the debate, lifting his head and saying sharply: 'That's enough! You heard your mother! Let's hear no more of it.'

Later that evening, the eldest brother, Kevin, had found Maud in tears on the outskirts of the forest and in his kindly, clumsy way, he had tried to persuade her that a name wasn't really important, it was no more than a label on a bottle, and what really mattered was what was inside.

Maud allowed Kevin to lead her home, but she was neither convinced nor consoled by his words. In her opinion, people and bottles should be labelled correctly, to avoid mistakes.

All this business over the name had been hurtful and terrible enough, but what had happened today made it appear as nothing by comparison. She sat at her window, torn between grief and anger, convinced that the gulf of misunderstanding which separated her from her parents had widened to such an extent that it was incapable of being bridged.

School had broken up that day for the long summer holiday and just as Maud was about to leave to catch the school-bus, Mrs Waring had taken her aside and made her the most wonderful, fabulous, stupendous offer. Mrs Waring, who always produced the school plays, had some connection with the National Youth Theatre in London; she and her husband were going to spend part of the holiday assisting with the production of a new play by Peter Terson. Would Maud like to come with them for a week, or even two? It would cost nothing in terms of accommodation, since they would stay with Mrs Waring's parents in Lewisham, and Maud could sit through the rehearsals, she might even be allowed to appear in the crowd scenes. They were leaving the next day, they would have asked her sooner but the idea had only just occurred to them; she was to explain all this to her parents and make sure that one of them phoned that evening to give their consent.

Maud went home brimming with the news, eager to tell her mother, confident that she would share her excitement. But to her dismay, her mother received the news with a doubtful, almost frightened, shake of the head, and to all Maud's entreaties, replied that she must speak with her father. When Mr Pickering arrived at 5 o'clock, his wife met him at the gate and they spoke together for some moments, looking occasionally at the house. Maud watched them in a turmoil of apprehension.

Her father washed himself at the kitchen sink, splashing the cool water over his thick, heavy arms and brick-red face, grunting as he did so. Maud stood at the door and waited for him to finish. He looked at her as he flung down the towel and said one word.

'No.'

'Why? Why can't I go?'

'I don't have to give reasons. You're not going. Let's hear no more of it.'

'You're too young, Maud,' said her mother, seeing the child's face. 'We can't let you go off with a stranger. Not to London. It's such a big place. Anything could happen. And all those theatre people—' She shook her head. 'When you're older—'

'Let's hear no more of it,' repeated Mr Pickering sharply.

Maud felt as though she would drown in tears, but she fought them back, too proud to show weakness, or to plead further. And now, as she sat in her room, a brown, freckled face pressed against the window, she made her decision.

She emptied the books from her school satchel, and packed it with a dress, some underwear, her best shoes, a toothbrush, and her mascot, a green mouse made of rags which Kevin had given her last Christmas. She removed the head from the china policeman, took out the money she had saved, a total of 74 pence, and knotted the coins into a handkerchief. Then she hid the satchel under the bed, out of sight.

She made a very simple plan. Early in the morning, before it was light, while the others slept, she would creep out and go to the house in Cawby village where Mrs Waring lived. She would wait outside the house until morning, and then she would simply knock at the door and say that she was ready to go to London. If necessary, she would lie, tell Mrs Waring that her parents had consented.

Cawby wasn't far away. Five miles if she followed the road round, only four if she cut across the forest. She decided on the forest. She knew the tracks well, and no-one would see her at that time in the morning.

It would be safer than the road. And she would be with her friends, the trees.

4

Shortly before 7 p.m. that evening, Gosford was shown into the office of the Chief Constable at police headquarters in Scarby. Besides the Chief Constable, two other men were present, his Deputy, Gordon Hale, and Detective Chief-Superintendent James Murray. All three men had glasses of scotch before them, but no attempt was made to include Gosford in the hospitality.

'Right, Chief-Inspector, let's have it,' said the Chief Constable brusquely.

A large, pink-faced man with greying close-cropped hair, he was not in a good mood and seemed determined to show it. He disliked the humidity; he had a dinner engagement which for once promised to be enjoyable rather than merely formal and official; and on the following day he was due to captain a team from the Scarby Golf Club in a challenge match at Blackpool, an engagement which he was determined to fulfil, whatever the demands of his high office. All these things were on his mind as Gosford began to explain the reasons for the meeting, but by the time Gosford had finished his account of the day's events, he was listening with close attention and some bewilderment.

'Tigers!' he said. 'You can't be serious, man! Where the hell did they come from?'

'We're running a check on that now, sir. So far none of the zoos or safari parks, or the circuses for that matter, have been able to help.'

'If these tigers exist—'

'They exist all right, sir,' Gosford said quickly.

'Have you seen them?'

127

'No, sir—but—'

'Has anybody else seen them—actually seen them?'

'Not to my knowledge, sir.'

'Then we'll go back to my question. If these tigers exist—'

'Sir, they exist,' said Gosford stubbornly and as the other man's face creased in a frown, he added quickly: 'Or at least, we have to act on the assumption that they do. They've already killed one man—'

'You can't even be sure of that. You found a body, yes—'

'We found the remains of a body, sir.' Gosford wanted to shout at the man, to move around the big desk and shake some sense of urgency into him, but he held back his anger, remembering that only an hour or so before he himself had been plagued with similar doubts. He went on quietly: 'Only an animal, a wild animal, could have killed Pickford. The leg was found—there were marks on the flesh, tooth-marks, made by an animal and only an animal. And there is other evidence. The dead sheep on the moor.'

'That could have been a dog,' said Murray, screwing his boxer's face into a frown.

'It would have taken a pack of dogs! And what about the deer? Just before I came here, I had a call from Peter Street, the District Officer of the Forestry Commission.' He stood up and walked across to a large wall-map of the area. The forest areas stood out clearly against the shaded brown marking the moorland; the main mass looked like two huge green lungs, one on each side of the road which ran roughly from north to south, and beyond this there were other, isolated blobs of green, spread out across the county like satellites of the main forest. Gosford pointed to the most southerly of the lungs.

'Street's workmen reported a very strange occurrence. All day long the deer have been trickling across the road, out of this area to the south, into this other part of the forest, here, to the north. Why should they suddenly take it into their heads to do that? It can only be that they have been scared off. And that ties up with what Birk found—the dead hind and the fawn.'

There was a long pause. The Chief Constable sipped his scotch thoughtfully and his two colleagues followed his example, as though they had been waiting for a signal to do so. The Deputy Chief Constable, a lean and cynical-looking man, with sharp, bitter eyes, lowered his glass.

'Who is this man Birk? What do you know of him?'

'Very little, sir,' said Gosford. 'He lives up at Stowcroft, that old house on the high moor. He's spent some time in India, he knows about tigers.'

'How much does he know?'

'I'd say he was pretty much of an expert, sir.'

'Have you checked on him?'

'No, sir.'

'Why not? I should have thought that would have been one of your first steps.'

'I haven't had much time, sir,' said Gosford quietly.

'You've only got his word about the hind.'

'What about Pickford's body, sir? I saw that.'

'With this man Birk. It seems to me that you allowed him to interpret what had happened—and swallowed his theories hook, line and sinker. Has it occurred to you, that he was the one who led you to the body?'

'The girl took us there—she showed us where she last saw Pickford.' A new kind of sweat rolled down Gosford's face, his cheeks reddened with exasperation and frustration.

'She took you to the road, that was all. According to your story, it was Birk who led the way into the forest. He seemed to know where the body would be found.'

'You're not suggesting that he—'

'I'm suggesting that we ought to know a damned sight more about the man than we do at present before we accept his so-called theories!'

It took all Gosford's will-power to answer without the anger showing in his voice. 'All right, sir. Let's forget Birk for a moment. We've still got a violent death on our hands. I admit I can't tell you—I can't prove—how Pickford died. But I saw what was left of him, sir—and if he wasn't killed by a wild beast, then we'd better start looking for a murderer with a meat-axe.'

There was a silence in the room, broken at last by Murray, the C.I.D. man. He shifted his body in the chair, his square muscular shoulders straining at the confines of his jacket, and said: 'I think I'd better get over to Whitford, sir, and set up a full investigation.' He turned to Gosford. 'What did you do about the body?'

'There isn't much left of it, sir, as I said. We sealed off the area, and posted two men as near the scene of the crime as possible.'

'What do you mean—as near as possible?' Hale, the Deputy Chief Constable looked at Gosford aggressively.

'Bearing in mind the risk, sir. If there are tigers on the prowl—'

The Deputy Chief Constable grunted and raised his eyes to the ceiling in an elaborate gesture of disbelief. The Chief Constable put his hands on the desk, examined them for a moment, and said, as though dismissing the meeting: 'Right. I think that's the line to take. For the moment, we'll treat this as a murder investigation. If it turns out to be otherwise—well, we'll deal with that if and when it arises.' He pushed back his chair and was about to rise when Gosford interrupted.

'Excuse me, sir, but I don't think that is enough.'

'Oh?' The Chief Constable gave him the look of a man who was holding on to his patience with some difficulty.

'I mean,' said Gosford, 'that it isn't enough simply to set up a routine murder investigation. It's got to be more than that. I was sceptical about this tiger business, sir—until I saw Pickford's body and spoke to Birk. But not any more.'

'We're back to the tigers, are we?'

'With respect, sir—yes, we are. I don't think we can discount the possibility. There are hundreds, thousands of tourists in the area, not to mention the residents. They ought to be warned to keep out of the forest and away from the moor. We can use the excuse that there's a fire risk. We should draft in more patrols to keep people away from the area. And we should get Birk to take in a squad of picked marksmen; if the tigers are there, he'll find them.'

'And start a full-scale bloody stampede!' said Hale scathingly. 'What are we going to do? Go on TV and radio and warn people off? The tourists might believe the yarn about a fire-risk, but the locals won't—especially if they see a bunch of men with rifles rampaging through the forest! Then the word will spread and we'll have a riot on our hands!' He paused, then continued more calmly: 'The way I see it, the first step is for Jim here to look into the situation as quickly as possible. Let's find out what we're looking for, before we do anything else. What have we got? A body, the remains of a body, found in the forest. Was Pickford murdered—or was he killed by wild tigers? For my money, the chances of him being the victim of a couple of marauding tigers have got to be in the region of a million to one. If we'd been told that tigers had escaped from a nearby zoo—then it would be a different matter. But we haven't. People don't go around losing wild animals, they just don't. If some tigers had got loose, we'd damn well know about it. And if we go off at half-cock and start screaming tiger in all directions, we could end up with egg all over our faces. No! In my view, we should proceed quietly, step by step. Let Jim carry out a preliminary investigation. If he comes back and tells us that he agrees with Gosford, all right. Then we can take the appropriate action.'

'Such as what?' asked Murray.

Hale shrugged. 'I wouldn't go as far as Chief-Inspector Gosford. No need to get the public uptight about it. We simply pick out a half-dozen sharp-shooters and send them in to flush out the blasted animals and kill them. No reason why we shouldn't put a few men on stand-by immediately, just in case. They could go in early tomorrow morning if necessary, do the job without too much fuss, and nobody the wiser. No panic, nothing.'

'Seems to make sense,' said the Chief Constable. He made circles on his chin with the back of his thumb, and stared thoughtfully at Gosford. 'What about you, Chief-Inspector?'

'There's a lot in what Mr Hale says, sir,' Gosford said diplomatically, though the doubt still showed in his tone.

'But you're not sure?'

'Well, sir, I don't know much about tigers. Next to nothing in fact. I'm just wondering how easy it will be to find them and kill them. It's a big forest. And shooting a tiger isn't like shooting a deer.'

'If there are tigers,' said Hale. 'Let's establish that beyond all doubt—that's what I'm saying. I just want us to avoid panic action.'

'Right!' said the Chief Constable, standing up. 'That's what we'll do. Jim, you get over to Whitford and take a look-see. Report back to me as soon as possible. Gordon—you organise a squad of a half-dozen sharpshooters and have them standing-by, just in case they should be needed. Gosford—put more men on patrol on the forest road. Keep people out as far as possible until all this is cleared up. But stick to the line you've already taken—the restrictions are being imposed because of the fire danger, no other reason. Clear?'

Gosford was already on his feet, his body stiffened into a position of attention. 'Right, sir.'

The Chief Constable relaxed, smiled, glanced at his watch. 'Fine. Now, I have to push off. But you know where to get me, Jim—Gordon—if I'm wanted. No need for you to rush. Have another drink. Give Gosford one, daresay he could do with it.'

Better late than never, thought Gosford. The Chief Constable gave them the brisk, satisfied nod of a man who feels that a potentially dangerous situation has been brought under control by dint of leadership and left the room.

'Scotch?' asked Hale, looking at Gosford.

Gosford put down the whisky in a single swallow and made his excuses. He was ashamed of what he felt to be his own weakness in the face of their arguments, annoyed that he hadn't stood his ground. But they were the boss-men, there wasn't much he could do against their combined opposition, and at least he'd warned them, if anything happened now, it would be on their heads.

'I'd best get back and find out what's been happening,' he said.

'I'll be right on your tail,' said Murray. 'Should be able to get out to the forest before the light goes.'

Gosford closed the door and waited for a moment. As he turned away he heard the Deputy Chief Constable's voice: 'Tigers! Christ, Jim—now I've heard everything!' And afterwards, a chuckle of derision.

5

Within five minutes of setting out on his search for Penny, and as his anger died down, Toby Waites remembered the brown manilla envelope and the photographs. The sense of shock was overwhelming, he could feel the colour drain from his cheeks, his heart pound with fear. The driver of a car behind hooted angrily as he suddenly pulled in to the side of the road and stopped.

The photographs, the photographs! Oh, God, oh dear God, if those photographs were to get into the hands of someone who knew him! He rested his forehead against the steering-wheel, trying desperately to order his thoughts. Had Penny found and taken them? He tried to picture the bedroom, the open trunk, the litter of magazines on the floor and the bed—but he could not recall seeing the envelope. On the other hand, he could not be

sure, he might have missed it. He had been so outraged at
the loss of the money that his mind hadn't really taken in
anything else.

He groaned aloud, shaking his head; tears of self-pity
stirred in his eyes. He'd been mad to keep the photographs, crazy, out of his mind. Another week or so and he
probably would have destroyed them, as he'd destroyed
others in the past. Somehow, he had always known, in a
part of his mind, that retribution would come one day,
that sooner or later God would visit him with punishment.
But why had He waited so long, so long? Some words from
Jeremiah echoed in his head, words that he had often
spoken in the chapel: *Thou has polluted the land with thy
whoredoms and with thy wickedness.*

He started guiltily and looked towards the nearside
window. A man was standing there, rapping on the glass;
Toby leaned over and wound down the window.

'Are you all right?' The man looked at him with an
apologetic smile.

'What?'

'Sorry. Saw you there, thought you might be ill. Sorry.'
The man moved away and Toby restarted the engine. It
was now more urgent than ever that he should find Penny.
She could keep the money, she could have every penny of
it, so long as he got the photographs back. The whore, the
whore, the Jezebel!

He covered the approach roads to Whitford, drove into
the town itself, doubled back two or three times, and as
the time passed, his desperation grew. Finally he turned
towards home; his one hope was that the photographs
might still be there, that he had overlooked them. And
there was also a slender chance that Penny might have
returned.

He stumbled up the stairs to the bedroom, but to his
horror he found that the magazines and the broken trunk
had gone.

'The police have been.' He turned and saw his wife

standing in the doorway, anxious eyes in a drawn and haggard face.

'The police!'

'They've found Penny. She's at the station. And they've got your money.' There was no bitterness in her voice, and no triumph.

'Why did they come here?'

'They took the trunk—your trunk. They said they wanted it for evidence.' She did not tell him that she had called the station to report the theft. His manner, the look in his eyes, was too frightening; he seemed like a man at the end of his endurance.

'Did they take the—the other stuff?'

She shook her head. 'No, I cleared it up before they came. It's in the outhouse, under the hay.'

He charged past her, and clattered down the stairs. She went to the window and watched as he emerged from the house and ran to the outhouse. When he came out a few minutes later, he seemed smaller, as if his body had shrunk within his clothes; he leaned against the door-frame with his eyes closed for a long time.

She called down to him: 'Toby.' He opened his eyes but he did not lift his head or move from the shed. 'The police,' she said. 'They want you to go to Whitford station as soon as possible.'

He gave a small, almost imperceptible nod, then turned away and walked with slow, deliberate steps away from the house towards the farm buildings. She busied herself in the kitchen for a half-hour, occupying her hands with routine tasks as an antidote to her thoughts. The telephone interrupted her and when she answered it, it was the police, a Detective-Sergeant Miller, asking whether her husband had returned.

'He's just come in,' she said.

'I'd like him to come in as soon as possible.'

'I'll tell him right away.'

She went out into the yard, stepping through the hens

who came clacking round at her approach and called her husband. When he did not reply, she looked into each of the buildings in turn.

She found him in the last one, the old barn. He was hanging from a rope attached to one of the main roof beams, his head slumped forward over the thick noose, and his body swinging in slow, even, little circles.

6

The sad remains of Tom Pickford still lay where they had been found silently awaiting detailed examination by the officers and experts of the County Police Murder Investigation Squad. The area around had been roped off and two policemen placed on guard. They found their instructions puzzling, for they had been posted along the edge of the road, at least a quarter of a mile from the scene of the crime, but they did not question them. They had seen enough, they were thankful to be separated from that gruesome place.

They had little to do, for what few cars there were passed through, their occupants giving the policemen no more than the odd, curious glance, and they saw no-one moving on foot. Each took a turn at patrolling the road for 250 yards or so in both directions, while the other waited by the blue-and-white police car.

Evening had brought little respite from the oppressive, almost tropical heat. The air was still heavy and humid, and the sun, as though it had abandoned its efforts to penetrate the forest, seemed to concentrate its strength on the narrow road, the white dust dancing and glittering in its yellow, slanted rays. The constables were in regulation summer kit, without tunics, but even so their skins were sticky with sweat, they felt lethargic, drained of energy.

The younger of the two, P.C. Parker, the bearded officer who had called at the Waites' farm earlier in the day, took his turn to rest by the car while his colleague, P.C. Collins made the routine patrol. He climbed into the front seat, lit a cigarette and relaxed, watching the road ahead and casting an occasional look at the rear-view mirror so that the arrival of any superior officers would not take him by surprise. He was a subscriber to a correspondence course in French, and as he drew on the cigarette he began to run through a list of the new words and phrases he had committed to memory the previous evening.

He spoke them aloud, practising the accent carefully, pleased that he had forgotten so little, when he became aware of a subtle change in the atmosphere. He tensed, the words fading in his throat; for no reason that he could understand, he felt suddenly isolated, vulnerable, surrounded by some unknown threat. The road ahead and behind was clear, he could not see his colleague, he was bewildered by this strange, prickling sense of danger. Slowly, very slowly, he turned his head towards the forest.

At first, he could not believe or comprehend what he saw. Two luminous, greenish-yellow eyes were staring out at him from the undergrowth, eyes that glowed with a ferocity so chilling that he felt his skin crawl with fear. There was no substance, no body, behind the eyes that he could see, they seemed to be fixed in the air. Then, gradually, he was able to make out the irregular white patches above the eyes, the pattern of short, broken, black stripes on a background of rufus red and white skin, the lips curled back over gleaming white teeth, until it all came together into a single vision, and he realised that he was looking into the face of a tiger.

Afterwards Parker was to speak of these few moments as if they were an eternity. It seemed to him as if time was frozen, as if he would sit there forever held by those glittering eyes. And then, slowly, the animal moved. The striped body rose gracefully from the screen of bushes, the great head turned almost imperceptibly from right to left and back again, and then it padded silently towards the car.

The hypnotic glare was broken momentarily, and Parker moved also, scrambling feverishly to turn up the windows, and lock the doors. He watched fearfully as the tiger circled the car warily, head down, as if it were scenting some unknown beast. It paused by the window, staring with cold insolence at the white face of the man within, and lifted one huge paw, pressing it against the thick glass. The door creaked under the pressure, and then suddenly, the paw was removed, and Parker saw the tiger turn and look down the road, its ears cocked, the ringed tail twitching ominously. A new fear needled his flesh, like an electric shock. There was no-one on the road ahead, no sign of Collins, but he was down there, and soon, very soon, he would turn back and come towards the car, towards the waiting tiger; and, as though on cue, at that moment, the sturdy figure of the other man appeared round a bend in the road.

Through the window, Parker saw the tiger lower its body into a crouch, as if preparing to attack. He closed his eyes for a second, gathering the will to act, and then he thrust the palm of his hand against the horn of the car, pressing it up and down in long, insistent bursts. He saw Collins stop in surprise, he caught a sideways glimpse, no more, of the startled tiger as it leaped for the cover of the forest, and then he turned the ignition key and accelerated the car forward, its engine roaring.

Collins had not seen the tiger, and after his initial surprise at hearing the blare of the horn, he had begun to run towards his colleague. He stopped, his square, ruddy face creased in bewilderment as the car jerked to a halt at his side, its tyres noisily spitting up dust from the loose surface. Parker pushed open the rear door nearest to him.

'Get in!' he shouted, 'get in!'

'What?' Collins stared at him.

'For Christ's sake, man, get in, get in!'

Collins frowned, pulled himself into the car with laborious slowness and sank back on the seat. 'What the bloody hell—' he began.

'The door! Shut the door. Quick! Quick!' Collins, catching something of the other man's urgency, slammed the door and locked it. Parker put back his head and expelled the air from his lungs in a sigh of relief. Collins waited for a moment, disturbed by Parker's distress, and then he drew some cigarettes from his pocket, lit two, and, leaning forward, held one to Parker's lips. The younger man nodded, sat back, and inhaled deeply.

'All right?' asked Collins quietly.

Parker nodded again, and pushed a plume of blue smoke through pursed lips. 'Sorry,' he murmured, 'sorry.'

'What happened, Ray? What is it?' asked Collins quietly.

Parker turned slowly to face him, frowning. 'What do you mean?'

'What happened back there? What was all that business with the horn?'

'Didn't you see it?' Parker looked at him aghast.

'What?'

'Christ!' Parker shook his head in disbelief. 'You must have seen it!'

'What? Must have seen what?'

'The tiger, the tiger!' It was the older man's turn now to stare back. 'Listen,' said Parker, making an effort not to lose patience. 'There was a tiger back there.' Collins twisted round to peer out of the back window. 'You won't see it now. I scared it off. It ran into the forest. Christ, Eddie, it scared the shits out of me! Thank God, I was sitting in the car. I suddenly looked up and saw these eyes, in the bushes. Then it came out, walked all round the car. It shoved its head against this window—here—God, it was huge—and the teeth—' He stopped, and drew on his cigarette. 'I thought he was going after you. That's why I leaned on the horn—'

There was a long silence. The interior of the car was

heavy with smoke, and Collins wound down one of the windows. 'A tiger,' he said. 'Ray—that takes a bit of believing. You have to admit—it takes some believing.'

'I saw it, Eddie. As clear as I see you. I'm not making it up.'

'No, no, I didn't say that. I'm not saying you made it up,' said Collins carefully, but Parker knew by his tone and the look on his face that he was not convinced.

'Listen,' he said urgently. 'Whether you believe me or not, I know what I saw. There's a tiger loose in there and we've got to do something about it!' A thought occurred to him, and he continued excitedly: 'That body we found— what was left of it! This could be the answer! Yes, that's it! That poor devil was killed by the tiger I saw! Eddie, you saw it too—a murderer, an ordinary murderer, couldn't have done that to him. It was a wild animal—a tiger!'

'I'm not sure—' began Collins doubtfully, and then he stopped suddenly, and lifted his head, listening.

The sound was more fearful than anything he had ever heard, and so close that it seemed to shake the car: a great, blaring, trumpet roar of anger that hung in the air like a threat. It was repeated three times, the birds rose in shrill complaint, and then there was a long, quivering silence.

Three full minutes passed and Parker was the first to speak, his voice no more than a whisper.

'Now do you believe me?' he said.

CHAPTER EIGHT

1

Jim Topping of the *Whitford Gazette* did not stay long at Burnwick Farm. The torn and mangled bodies of the dead sheep were laid out in one of the barns, with the distraught farmer hovering and cursing over them. He was still convinced that this orgy of killing was the responsibility of a mad dog or dogs, he could think of no other explanation which would fit the circumstances, but Topping, after one look at the massacre, felt more certain than ever that the answer lay elsewhere and that he was on the track of a sensational and extraordinary story. It was all beginning to come together but he was experienced enough to realise that too much was based on supposition and deduction. He needed more hard facts, but how to get them, that was the problem.

He said nothing of this to the farmer, simply made a few sympathetic noises and put on a show of noting down the man's fierce comments about the criminal laxity of some dog owners, and when the photographer had taken a series of shots, he made his excuses and hurried back to the office.

Topping didn't stay long at his desk either. Before leaving for Burnwick he had directed Colin Essex, the only other staff reporter available, to the Whitford police station with orders to report any unusual happenings.

Essex, a serious young man who regarded his job with the *Gazette* as one of great social responsibility, was waiting in the outer office for Topping to return. He reported that police activity in Whitford appeared to be running at an abnormally high level, although the police themselves continued to deny that anything of unusual importance was taking place.

'The sergeant just keeps stone-walling, Mr Topping,' he said, making it plain by the indignation in his tone that, in his view, this was no way to treat an accredited representative of the Fourth Estate. Not for the first time, Topping inwardly cursed the management of the paper in general and Mr Dailey in particular, whose penny-pinching meanness and lack of vision would not allow him to employ an experienced senior reporter. All they seemed interested in was the number of column inches of advertising, the pages of classified advertisements which made up the bulk of the paper.

Topping could visualise the scene at the police-station, see Sergeant Miller waving Essex away, even hear the Sergeant's words in his head: 'Look, sonnie, there's nothing to tell you. When there is, I'll let you know, all right? Until then, just piss off and let me get on with some bloody work.' He would not have been surprised to learn that this mental reconstruction of the incident was almost 100 per cent accurate.

'The police are bastards, lad,' he said with a sigh that echoed many years of experience. 'When they want the press, butter wouldn't melt in their mouths. When they don't, they treat us like toilet-rolls.'

'They wouldn't treat someone from *The Sunday Times* or *The Guardian* like that,' said Essex with feeling. He spoke the names as Jason might have referred to the Golden Fleece; a job with either of them represented the summit of his immediate ambition.

'What is going on down there then?' asked Topping. 'Why are they playing so hard to get?' He took a cheroot from the tin on the desk, went to light it, then remembered that he had promised himself to keep his consumption down to five a day and that he had already exceeded this self-imposed ration. He put the cigar and the lighter down, then sat back and fanned himself with the latest press release from the Whitford and District Conservative Society. But he was soon sitting forward again, listening intently, for Essex had plainly not been idle.

'I think there's something big going on—really big, Mr Topping. First, they brought in a girl named Waites. Penny Waites.' Essex consulted a little black notebook. 'Lives at Little Chase Farm, near Cullington, with her uncle. She came from Scarby, in a police-car with a W.P.C.'

'Why are they holding her?'

'To assist with enquiries. I don't know, of course, but I reckon it could be something to do with Mr Pickford. You know about him, of course.'

'Of course,' said Topping. Like most newspapermen he did not relish the idea that he was less well-informed than others, especially people on his own staff, so the lie came easily, quickly.

'All the same,' he continued smoothly, 'I'd like you to give me the facts about Mr Pickford as you know them.' He smiled, and decided to light the cigar after all.

'What I heard is that he hasn't been seen since last night. Didn't go home, didn't show up at his office in the Town Hall this morning. And they found his empty car in Watts Lane near Cullington. That's all, really.' Christ, thought Topping, how the hell did I miss that one? The Deputy Borough Treasurer missing, a girl being questioned about him! The trouble is, he told himself, reproachfully, you've been so obsessed by these bloody tigers that you haven't allowed yourself to think of anything else. 'What else happened?' he asked. 'Apart from this girl?'

Essex briefly outlined the other comings and goings of the afternoon, culminating with a report of the arrival at Whitford station of a party of officers from County Police HQ, led by Detective Chief-Superintendent James Murray. They had spent only a few minutes at the station and then set off again, heading in the direction of the forest.

The forest! Every damn thing seems to lead back to the forest, thought Topping. A few seconds ago his belief in the existence of the tigers had weakened, but now it hardened again. One way or the other he had to get at the truth, if only to settle his own mind. He pushed back the chair and stood up.

'Good,' he said, 'you've done a bloody fine job. Now, I want you to do something else. You're not busy this evening?'

'Nothing I can't drop, Mr Topping.'

'Have you eaten?'

'No. But—'

'A good journalist never works on an empty stomach. Go and get yourself something and then come back. Don't take too long.' And as Essex moved to the door, he added: 'Do you like the circus?'

'Yes.' The tone was hesitant. 'At least, I used to—'

'Good. Because that's where you're going.'

He enjoyed the look of surprise this brought to the young man's face. A moment later Lucy tapped at the door and came in. She looked a little weary.

'I've checked, Mr Topping. Every zoo and safari park on the list. Nobody's bought any tigers in the last two days.' She paused and added, with a little frown: 'You weren't having me on, were you?'

'Lucy!' he said, in mock horror. 'Why would I do a thing like that?'

'Only it seems so silly, I mean, a lot of the people just laughed. I didn't know what to say. I mean, I couldn't tell them why I was asking, because I didn't know, did I?'

'Would you like to know?'

'I wouldn't mind.'

'Well, I'm not absolutely sure myself. But I am about to find out. You sit there and listen.' He guided her to a chair and went back to the desk. As he picked up the telephone and dialled a number he smiled reassuringly at her. She gave a little deferential, uncertain smile in return and nervously crossed her legs under the short skirt. He caught a momentary glimpse of smooth, brown thigh and thought, Christ, darling, don't do that, not in this weather, it gives me ideas. She must have sensed his reaction, for she hastily

144

dropped her legs into their former position and tugged at the hem of her skirt.

By this time, he was through to Whitford Police station and his mind was on other things. 'Jim Topping, *Whitford Gazette*. Put me through to Chief-Inspector Gosford please.'

'Can I help you, Jim? Sergeant Miller here. Mr Gosford is tied up at the moment.' The tone was wary but civil, placatory.

'I don't know whether you can, sergeant.' Topping winked at Lucy over the desk. 'Actually, I'm writing a piece for one of the London dailies about the tigers which are loose in the forest and I just wanted to check a couple of my facts.'

Lucy's jaw dropped in surprise, and there must have been a similar reaction at the other end of the line, for there was a long pause before Miller came back again.

'Look, Jim—I told you when you rang before. We have no knowledge of any tigers. I know there have been rumours—'

'Sergeant,' said Topping softly.

'Yes?'

'Put me on to Gosford, will you? I have to file this story in the next fifteen minutes. If you don't know, I'd like to check with someone who does.'

There was another short silence, and then Miller said gruffly: 'Hold on.' Topping relit his cheroot and waited, smiling at Lucy and wondering whether she was as innocent as she appeared. A minute later, he heard Gosford on the line, asking him brusquely what he wanted. He repeated what he had already told the sergeant, trying to make it sound casual, normal, but aware that his whole body was tensed, as though in anticipation.

'Where did you get hold of your information, Mr Topping?' asked Gosford.

'From various sources, Chief-Inspector. Naturally, if you categorically deny the story—'

'Mr Topping, before you write anything, I think it would be a good idea if you and I had a talk.'

'I'd like that, Chief-Inspector.'

'Could you come straightaway?'

'I'll be round in a few minutes. One quick question, Chief-Inspector, before you hang up. Naturally, my concern is with the public. Can you tell me why the police have not yet issued a statement warning them of the danger?'

'I'll expect you in a few minutes, Mr Topping.' Gosford hung up abruptly. Topping listened to the buzz of the telephone for a moment, then dropped it back on the cradle with a flourish.

'What did they say?' asked Lucy.

He spread his hands, pleased with himself, pleased by the note of awe in her tone. 'They told me all I need to know, love. I called their bluff that time.'

'You mean, there really are tigers in the forest—wild tigers?'

'Lucy, this is between us, you understand?' She nodded her head. 'We're on to one of the biggest stories of the past 50 years, and we're going to keep it to ourselves for as long as we can. Tomorrow every newspaper in the country will have a man in Whitford. Tonight, before they get here, we are going to tie up as many angles as possible. You listen and learn, love. Uncle James will demonstrate the gentle art of milking a story. Now, I want you to look up the private address of a Mr Thomas Pickford and let me have it. When I've seen the police I want to go and talk to his wife. And I shall need you to stick around, handle the telephone. You might have to stay late. That all right?'

'Yes, of course, Mr Topping.'

She hurried away. As the door closed, he sat back in his chair and closed his eyes. It was a long time since he had felt so exhilarated, he knew from Gosford's attitude that his instincts had been right and that he was on to one of the biggest stories of his life.

He opened his eyes and stretched his arms and then ignoring the half-smoked cigar in the ash-tray he lit another one.

2

'I'm afraid,' said Gosford, 'that the press are on to it!'

There were four other men in the office: Hale, the Deputy Chief Constable, Murray, the top C.I.D. man from Scarby, Detective-Inspector Banks, his aide, and David Birk. The Deputy Chief Constable sat in Gosford's chair at Gosford's desk as though by right. He had driven from Scarby to take charge of affairs and he was in a bad temper. There could no longer be any doubt that one tiger at least was at large in the area, which meant that Gosford, a subordinate officer, had been right and he had been wrong. He was not the kind of man to accept such a circumstance with any grace and he made it plain by his attitude; Gosford might be the officer in charge at Whitford, but he, Hale, was the boss, and he intended to run this particular show.

'The press? Who tipped them off?' he asked sharply. 'You were told to keep the lid on this thing!'

'I don't think he could have got it from here, sir,' answered Gosford. 'I gave strict instructions.'

'Someone must have talked.' Hale's eyes moved to David Birk, who was sitting quietly at the back of the room. 'You spoke to the District Officer of the Forestry Commission, Mr Birk. Did you tell anyone else of your theory?'

'No.' He spoke quietly, ignoring the brusque, almost offensive tone of the question. Hale seemed about to challenge him again, but the look in David's eyes deterred him, and he merely grunted and looked away.

'What do we do about the press, sir?' asked Gosford.

'I thought I'd already made that clear! At this stage, I don't want the media poking its nose in, spreading rum-

147

ours, stirring up the public. With any luck, we'll have the whole thing resolved in a few hours, and then the press can do and say what it damn well likes! Until then, they'll be kept out of it. Who is this fellow—what's his paper?'

'Topping. He's the chief reporter of the *Whitford Gazette.*'

'Then there's no problem, is there? It's a weekly, doesn't come out until Friday, by which time our problems will be over.'

'It doesn't quite work like that, sir. Most of these chaps also work as stringers for the national papers, and they have links with TV and local radio.'

'I know how they work, man. But this man, Topping, is an employee of the *Whitford Gazette,* right?'

'Yes.'

'Then we can fix him through Dailey, the man who owns it. I know him, he'll co-operate. See this reporter, find out how much he knows, and warn him that if he mentions one word of it to his London contacts or to anyone else, he'll find himself out of a job. Clear?'

'Is this a private discussion or may anyone join in?' The voice came from the back, from David Birk, and the others turned to him.

'It's open to everyone naturally, Mr Birk. That's what we're here for,' Hale said silkily. 'You don't agree with my approach to the press, I take it?'

'Do you want a candid opinion?'

'If you insist.'

'All right. No, I don't agree. First, I was under the impression that the police were in business to put down blackmail, not promote it on their own account. Second, I believe that you should seek the co-operation of the media. You're going to need it. And finally, I think it's time you stopped worrying what the papers will do or say and started talking about tigers.'

The silence that followed crackled with tension. None of the officers in that overheated little room had ever heard

148

the Deputy Chief Constable spoken to in that way, or would have dared challenge him in similar fashion. In normal circumstances they could have predicted Hale's reaction, the savage sarcasm, the words sharp as swords, with which he had so often reduced stern and efficient men to a state of quivering nervousness. But this was different. Birk was an outsider, beyond the reach of Hale's authority; but more than this, there was some force of personality in the man, an authority in those extraordinarily sharp, blue eyes which perhaps even Hale would be forced to recognise.

The Deputy Chief Constable had turned his head away and was looking down at the desk, fidgeting with some papers. When he looked up at last, his eyes glittered like frost, but his voice was controlled and even. 'You're an expert on the press and public relations also, are you, Mr Birk?'

'No.'

'No? Well, we do have some experience. Extensive experience. And that experience tends to prove that the newspapers invariably get it wrong. As does television. They are not so much interested in the truth, in the facts, as in sensation. And it happens to be my view—as a senior police officer—that to have this present situation treated sensationally could be dangerous in the extreme, I am not prepared to see that happen, and I am prepared to take whatever steps are necessary to see that it doesn't happen.' He paused and turned to Gosford. 'Chief-Inspector, I asked you a question. Are you quite clear about my instructions on this matter?'

'Yes, sir, I am to ask Topping not to publish any story which bears on this subject of the tigers.'

'No!' said Hale sharply, and he glanced at David. 'You won't ask. You will tell him not to publish. You will warn him of the consequences if he refuses to co-operate. And if he chooses to go ahead regardless you are to inform me and I will speak to his employer.'

'Yes, sir,' said Gosford. He wanted to argue, to agree with David Birk, but he felt out-numbered, helpless. Hale was a bitter man, whose applications for the post of Chief Constable in other counties had been turned down on three occasions. He believed that he had been rejected in favour of inferior, establishment figures and in private conversation, made no secret of his resentment. No-one had ever dared suggest that the fault lay in himself, in his own jealous and embittered nature, and not, as he claimed, in his humble background. He would not have listened, it was not a subject on which he was capable of being rational or objective, the frustration had gone too deep and soured his outlook.

Gosford had worked in Scarby under Hale at one time and learned to recognise the man's moods, he knew that at certain times it was impossible to hold him in reasonable debate, and certainly dangerous to cross him, for he virtually ran the County force, and was quite capable of blocking a man's promotion. Even so, his own lack of resolution made him feel a certain guilt, and he looked across at David, a tentative, unspoken apology in his eyes: but David responded with a little, enigmatic smile that might have meant anything.

'Well, gentlemen,' said Hale, with the air of someone who has made his point, 'now we have disposed of that, perhaps we can get back to the main problem. Mr Birk, I understand that you are of the opinion that there could be two tigers at large in the forest?'

'There are two,' said Birk. 'I heard them—two distinct and separate calls. One is probably female, a tigress.'

'So far, of course, we have only definite proof of one. The tiger seen by P.C. Parker. However, you are the expert, and we'll defer to your opinion. We will operate on the assumption that there are two animals to deal with. Have you any idea where they could have come from?'

'None. Does it matter? The point, surely, is that they are there.'

'Mr Birk, it matters very much. According to our enquiries, no tigers have escaped from captivity in the last day or so. It is possible that someone—God knows who—managed to get possession of the animals and then deliberately released them. That person must be found. I'd say he was in a pretty fair way to being charged with murder. I was wondering whether, with your contacts, you might be able to help us. After all, it can't be easy to get hold of a couple of tigers, they're not the sort of things you can walk into a shop and buy, are they?'

This brought a dutiful chuckle from Detective-Inspector Banks, and an uncertain smile from his superior, Detective Chief-Superintendent Murray, who was clearly uncomfortable at the turn the conference was taking. Gosford did not respond; he was watching David Birk, trying to read the man. David seemed to be the coolest person in the room, untouched by the heat, and again as at the house on the high moor, Gosford was fascinated by his immense repose. But now there was something else there, a tension crouched under the stillness, and in a leap of intuition, he saw and understood what it was. He had seen a tiger only once in his life, at the London Zoo, many years before, but now, suddenly, he saw it again on the screen of his mind.

He had watched the great beast pacing the cage, lithe, majestic, powerful, turning at intervals to cast cold, contemptuous eyes on the puny, human faces which had gathered to stare, and he had turned away in shame, horrified that man should make a spectacle of a creature so noble and magnificent.

David Birk reminded him of that caged tiger at this moment. The eyes, clear and compelling, seemed to be looking out in the same way, as from behind iron bars, at a pygmy world to which he was a stranger, there was the same feeling of rippling power coiled beneath the calm exterior.

He forced his thoughts back to the meeting as Hale, in

response to David's silence, said: 'I take it you can't help us in that respect. Pity—but I daresay we shall manage.'

David lifted his wrist, looked with pointed deliberation at his watch, and stood up. 'If you'll excuse me,' he said and moved in his easy, laconic way to the door.

'You're not leaving us, Mr Birk?' asked Hale, and there was a slight sneer in the tone.

'I've things to do.'

'They can't wait?'

'No.'

'Well,' said Hale, 'thank you for giving us your time. I hope we shan't need to intrude on it again. At first light tomorrow morning we shall be sending in a squad of sharpshooters to pick off your tigers, and hopefully, that will be the end of the matter.'

David twisted the door-handle, the door opened a little, and then he snapped it shut and turned back to face the others.

'For God's sake,' he said earnestly, 'be careful what you do. At least one of these tigers has tasted human flesh—that means you have a man-eater on your hands, possibly two. And hunting tiger isn't like culling deer, believe me. They could kill two or three of your sharp-shooters before they have a chance to cock their rifles. You won't be doing the hunting—it will be the tigers, and there's no animal, human or otherwise, to match them at that game. You may not find them in the forest—if the deer have moved on, they'll move on too, looking for a kill. If they are still there, you may only succeed in driving them out on to the moors—do you want that? Are you prepared to evacuate all the isolated homesteads out there, even some of the villages? Because if they leave the forest, that's what you'll have to do. It's going to take a bit more than a half-dozen sharp-shooters, I assure you. Out in India, my father once tracked the same tigress, on and off, for nearly three years. In that time, she accounted for over five hundred human beings, men, women and children.'

'Mr Birk,' said Hale, 'this isn't India.'

'You know it,' said David, 'I know it—but do the tigers know it?'

3

'You know your trouble, shall I tell you your trouble? You never know when to draw the line! You just can't say no, can you! Do you realise what an exhibition you put on tonight? Everybody noticed it, everybody was talking about you! And they knew why we left early, they didn't believe my feeble excuses.'

Ellen Fitch screwed up her face as she glanced at her husband. His thin lips were moving angrily as if powered by clockwork and above the toothbrush moustache his angry, little eyes glared at the winding forest road, as though it were a personal enemy. It was all too familiar, she could have reproduced his monologue from memory, and she turned away with a sigh. She had learned by constant practice, to switch off whenever her husband launched himself into one of his long tirades and she did so now; she smiled smugly to herself, remembering with some astonishment, an incident at that evening's barbecue when she had left the garden and gone into the house in search of the lavatory. She found the downstairs cloakroom occupied, and Lou Unstead her host, coming from the kitchen at that moment, had taken her hand and led her upstairs towards the main bathroom. And then, on the upper landing, out of view of the hall below, he had suddenly swung her round and pulled her towards him. It was quite amazing really, the last thing she had expected to happen. She could still feel the moistness of his lips, smell the faint but not unpleasant odour of tobacco on his breath and—most incredible of all—his hand pressing her breast, then sliding down her long white skirt, to fumble urgently between her thighs. And she made no protest, she had felt herself respond—with Lou, of all people, one of their oldest friends! Of course, he had drunk too much, as she had; in the morning he would have forgotten the incident, or be too ashamed to mention it. All the same, she wondered if he would telephone, wondered what she would say if he did. The thought of an affair excited her, in the past year or so she had longed with increasing frequency for something, anything, which would enliven the grinding, suburban monotony of her life, but would she have the courage to go through with it? She had been faithful to Gilbert for 15 years, since their marriage, but after all, people looked at these things in a different way now, they were more broadminded. Here, for example, in the forest; this would be an ideal place to meet, they could lose themselves here. She saw herself parking her little Mini off the road, under the trees, where Lou would be waiting in his Rover 2000—

The car began to jolt and jar as it reached a bad piece of road and her dream was drowned in a sudden wave of nausea. Her stomach began to heave, cold sweat broke out on her forehead.

'Gil—you'll have to stop.'

'We can't. You heard the police warning. We're not allowed to stop on the forest road.'

'I'm going to be sick!'

'I'm not surprised! After what you put away—'

'Gil, please—quick, quick!'

With a sigh of resignation, he pulled off the road. She had the door open almost before he braked to a halt, and tumbling out, she ran towards the shelter of the trees. Her husband shook his head in disgust, and reached into the glove compartment for the little tin of lemon sweets; he had drunk only two glasses of the red wine that evening but his throat felt harsh and dry.

As he took off the lid, he heard the scream, long, drawn-out, shrill with terror. The tin dropped from his fingers, scattering the sweets over the floor of the car, as he stared, white-faced, towards the forest. There was no sign of Ellen, but the scream still seemed to echo on the sultry air. He scrambled out, and ran to the edge of the trees, calling her name. The thick undergrowth just ahead was quivering as though in protest, and suddenly it opened out and the tigress appeared.

She glared at the man, her eyes glowing with menace, her tail swishing and beating against the bushes. She held an odd, doll-like figure in her powerful jaws, and it took Gilbert Fitch a long, horrified moment to realise that it was Ellen, his wife. Her torn skirt drooped over the animal's front legs like a grotesque curtain, her head swung from side to side; one breast was exposed, and where the other should have been there was a raw and bloody gap. And as the man and the tigress faced each other, the woman moved, one arm pushing feebly at the body of the tigress as she tried to ease the grip of those grim, white teeth. She was trying to speak, to call out, a stream of incoherent words dribbled from her mouth.

Gilbert Fitch bore no resemblance to the conventional hero or man of action. Small, neat, precise, he had built a solid and fairly successful practice as a chartered accountant largely on his reputation for caution, and for painstaking almost finicking attention to detail. No-one who knew him would have described Gilbert as imaginative or quick-witted; the principal complaint of his associates was that to screw a decision out of him was akin to undertaking a major dental operation.

Yet in this instance he acted immediately, and with immense courage; not from any conscious sense of bravery but simply because he felt outraged. He might have reacted thus if someone had walked naked into a church service, or wantonly disarrayed his filing system. Blazing with anger and indignation, he seized a loose branch which was lying at his feet, and advanced on the tigress, shouting the sort of stern warnings one might address to a recalcitrant dog. The tigress stared back, puzzled by this unexpected defiance; she could not forget her fear of men, she had lived with it for too long.

Had this man turned and fled as Tom Pickford had done, had she caught the scent of fear, she might have attacked; but he was advancing on her, making sounds similar to those she had learned in her days of captivity, and the old disciplines stirred in her blood. She backed away a little, but this only seemed to encourage him, for he came on, brandishing the improvised staff as, in different circumstances, he might have brandished his umbrella. She opened her jaws, dropped the woman to the ground, and stood back, hissing at the man, crouching down as if she were about to spring. Fitch was only three or four yards away now, and in a final, reckless gesture, he threw the branch at the face of his adversary. The tigress brushed the missile aside as if it were no more than a toothpick and for another long moment beast and man faced each other.

The man was looking straight into those cold amber eyes, and below them he could see the fierce, canine teeth bared in a snarl. The strong animal odour of the beast pricked at his nostrils, and suddenly all his fear came back, quenching his courage; he felt unable to move, he stood rooted to the earth in blind terror. But by some miracle, it was the tigress who was the first to break. She backed away, hissing and snarling, then turned and leaped away, disappearing into the gloom.

Fitch fell to his knees, shuddering and sobbing with relief and it was a long time before he regained control of himself. A low moan from the torn body of his wife roused him at last. He stooped over her and she looked up at him with dull, shocked, uncomprehending eyes; his hands shook as though with fever as he tried to draw the clothing over her piteous wounds. He recalled the injunction that someone so seriously injured should not be moved, but it was impossible to leave her in this place while he went for help and too dangerous to stay.

With difficulty he lifted her up in his arms, murmuring

gently to her as she groaned in pain, and stumbled back to the car. He laid her on the rear seat, pillowing her head on his folded jacket and covering her as best he could with the tartan-patterned car rug.

He had to rest at the wheel before driving off, gulping desperately for air, chest heaving, heart pounding, streams of sweat pouring painfully into his eyes and down his face. He felt a warm stickiness on his chest and looking down he saw that his shirt-front was darkly stained with blood.

He drove faster than he had driven in years to Whitford Cottage Hospital, and then, as the kindly, efficient nurses wheeled her away, shock and exhaustion overcame him. He lay stretched on a couch staring blankly at the ceiling, and to all their soft-spoken questions he replied with a slow turn of the head, as if the answers were beyond words.

After a while, the doctor on duty injected a strong sedative and left him to sleep.

4

'So that's how it is,' said Topping. He ran a tentative finger over his upper lip, his eyes on Gosford. The conference had broken up a few minutes before, the Deputy Chief Constable was on his way home to Scarby (having indicated that he would be back at dawn the following morning) and the two men were seated in Gosford's office.

'That's how it is, I'm afraid,' said Gosford. 'We want the story kept under covers for the time being.' He didn't like what he had to do, and it showed in his defensive manner.

'This wasn't your idea, was it?' said Topping, watching him keenly.

'I'm making an official request Mr Topping,' Gosford replied, sidestepping the question. 'I'm asking you to co-operate. For obvious reasons, we don't want the public alarmed unnecessarily.'

'You do know that rumours are already circulating?

We've had a half-dozen calls asking if there is any truth in the story that some wild animals are loose in the forest.'

'So have we. But we can contain that. Most of the callers are treating it as a joke.'

'A joke! My God!'

'We're a media-minded nation, Mr Topping. You ought to know that. If it's not on the BBC or ITV we don't believe it.'

'And Tom Pickford. What about him?'

'We're issuing a statement.'

'Will it say that he was mauled and killed by a tiger?'

'We've no proof that he was—at the present.'

'It's a pretty fair deduction, isn't it?'

'Between you and me—yes, it is.'

'You haven't caught the tigers yet, have you?'

'No.'

'So how can you be certain that there won't be another Tom Pickford? There are hundreds of visitors in the area, hundreds, coming and going all the time—your tigers could be making a meal of any one of them at this moment.'

'We're doing what we can to keep people away from the forest.'

'Eighty thousand acres of it? Not to mention fifteen square miles of moorland. You have to be joking. The public should be warned, Chief-Inspector, and you know it.'

'They'll be warned, if and when it's necessary,' said Gosford stiffly.

Topping shook his head slowly. 'No. It's not on. Sorry. You do your job in your own way, I'll do mine. Sorry.' He put a match to a stub of cheroot, screwing up his eyes and lifting his chin as he held the flickering flame.

Gosford got up and walked to the window. He moved slowly, he felt depressed, leaden, without energy. The sounds of the evening drifted in; the strident note of a motor-cycle rising to a pitch and fading into the distance, the quieter hum of an occasional passing car, faint music and a burst of laughter from the garden of a public-house nearby.

This time yesterday, he thought, I was complaining of the boredom of the job, the stifling routine, praying that something would happen, longing for a challenge. Well, since then, the skies had opened, it was showering problems on his head. Two tigers had appeared out of nowhere and, in consequence, one man had died a terrible death in the forest, another had killed himself, and neither of the men had been what they seemed. The coming of the tigers had ripped away the façade of their respectability: the first had been running an affair with some poor little scrubber who, at this moment, was being interrogated in the back room and who would probably end up with a charge of theft round her neck; and the second, in between sermons, had not only indulged in some peculiar practices with young girls, he had actually recorded his hobby in glorious Kodachrome! Who was the other man in those photographs, who and what would they uncover when they started to chase down that particular hare? And that still left George Leppard! Had he lied about Tom Pickford's movements simply from motives of friendship, or was there something deeper, a local government fiddle of some sort— and into what murky waters will that lead us?

And all this in less than 24 hours! Out there they were watering their gardens, sipping cool drinks, playing bowls and tennis and golf, talking about the heat-wave, holidays, inflation, passing on the strange rumours about wild animals being at large in the forest with a laugh and a shake of the head. What other secrets would they yield up before it was finished, what additional tribute would they have to pay to the tigers?

The challenge had come with a vengeance and as a policeman he ought to be feeling excited, stimulated. But he felt only weariness, a sagging lethargy of mind and spirit. Left

159

to himself, he was positive that he could have handled the situation, and would certainly have approached it in a different way; but they had taken it out of his hands, Hale had descended from above and assumed command, issued the orders. The conference had depressed him, the long, irrelevant discussions, the arrogance of Hale, the assumption that rounding up the tigers would be an easy matter. The only concession the Deputy Chief Constable had made after David Birk's tirade was to double the number of sharp-shooters, that was all!

Gosford felt in the marrow of his bones that Birk was right, he had wanted to get up and applaud his speech. Then why hadn't he done so? This was what oppressed him most of all. It was wrong, all wrong! To follow Hale's line could, and probably would, lead to further tragedy but he had meekly accepted it, he had sat in virtual silence, making no protest. Why, why, why? All right, he would have been over-ruled at the end, there was little doubt of that, but at least he would have made his point for the record, he might even have won over some of the others. But he hadn't had the guts to do it!

The truth of the matter was that he was afraid of the Deputy Chief Constable, afraid of his influence and of what he could do to his career. It was as simple and shameful as that. What made it worse was that he had little or no respect for the man: once, a long time ago, Hale had been a good policeman, they said, but that was true no longer. Something had happened to him over the years, the bitterness and cynicism had driven out the humanity, almost all his judgments were clouded by his conceit of himself. Strange how a man could be flawed in such a way, how a spark of weakness could grow into a fire which consumed him from within, leaving only the husk to remind people of what he used to be. Gosford was a policeman to his fingertips; he could conceive of himself doing no other job, and he truly believed that he was a member of the finest force in the world. Yet even in the best organisations, it seemed, there had to be a Hale; there had been just such a man, an officer, in his regiment in Korea.

And what had he done? Nothing, precisely nothing. He had simply bowed his head, taking the line of least resistance. Yes, sir—certainly, sir—of course, sir! He was a time-server, a boot-licker, a yes-man, concerned only to protect his own skin, to curry favour with a man he despised!

He pressed his thumbs against closed eyes for a moment, as though to erase this picture of himself, and then turned back to Topping. 'You know what will happen if you use this story, don't you?' he said wearily.

'Tell me,' Topping said.

'It's not a joke.'

'Who's laughing?'

'You could lose your job.'

Topping laughed softly, mirthlessly. 'I see. Be a good boy, or you don't eat, is that it?'

'This is a small town, Topping. A closed community. The top people live in each other's pockets. And they like to keep in with the police.'

'Like Mr Dailey, for instance?'

'Draw your own conclusions.'

'Christ, Chief-Inspector, is it that important? Is it?'

'Some people think it is.'

'Some people meaning Mr Deputy Chief Constable Hale?' Gosford didn't answer. 'Of course. He has handed down the ruling, and ordained that it should be observed. He runs this county, his orders must be obeyed by all and sundry. And if you step out of line—' He drew a finger across his throat and made a sucking noise with his gums.

'He could just be right about this,' said Gosford weakly.

'Balls!' said Topping. 'The man's a bloody fascist, or next door to being one. He can't see beyond his own ego. Well, he may be able to crack the whip and put Dailey through the hoop, he may scare the pips off your shoulder, but he doesn't own me! And don't get the wrong idea. I'm no moral crusader. I've been around too long, I can be bought, I know how to compromise. I could tell even you things about the people in this town that would make your hair curl. Why don't I print them? Not just because of Mr Dailey, believe me. It's because I have to live here, I like my job, I'm too long in the tooth to pull up stakes and start over again—even if I could. But it's my own decision, do you understand that? I don't like being told what I can or can't write about, I don't take kindly to that at all, especially when it comes from someone like Hale and is backed up by as juicy a bit of blackmail as I've come across in a long life. And there's one other point—probably the most important of all. Actually, I'm a good newspaperman—inconsistent maybe, that's my trouble—but when I do put my mind to it, I'm good. I got on to a great story today, Chief-Inspector, largely through my own initiative, and that doesn't happen often in a lifetime. To me, that story is something special, can you understand that? I want to see it in print, with my name on it. Call it pride, if you like, I've never seen anything wrong with a bit of pride, as long as it's not overdone. And money, of course, there'll be good money in it. I'm not ashamed of that either. I'm a professional, I started as a penny-a-liner, I've never worked for love in my life.' He paused and laughed apologetically. 'Sorry. Sorry. Didn't mean to bash your ear.'

'I enjoyed it,' said Gosford ruefully.

There was a tap on the door and Sergeant Miller came in. He glanced quickly at Topping, and then turned to Gosford and said in a low voice: 'Can I have a word with you, sir?'

'What is it, sergeant?'

'Something's come up. Very urgent.'

Gosford excused himself and went out into the corridor with Miller. A minute or so later he came back, his face grey, the skin taut over his cheekbones, his eyes dull with fatigue. Topping watched as he moved wearily to his desk, and then Gosford straightened his shoulders and seemed to take command of himself. 'The public should be warned—

isn't that what you said? So what are you waiting for?'

'What's happened?'

'I wasn't joking about Hale. He means business.'

'Sod Hale. I've told you how I feel. What's happened?'

'A woman was admitted to the hospital a half-hour ago,' said Gosford slowly. 'They're puzzled—and I don't blame them. They can't get any sense out of her husband, he's in a state of shock. But the surgeon—these are his actual words—the surgeon said he'd never seen anything like it. He said it looked as if she'd been savaged by a wild beast.'

Topping nodded slowly, and took a deep, sad, breath. 'I'll see that the nationals get the story. And I'll tip-off the BBC. But you should get the rest of the press boys in and brief them.'

'I'll do that.'

'What about your job—what will Hale do to you?' asked Topping.

'I'm past caring.'

Topping nodded and leaned forward to stub out his cigar in an empty coffee-cup and without thinking Gosford shouted angrily: 'No!'

Topping looked up, startled, and shrugged an apology.

'Sorry,' he said. 'It is a filthy habit.' He dropped the cigar into an ash-tray and stood up. 'You look whacked, you need to put your feet up for an hour or so.'

'No way,' said Gosford with a smile that was no more than a movement of the facial muscles.

Topping went to the door, raised a thumb in a gesture of approval, and moved out. What was that for, thought Gosford? Because I've decided to do something at last? God in heaven, does someone have to die, or be torn to bits before we can make up our minds to act?

CHAPTER NINE

1

David Birk did not find it difficult to elude the police patrol. Half a mile past the control point he drove the land-rover off the road and into the forest, where it was screened by the tall undergrowth. The dog, Buster, who was stretched out behind David, opened his eyes and lifted himself expectantly.

'No, boy. Stay. This is no job for you. Stay,' said David.

Buster settled down again without protest, dropping his head on his front paws, but the look he gave the man seemed to be reproachful, concerned. David took a small pack, a coil of rope, and the 270 Winchester from the luggage area, locked and checked the doors, and moved into the forest, heading towards the low ground where he had found the remains of the hind and the dead fawn.

He calculated that there was an hour until dusk, an hour at the most; there was a strong possibility that even now the tigers would be on the prowl, and he moved cautiously, pausing every now and then to survey the way ahead, or to examine the soft earth for the tell-tale pug-marks.

At length he reached the crevice with its dank marsh, and was relieved to find that the remains of the hind and her dead calf were still lying there, untouched. He had already selected the tree he planned to use, a sturdy birch, from whose upper and middle branches he would have a dominating view of the area.

First, he unloaded the rifle, laid it at the foot of the tree, and tied a length of cord to the trigger-guard. Then he began to climb, moving with the apparent ease of an expert, until he reached two strong, almost horizontal branches about thirty feet above ground level and well covered by foliage. He tied the end of the rope to one of these, and bound it round the other, criss-crossing back and forth, until he had fashioned a rough cradle or machan, strong enough to bear his weight. A double strand of rope fastened in similar fashion lower down provided support for his feet, so that it was possible for him to sit easily between his branches.

He pulled the surrounding branches down so that they hid the machan, tied them into position with a length of cord, and cut a small opening in this protective screen so that he had a clear view of the area below. Next, with infinite care, he ran the cord attached to the Winchester through his fingers, and hauled the rifle up into the machan. He reloaded it, tested the field of fire, made one or two minor adjustments and then, with his back firm against the trunk of the tree, he settled down to wait.

The odds, he realised, were against his plan. He was banking on the possibility that one, at least, of the tigers would return to the remains of the kill, but he knew also that what was left down on the ground was not enough for a hungry beast, and that the tigers might easily be diverted by a more satisfying target. And again, if they got wind of his presence, if he betrayed himself by the slightest sound or movement, they would not approach the kill. The tiger was a curious blend of courage and caution, as he knew only too well; even in India it was almost impossible to predict its behaviour and often fatal to generalise about it. He had known a tigress return to the scene of her kill and wait in the bush for hours on end, simply because some sound or scent had aroused her suspicion. Captivity might have blurred the natural cunning of the tigers in the forest below, and consequently made them more vulnerable, but by the same token, it was also more difficult to predict how they would react.

He wished he had given himself more time. He would have preferred to stake out a live bullock as bait, and either sit up over it, or track the tiger by daylight after the bait had been taken. But it was too late for that now, he had to make do with things as they were. The light worried him. It would be dark soon, very dark, for little or no moonlight would penetrate the thick, leafy roof formed by the tops of the closely bunched trees. He could only hope that the birds and the forest creatures would give him some warning of the tiger's approach, and that he would get at least one clear view of those luminous eyes....

The ropes creaked as David pulled out his pipe, put it, unlit, into his mouth, closing his teeth on the stem, and allowed the silence to surround him again. Gradually he became aware of the secret sounds which made up that silence; the slight rustle of leaves, whispers from the undergrowth, the murmuring of insects, until it seemed that the air itself was quivering and humming like electric wires. The tree stood motionless, rooted in the earth, yet it was vibrant with life, as though some hidden force, welling up through the spreading roots was flowing out of the branches into the sky beyond. David could feel that force in his own flesh; he closed his eyes momentarily overcome by a sense of mystery and wonder. It was as though he had entered a great and soaring cathedral and was enclosed by its deep tranquillity; or that he had renewed some ancient, necessary partnership and in doing so touched on some profound truth. It was a moment which always came when he was alone in the forest, among the communion of trees.

This was largely a man-made forest. A tiny gesture of conscience for the senseless butchery the human race had perpetrated over the centuries, for all the trees it had murdered? Perhaps, thought David—and perhaps it also represented a tardy realisation by man that he owed what he was to the tree and that without it he could not long survive? The first human beings had been cradled in the primeval forests, and since then the tree had served and sheltered man, absorbing his poisons, warming his hearth, nurturing and renewing his soil, giving of its life and substance in a thousand ways. But if man failed to learn the lesson, if he continued wilfully and thoughtlessly to exploit and abuse the tree, then nature would exert a terrible revenge on his children and his children's children...

It was dangerous to drift away on this tide of thought, what he had to do demanded his utmost concentration, and with an effort he brought himself back to his present task. He checked his watch and then, remembering those fierce, keen eyes which could pick up the slightest movement, he unfastened the strap and slipped it into his pocket. A flash of the dial as he moved his wrist and he might well lose his quarry.

It was 8.45 p.m., almost dusk. This was the time of the tiger, when he lifted his great head and began the long prowl for food.

David took a deep breath, filling his lungs with the strong, musky, resinous air. He felt an enormous sense of well-being as he settled back again, at one with the forest and its whispering stillness.

2

Freed of the despondency which had sapped his vigour and depressed his thinking earlier in the evening, Gosford acted swiftly. He summoned to his office the local representatives of the BBC and Independent Television, together with a half-dozen other assorted journalists, and briefed them fully on the situation. Within a half-hour the first bulletin went out over the local BBC radio network, and listeners were asked to stay tuned for further announcements. The Whitford police station was a small, fifty-year-old building, and the spare office on the first floor had already been taken over by Detective Chief-Superintendent Murray and his team from Scarby C.I.D., so Gosford commandeered the rest-room at the rear of the ground floor and turned it into an Information and Press Room, placing the young Sergeant Sanders in charge. It had only one telephone, and was not really adequate, but it had the advantage that the journalists could get to it through the car-yard without cluttering the front entrance or the main station office and Gosford decided it would have to do.

Every available man was told to report in, and all leave cancelled. The official transport consisted of three police-cars, all of the Austin 1100 type, and one Ford Thames utility truck, and when these had been deployed, the men's own private cars were pressed into service. Gosford gave orders to seal off the two main lines of approach to the road running through the forest; all vehicles, other than those specifically authorised by the police, were to be turned back or diverted. Other officers, working in pairs, were told to cover the many isolated homesteads and farms in the area, and since the long school holidays had just begun, they were instructed to lay special stress on the need to keep children indoors or under close supervision.

The numerous camping and caravan sites presented a special problem. Gosford recognised that it would be difficult to get these cleared at short notice and at such a late hour; all he could do for the moment was to see that the people in charge were warned of the possible danger, and urged to stay on the alert. He told the officers concerned to suggest that each camp should keep a large bonfire burning all night. Finally, he made contact with Peter Street, the District Officer of the Forestry Commission and secured his full co-operation. All working parties were to be withdrawn from the forest until the crisis was over, and Street undertook to alert the inhabitants of the village of Lyndholme, most of whom were employees of the Commission and their families. Some of the men were trained marksmen who were called upon at certain times to cull the rapidly-growing deer population, and Street proposed that they should be organised into guard patrols. Since Lyndholme was almost entirely sur-rounded by forest and therefore presented special problems, Gosford readily agreed to the suggestion.

Throughout this hectic period of decision-making, Gosford was conscious that the steps he was taking were purely defensive. The basic problem was to find and destroy the tigers, and in this respect he felt woefully inadequate. He had no confidence in the proposed dawn sweep by a squad of police sharp-shooters, but he was forced to admit that he had no positive alternative to put forward. He needed David Birk, he needed his expert advice, and when he was satisfied finally that he had disposed his pathetically small resources to the best possible advantage, he despatched a police motor-cyclist to the high moor, with instructions to ask David, as a matter of urgency, to come back down to Whitford and help organise the tiger-hunt.

He knew that a long, hot, steamy night lay ahead of him, and he decided that it would be sensible to slip home for a half-hour and freshen up with a shower and a change of linen, but as he reached for his jacket the door opened and Detective Chief-Superintendent Murray came in. The two men had worked together before, they knew and liked each other. Murray combined the ruddy, outdoor look of a ploughman with the build of a weight-lifter; his heavy body seemed always to be about to burst through the confining influence of his clothes. He was not an imaginative man, but what he lacked in flair he made up for by tenacity, dogged untiring energy, a capacity for organisation, and a plain, uncomplicated, logical mind.

'Charlie,' he said, 'I was in my hotel room five minutes ago and I switched on the radio. The BBC have the whole story.'

'I know,' said Gosford. 'I gave it to them.'

'The Deputy Chief Constable left specific orders—'

'Yes, I heard them. But since then we've had another attack. A woman—she may be dead by now for all I know. From all accounts she hasn't much chance.'

'Why wasn't I told? I was at the hotel, two minutes away. You could have sent word.'

'Yes, yes. I know. I'm sorry—but I've had other things on my mind. I've got a C.I.D. man at the hospital hoping to get a statement from the woman or her husband. But, Jim, we already know what they will say. She was pulled down and mauled by a tiger—there's no other answer. And Hale or no Hale, I'm just not going to sit here on my backside and let it go on.'

He went on to outline the measures he had put in hand. The big man, squatting uncomfortably on the edge of the desk listened quietly, nodding occasionally, his face grave and serious.

'Why didn't you contact Hale and tell him that the situation had changed?'

'There was no time.'

'There's always time, Charlie. Especially if you want to go against orders.'

'All right.' Gosford crunched a sheet of paper in his fist and stood up. 'I didn't contact Hale because I know he would dig his heels in. He's determined to do this thing his way, and he won't be budged, he won't listen to reason.' He threw the ball of paper into the waste-bin, and faced Murray, as if challenging him to contradict.

The square, rugged face broke into a slow, wry smile as Murray heaved himself up into a standing position. 'O.K., Charlie, O.K. It just occurs to me that you've already got two tigers on your hands. Now you've made it three. And I reckon I'd sooner tackle the two in the forest than take on Hale.'

'I shan't involve you,' said Gosford. 'I acted on my own initiative, I take full responsibility.'

'You're a liar,' said Murray bluntly.

'What?'

'I've been here all the time. You consulted me at every stage and I gave my full approval.'

'No, Jim,' said Gosford. 'Thanks all the same. To tell you the truth, I don't really care. If Hale cuts up rough—'

'He will! I'll lay my pension on it.'

'Then I'll put in my papers. I'll quit. No, I mean it. There's a limit. I've done my last bit of boot-licking.'

3

There seemed to be nothing else moving in the forest. The tigers pushed their way sullenly through the undergrowth, turning in great circles in their hunt for food, and as time passed their frustration grew. On two occasions they approached the road, with the intention of crossing into the thick woodlands to the north but they were driven back by the noise of cars, the strong beam of headlights, and by their own uncertainty. Ranee, the tigress, could still taste the blood of the woman, feel it on her teeth and tongue, and, in consequence, her appetite held a sharper edge, her resentment went that much deeper. Whenever Mohan came too close she turned on him, spitting and hissing in anger, and once, when he brushed against her coat, she tore so painfully at his flanks, bringing blood, that he drew away. She stalked away in disdain; weary of her moods yet afraid to make a challenge, he let her go.

The wound in his side was superficial but nonetheless painful, and he lay down in the cool softness of a hollow, licking the scratches, until the throbbing ceased. It was as he lay there that memory or instinct told him that he knew this place, that he had been here before. The land sloped downwards, the earth was moist; it was near here, just below, that he had found the hind and her fawn. He sucked noisily at his lips, remembering the warm blood, the tenderness of the flesh, feeling the flavour rise tantalisingly in his throat.

He rose, bracing himself, and in obedience to instinct yet again, he released a deep, rolling roar, as if to warn the forest and its creatures that he, Mohan, the tiger, was on his way and that they should stand aside. He waited, but apart from the frightened fluttering and calling of the birds, there was no response of any significance, and head down, body flattened into the stalking position, he began to move through the brittle undergrowth. In twenty-four hours he had learned much; his footfall brought no tell-tale crackle from the dead and brittle twigs or the dried leaves underfoot, and the natural camouflage of his skin merging with the patterns of the forest, made him almost invisible.

The tigress moved in the opposite direction, padding forward, alert for any sound or scent which might suggest food, or threaten danger. In addition to hunger, she was conscious of movement in her heavily swollen stomach, of the live weight of her unborn cubs. She came at last to a point in the forest where the undergrowth began to give way to grass and the trees stood in more open order, and she was about to turn back when she heard the murmur of voices. Desperation made her bolder, and using what cover she could find, she edged forward until she reached a semi-circle of hazel-bushes and bracken at the fringe of the forest. The voices were louder now, and through the tangle of leaves and branches she saw the outline of buildings and the square-shaped yellow gleam of lighted windows, a gentler version of the great lights she had known at the circus. Between the forest and the buildings a huge bonfire sparked and crackled, tossing flames of red and yellow into the darkness, and around this men were gathered, talking together in low voices, occasionally looking towards the trees.

They were only thirty or forty yards away, a matter of seconds if she launched herself at speed, but the fire was too intimidating, the men too numerous and too closely bunched; her whole being was concentrated on the need to appease the hunger which hammered at her body with growing intensity. From time to time, the men moved away in pairs from the protecting circle of fire, and in this she saw her only hope. If one man isolated himself from the others, if he wandered into the darkness, she would be waiting. A few seconds, that was all she needed.

Away in the distance she heard Mohan roar and she pressed herself into the ground, waiting until the echoing sound faded. For a few moments the men fell silent also, and then they began to shout, calling to each other, drawing closer to the fire, and pointing to the forest.

As they settled down again, Ranee lifted herself and began to circle the area, seeking a line of approach which, though further from the fire, would bring her closer to the buildings and the men on patrol; two or three hundred yards on she found a spur of forest jutting out from the main body of trees like a huge finger, where the tangle of bramble, the tall ferns, provided almost perfect cover. The bonfire was almost hidden from view at this point, but she could see its glow hanging in the air, and, more important, she could still hear the rise and fall of the human voices.

The tangle of bramble bush and the tall ferns provided almost perfect cover. Ranee settled back on her haunches, her eyes fixed on the perimeter of darkness between the forest and the village.

4

When Gosford arrived back at the station after his brief visit home, he was met in the car-yard by his deputy, Police-Inspector Melvyn Somers, who had been called in from leave.

'Trouble, sir,' Somers said blandly. A young man of calm and equable temperament, he was seldom ruffled; the greater the pressure, the more amiable and relaxed he became, a characteristic which, though it had its undoubted merits, could at times be irritating. Gosford found it so now. When Somers spoke of trouble it was almost impossible to tell from his manner whether he was referring to mass murder or an act of petty larceny, since he used much the same expression to convey either possibility.

'In the forest?' he asked sharply.

'No,' said Somers. 'Not that. It's the Mayor. He's at the Town Hall—wants you to ring him as soon as you can.'

'Yes,' Gosford said wearily. 'I slipped up there. Should have called and put them in the picture.'

'You can't think of everything.'

'Anything else been happening?'

'Everything. Phones jammed with callers, a queue of people in the outer office. All wanting to know about the tigers, naturally. Hotel keepers, pub landlords, all the tourist trade people, to tell us that we're going to ruin their business with these panic measures. Animal lovers insisting that we should take the tigers alive and unharmed. Oh, and one old duck who said that the tigers had been sent by Almighty God to punish us for our sins.'

'She could well be right,' said Gosford. 'Any word on David Birk?'

'No. Cotton came back ten minutes ago. Apparently Birk didn't go home when he left here. And no-one seems to know where he is.'

'Damn.' He drew a deep breath. 'Any news from the hospital?'

'The woman died on the operating table, sir. Her husband is still in a state of shock, and has said nothing.'

Gosford nodded slowly, as though he had known this would be the answer, moved to the door leading in from the car-yard and paused. He had held back one of the questions uppermost in his mind, he was reluctant to ask it now, but it had to come out.

'Any word from HQ, from Scarby?' He did not mention Hale by name, but that was the purport of the question, he knew it and Somers knew it.

'Oh, yes,' said Somers, casually, 'there was a message. From Mr Hale. You are to report to the Chief Constable's office in Scarby at 12 noon tomorrow.'

'If I'm awake,' said Gosford. 'Was that all?'

'No. Not quite. Hale instructed me to inform you that

174

you are suspended from duty until the interview. I was told to take over.'

'The bastard!' said Gosford quietly. 'The bastard. He can't do that, he can't do it.'

'I took the call,' said Somers cheerily. 'No-one else knows about it. Pity I shan't see you until the morning to tell you, isn't it? Ah, well, it all makes a change from indecent exposure, doesn't it, Charlie?'

Before Gosford could say anything further, he was gone. Gosford shook his head, amused in spite of himself, wondering if there was any possible combination of circumstances which could shake the man's iron affability. Then gathering himself with a conscious effort, he opened the door and went inside. One minute later he was put through to the Mayor of Whitford, a man whose benign senatorial manner and mane of flowing milk-white hair had caused him to become known in the town as The Silver Prince. As if determined to belie his reputation, he launched into a sharp and non-benign attack.

'What the hell do you think you're playing at down there? Do you know when I heard about these blasted tigers, Chief-Inspector? An hour ago! Do you know where I heard about 'em? At a bloody charity function! I'm on my feet talking and the chairman passes me a note!'

'I'm sorry, Mr Mayor,' said Gosford. 'I ought to have put you in the picture of course, but things have been a bit hectic, as you can imagine. I had to act quickly.' As he spoke he was thinking, with a certain sadness, a man and a woman are dead, two of your citizens, Mr Mayor. Couldn't you have spared one word for them?

'Not so hectic that you couldn't find the time to go home!'

Gosford ignored this. 'Did Inspector Somers give you a full breakdown of the situation and the steps we've taken?'

'He did. But I think I'm entitled to hear it from you.'

All right, all right, thought Gosford, you shall have your

pound of flesh. He went over the day's events as briefly as he could, finishing with a summary of the emergency measures. When he came on the line again, the edge had gone from the other man's tone.

'Incredible. Unbelievable! And you really think that all these measures are necessary?'

'I doubt if they go far enough, Mr Mayor.'

'What about the army? Do you think we should call on the army for help? Trained men, weapons, and so forth?' He sounded a note of responsibility now, a military man coiled for action.

'It may come to that,' Gosford said cautiously. 'We're sending in a squad of marksmen at dawn. If they don't flush them out then—yes—we're going to need all the help we can get.'

There was a silence at the other end, and then the Mayor said: 'Right, Chief-Inspector. You know that you can rely on my full support—and the support of everyone here. I shall make a public announcement to that effect, so that there is no doubt in the public mind. Just one thing though—we would like to be kept in touch and consulted where possible. We have our responsibilities too, you know.'

'I realise that, sir,' said Gosford politely. 'I'll see that you are regularly informed.'

As he hung up, Somers came in with a cup of tea. 'Personal service,' he said, setting it down with a flourish. 'How was the Mayor?'

'Nasty at first. But you'll be glad to know that we now have his full support.'

'That's nice. Well, just to make your evening, I've had Piers Holroyd, our friendly, local, neighbourhood M.P. on the line from his holiday cottage in Cornwall, asking what we're doing to protect his constituents. He's writing to the Prime Minister urging him to bring in tighter control on all wild animals kept in captivity in this country.'

'That'll be worth a par or two in the papers and an in-

176

dignant interview on the telly. They never miss a trick, do they? The Mayor's issuing a rallying call to the public, would you believe!'

'From a safe distance, no doubt.'

'Mel,' said Gosford, 'you're too young to be a cynic. Leave it for your elders and betters.'

The telephone rang at that moment. Gosford reached for the receiver with one hand, and his tea with the other. The conversation was one-sided; he asked two or three questions, and then said briskly; 'I'm on my way, Peter!'

He hung up slowly, put down his cup, and stood up. 'Peter Street, the Forestry man. Calling from Lyndholme village. I'm going out there now. A young girl is missing.'

As Gosford went out into the car-yard, Detective-Sergeant Bawden drove in and parked. A man of middle-age, his face a dull yellow in the lights that ringed the yard, was helped out of the rear of the car by Bawden and a constable in civilian clothes, and he stood there, his head sagging, as Bawden left them and came across to Gosford.

'What have you got there?' asked Gosford.

'A big one, sir, a very big one. I've been checking on those pretty pictures you brought back from the Waites's cottage,' said Bawden.

'And?' Gosford did not add that he had forgotten all about them.

'One of the men in them was Waites himself—'

'The suicide.'

'Yes, sir. And chummy there is the other fellow.'

Gosford looked over at the other car again. The man's head was still down, his body seemed to have shrunk within his clothes; he stood like some dumb animal awaiting a word of command from his master. He lifted his face momentarily, looked at Gosford with quick, terrified eyes, and then his head dropped again.

'Are you sure?'

'No doubt, sir. The girl put us on to him. And we found

177

all the gear at his place, cameras, lights, the lot. Plus some more photographs.'

'Is he a professional photographer?'

'No, sir. He's a teacher up at the school.'

'A teacher?'

'Afraid so. What's more, I think at least two of the girls there were involved, maybe more. The girl in the photographs you saw—she's a kid at the school. Just turned thirteen. He's been teaching her maths—and other things on the side. Seems to be quite a racket. This fellow was not only doing it for pleasure—he was selling the stuff to the porn merchants in Leeds and London.'

'You know something?' said Gosford. 'You want to know something? I prefer the tigers. At least they don't pretend to be civilised.'

5

Maud Pickering had not been told about the tigers. When her mother looked into the bedroom after hearing the first news bulletin, the girl appeared to be asleep and there seemed to be no point in waking her. Later on, Maud heard sounds of unusual activity in the village and saw a group of men, her father and elder brothers among them, holding flaming torches and building a huge bonfire. Some of the men appeared to be armed.

She was intrigued, the situation appealed to her sense of the dramatic. All kinds of possibilities surged through her mind; in the end she settled on the view that the intense activity outside could only mean that a very dangerous criminal, perhaps an escaped convict, was at large. Her principal concern, however, was her own plan to go over to the village of Cawby, to the house of her teacher, Mrs Waring, and how this new situation would affect it. She was a determined young lady and it occurred to her that, in some ways, this strange twist of circumstances might work to her advantage. Her family would be too pre-occupied to think about her, she might never have a better opportunity to slip away unnoticed.

On the other hand, she couldn't leave it until dawn, as she had originally intended. The men might still be out in force, the danger of discovery would be that much greater. No, she would have to leave under cover of darkness, keep well away from the bonfire, and get into the shelter of the forest as quickly as possible. She knew it well, it held no fears for her. Once there, she could rest before making her way to Cawby.

And the criminal? If indeed there was a criminal on the loose, she would have no difficulty eluding him in the forest, that is if she wanted to do so. She imagined him as a sad, misunderstood person, and inclined to the thought that she would like to talk to him, help him. She saw her-self as his only friend, standing with him against society, helping him perhaps to escape to Australia and start a new life.

Her mind filled with these interesting thoughts, she dressed, and with the heavy school satchel over her shoulder, went out on to the landing. From the stairs she saw that the front-door was open; her mother was outside, standing by the gate, talking with some neighbours. Maud crept down, and went through the kitchen to the back-door, pausing briefly on the way to take an apple from the dish on the dresser.

The garden was deserted. In the sky beyond the house she saw the sparks floating up from the bonfire, heard its fierce crackle, the murmur of voices. She slipped the bolts on the gate in the back fence, and closed it quietly behind her as she went through to the patch of communal allot-ments on the other side.

The air was sluggish and heavy with heat, the night had brought little change. She could feel the sweat on the nape of her neck, her heart was pounding with excitement. She circled the allotment, came out on to a stretch of rough pasture-land, and eventually reached the dusty lane which marked the edge of the forest.

Suddenly she heard the crunch of footsteps and she crouched down in the shelter of the hedgerow, her teeth clenched, holding her breath. Two men, shotguns in their crooked arms, came along the lane, moving towards her. Luckily there was only a sliver of moon, but even so she turned her face away, lest its tell-tale whiteness should betray her. The men moved with maddening deliberation, talking quietly together. She felt an insect crawling up her bare leg, tickling her skin; she dare not move and it was as much as she could do not to cry out. But at last the men went by and soon their footfalls were no more than distant whispers.

She brushed the insect away, stood up, and still determined to maintain the drama of the situation, looked down the hill towards the village and its glowing lights. It's been my home, she thought, I was born there; but now I am leaving it, perhaps for ever, perhaps I will never come back!

'Farewell!' she whispered. It was one of her favourite words, so much better than an everyday word like goodbye. A moment later, she entered the forest.

It was almost an hour after this that her mother went to Maud's bedroom and found that she had gone.

6

David judged that it must have been about an hour after he heard the distant challenging roar that the tiger came. It was almost pitch-dark, only an occasional pallid ray of moonlight penetrated the thick umbrella of the treetops, he could see nothing, but he felt in his blood that the quarry was close at hand. Long minutes passed and then he recognised the faint, distinctive, protracted sniffing which confirmed his instinct; unlike most animals, the tiger has an inferior sense of smell, and this one was clearly exerting himself in an effort to pick up a scent. It also marked him as an amateur, thought David; a jungle tiger, who had never known captivity, would not have been so incautious. He estimated the distance to be thirty yards or more. For the twentieth time he lined the rifle up on the spot where he knew the body of the calf to be lying; it was akin to guesswork in that darkness, he could only hope that he had got it right.

The tiger was edging closer now. David registered a half-dozen sounds, tiny whispers of protest from the under-growth, which would have been imperceptible to the ordinary, untrained ear. Twenty yards now and the tiger was making a low intermittent growling sound, like the purr of a domestic cat but harsher and more grating. It was beyond David's experience—he had never known a tiger make his approach in so incautious, even amateur fashion. The animal was apparently satisfied that he had found the remains of last night's kill, and that there was no danger, for the growling grew louder and the thicket crashed and snapped as he forced himself through.

He padded across the crevice towards the marsh.

David could hear but see nothing of him, so perfect was the cover of the night and the dark forest. The tiger brushed aganst the tree as he passed, and a tiny tremor seemed to shake the trunk while the leaves around the machan responded with a whispering, gentle rustle. David could feel that the tiger had stopped as though these faint noises had aroused his suspicions. Then he heard him sniffing at the remains of the hind and a moment later the crunch of bone.

There was no tension in David. One of his chief quali-ties as a hunter was an ability to remain relaxed, supple, free of that tightening of the muscles which, at the moment of decision, can cause the best marksman to make a poor shot. All the same, with a part of his mind he was willing the tiger to move, to approach the dead fawn, and to turn so that, for just one second, he could see those clear, lambent eyes.

The tiger growled again, a low threatening rumble which was half-complaint, half-anger, and moved on. David was almost sure that he could see the rufous red outline of the body, the flash of white stripes, as the animal stalked towards the fawn, and hovered over it, but he knew that it could only be imagination, the wishfulfilment of his mind.

His finger lay against the trigger of the Winchester. He had loaded one 160 gramme bullet only, knowing that this single shot was all he was likely to get, and then only if luck was with him. And luck meant that the tiger had to turn, he had to look into those eyes.

The world, time, all movement, seemed to have stopped; the earth was concentrated in this tiny space, his life had shrunk to this single minute.

And then Mohan turned and lifted his head, looked towards the tree, as though he had sensed the presence of the man. The eyes seemed more green than amber now; curious rather than vicious, they glowed like emeralds suspended on a curtain of the darkest velvet.

As David squeezed the trigger, the eyes glittered and moved, leaving only the darkness. The screaming roar of pain and anger which followed told him that the shot had gone home, but to what effect he could not be sure. A moment later the tiger appeared to crash through the nearby thicket and for the space of a heartbeat he was sure that he had only wounded the beast, that it was making good its escape. But then he heard a thud as of a body falling and his hopes rose again.

He waited in the machan for a measured thirty minutes. He knew that even a badly-wounded tiger was capable of returning to the attack, and he was conscious that the tigress had still to be met and matched and could be somewhere near. At the end of this waiting time he lowered the rifle and climbed down. He reloaded the Winchester, and taking a flashlight from his pack, he searched the ground. There was a splattering of fresh blood near the body of the calf, and gleaming blood spots led to the thicket, towards which he directed the torch.

The tiger lay slumped near the decomposing trunk of a fallen tree as though he had dropped on it in his attempt to leap through the thicket. He was motionless and appeared to be dead, but David held back; he had known a tiger which had taken a bullet in the head, splintering part of the skull, yet it had not merely survived, it had lived to terrorise a village for two years.

He picked up a heavy piece of wood and threw it at the still and silent animal. The missile struck Mohan on the mouth, but he did not stir, and after repeating the test once more, David moved closer, and saw, with a twinge of pity and of guilt, that there was no need for further caution. By a combination of luck and judgment the heavy bullet had entered below the shoulder at an angle which carried it into the heart.

In the white beam of the flashlight, Mohan with his magnificent head lying across the fallen tree, his body cradled by the soft earth, seemed to be sleeping.

He had known freedom for 28 hours.

At least, thought David, at least he found his forest at the end, and finished there, among the trees.

CHAPTER TEN

1

In normal times the great majority of people in Whitford went to their beds around 10 p.m. and rose early. They were inclined to boast of this practice, seeing it as a virtue.

But this was not a normal time. The unusual, almost tropical heat made sleep difficult, children were restless and fractious; their parents, no less irritable, sat fanning themselves in garden or sitting-room and, following the long-established adage that the hotter the brew the more cooling its effect, made and consumed gallons of tea.

Everywhere the talk was of the man-eating tigers. In the town and its satellite villages, in the streets, pubs, clubs, homes, on the telephone, over fences, at gates, from open windows, they sweated and picked over the events of the day, finding in this dramatic situation a new camaraderie. It was, as several people remarked, just like war-time, with Whitford as a front-line town. Inevitably, the stories grew and multiplied as they were passed from tongue to tongue, like one of those party word games which start out with a sliver of fact and end up as a work of fiction. It wasn't just two people who had been savaged and killed by the marauding beasts but four, five, six, a dozen. The police had been seen to visit a camping site, and this piece of truth was rapidly embellished until it became the story of an attack in which three children had been mauled and one actually carried off into the forest. It was reliably reported that entire herds of sheep and cattle had been wantonly slaughtered by the man-eaters.

Although no official statement had been made about how the tigers came to be at large, it was soon known that they had been deliberately released, and this became a prime object of speculation. The crime was variously laid at the door of the Provisional I.R.A., the Japanese Red Army, the Palestinian guerrillas, fanatics sent up from London, hippies, and similar way-out groups, but the most popular theory, the one which gained most ground, was that the release was the work of a madman, probably someone actually living in or around Whitford who nursed a grudge against the community.

Bernie Pullen heard some of these stories while he was waiting at the hospital for his girl-friend, Libby Fitch. He felt himself to be in a privileged position, since her mother was one of the victims. He had never actually met the family, he had formed the impression that he would not be welcomed at their home, but what did a little thing like that matter at a time like this? He waited in the reception-area, gravely discussing the situation with a hospital porter and anyone else who cared to join in, enjoying the sensation of being near the centre of things for once in his life.

He was a little put out when Libby, ashen-faced and in tears, came through with an aunt and uncle who informed him with cold politeness that they would be taking Libby home with them. She didn't lift her head, didn't even say goodbye or thank you for waiting! Charming he thought. After all, wasn't he the one who had heard the news on the radio, and been the first to tell her, the one who had rushed her to the hospital on his motor-cycle? And then to be coldly brushed aside! Charming!

Avoiding the porter's eye, he went out to the car-park and started up the Yamaha. There was only one thing to do—go back to his mates at Mrs Mac's café, and as he opened up along the Bardney Road, he began to work out what he would say to them.

He stacked the motor-cycle with the others at the rear of the little café, took off his crash-helmet, loosened the studs on his leather jacket and went through the back door into the steamy noisy room beyond. He moved slowly, and when he reached the inner-door he stood there, casually swinging the helmet and looking round.

It was a good moment. There'd been times, he had to admit, when his association with Libby Fitch had brought him nothing but grief. Some of the mob had been suspicious of this turgid little bird with the cut-glass accent and the square deep-pocket parents, they'd sent her up rotten and him with her. But he'd stuck with it, played it cool, and now it was all going to pay off. Yes, it was a good moment, the best!

The buzz of conversation dwindled into silence, someone even switched off the juke-box, and they surrounded him, as if he was a star or something, plying him with eager questions. Rick and Wayne, his closest friends, shoved some of the others aside, and made a place for Bernie at a centre table. Pearl put a cup of Mac's horrible black coffee in front of him and said: 'Wait a sec, Bernie. I'll take the curse off it.' She laced the thin, light-brown liquid with a generous dose of Jamaican rum.

'How's Libby?' asked Rick.

'I took her home.' The others nodded sympathetically. 'Cut up. I mean, only natural. It hit me too, know what I mean? Really shook me.'

'Well, it would, wouldn't it?' said Pearl.

'Be all over the papers tomorrow,' said Wayne.

'Yes,' said Bernie, 'there were a couple of blokes up at the hospital. Took Libby's picture. Wanted to chat her too, but I put the bar on that. She'd had enough, know what I mean? I run her home.' He spoke with quiet authority and they looked at each other, nodding and murmuring agreement.

'She's not alone, is she?' asked Pearl.

'What do you take me for!' said Bernie indignantly. 'I wouldn't be here if she was, would I? No, her auntie came over, going to stay with her.'

'Poor little cow!' said Rick.

'Did Libby, I mean, did she say anything like?' said Pearl. The initial ritual of sympathy was over, the time had come for some hard information. To make the point clear Pearl added: 'We only know what we heard on the radio, know what I mean?'

'It was the tigers, wasn't it? It was the tigers who got Libby's old lady?' said one of the girls, impatient for an answer.

'Why don't you shut up, Rhoda!' snarled Wayne.

Bernie flicked open his jacket, ran the back of his hand over the sweat on his forehead. 'Christ,' he said, 'it's like an oven in here.' They waited while he drank the coffee. He put the cup down slowly, shook his head in the manner of a man who feels that mere words are inadequate and said slowly: 'She never had a chance, you know? I chatted one of the porters who saw her when they fetched her in. He'd never seen a sight like it. Half her face torn away for a starter. And ripped open all the way down, neck to waist, blood and guts all over the place. This old boy said he'd never seen anything like it, know what I mean?'

'Poor cow,' said Rick.

Pearl poured some more rum into Bernie's cup and pressed his elbow, to indicate her understanding of his feelings. She laced the other cups that were held out to her and took a strong, fortifying swig herself.

'Poor cow,' Rick said again.

'What about the old man, Mr Fitch?' asked Pearl.

'Spark out. Shock, know what I mean?'

'No wonder.'

The excitement, aided by the rum, was beginning to work on Bernie. 'I'd like to lay my hands on the bastard who let them out. Tigers! I'd give him bloody tigers, know what I mean? Give me five minutes alone with the bastard!'

'I heard—' began the girl called Rhoda.

'Didn't I tell you to shut your gap?' said Wayne.

'All right,' said Rhoda, 'if you don't want to know, I'm not going to tell you, am I?' She shaped her lips into a sullen pout.

'Tell us what?' said Wayne scornfully.

'I thought this was supposed to be a free country, you know? But if I'm not entitled to speak—'

'For Christ's sake!' said Rick. 'What are you mouthing on about?'

'Nothing. Nothing. Only I heard—I did hear—that it could be that bloke who lives up on the high moor. Any road, he was seen down at the nick this afternoon.'

There was a silence. She had won their attention now and was enjoying it.

'Who?' Wayne demanded.

'I don't know his name, do I!'

'I know him.' The voice came from the counter, and they turned towards it. Mrs Mac was standing by the urn pouring more coffee, her wispy grey hair damp with steam, sweat bubbling on her flushed unhealthy-looking cheeks. She wiped the sweat away with a grubby tea-towel and squinted across at the group gathered around Bernie.

'Took that old house. What's it called—Stowcroft. Took it about a year ago. Lives up there on his own. Queer sort of bloke, I mean, must be to take on that place.'

'How does he come into all this?' asked Rick belligerently.

'Listen, don't ask me! All I know is what I'm told. One of my regulars went up there once to do a job—plumbing. Said the bloke's got pictures of himself with tigers all over the place. He's a right bleeding mystery, if you ask me. Comes into town once in a blue moon, hardly says a word to a living soul. Nobody knows who he is, how he lives, what he does up there. Work it out for yourselves, I mean, work it out.'

'Yeh!' said Rick, 'yeh. You could be right.'

'You mean—they took him to the nick and then let him go?' said Pearl indignantly.

'That's what it looks like, don't it?' said Rhoda. There was a long thoughtful pause.

'You said queer. What did you mean—queer?' asked Wayne.

Mrs Mac cackled mirthlessly. 'Well, he ain't got a woman up there, has he!'

There was a little silence. Rick turned slowly towards Bernie. 'How about it, Bernie?' he asked quietly.

'What? How about what?'

'How about we go up there and ask this feller a few questions like?'

'Great,' said Pearl, 'great, great!'

'We won't get through,' Bernie said. 'The forest road has been blocked off.'

'So what!' said Wayne. 'We can go up the old road and come in from the Scarby end.' And as Bernie still hesitated, he added: 'For Christ's sake! A minute ago you were telling us what you'd do to the bloke if you could lay your hands on him!'

'But he might not be the one.'

'O.K. O.K. O.K. So we ask him a few little questions like, and if he gives us the right little answers—no problem. We kiss him goodnight and leave.'

'And if he don't—I mean—if he don't—?'

'We'll leave that up to you, know what I mean? You'll work something out. It's your show, Bernie.'

Pearl took Bernie's arm. 'Come on,' she said, 'I'll jockey up with you tonight.'

2

From the cover of the spur of forest, Ranee had a clear view of the curving, dusty road which led down to the village. She lay there and watched two men reach the summit of the hill only about two hundred yards away; her nostrils flared in anticipation, but to her disappointment the men stopped and turned back again. They were separated from her by the road and by a stretch of heathland; if she attacked, she would have to do so in the open, nearer to the great light at the bottom of the hill where she had seen the buildings and the other men, and caution held her back.

But she was growing more desperate, the hunger was grinding in her body like mill stones, and some time later, when two other men appeared, moving along the same route as the others, she began to edge forward, bracing herself for an assault. These men paused at the summit, and then they also began to return the way they had come, presenting their backs to the tigress. Poised for the swift dash across the intervening space, Ranee hesitated; her eyes had registered a movement near some bushes to one side of the road, and she sank down again, curious and watchful.

The men passed on, walking slowly towards the village, Ranee could hear the low buzz of their voices, and knew that soon they would be out of safe range, too near the other men and the fire. She lifted herself once more, and as she did so there was a further movement by the bushes and a moment later Maud Pickering scuttled across the road, over a patch of rough common, and disappeared into the forest.

The tigress turned and headed back through the jutting finger of woodland in which she had been sheltering, moving in a line which would keep her parallel to the running girl, not more than about two hundred and fifty yards apart; as she penetrated more deeply into the forest, where the undergrowth thickened she began to narrow the gap and increase her speed, until at last she saw the girl again, moving forward with determined steps.

Ranee padded behind, walking now, sliding noiselessly through the bracken and bush, gradually reducing the distance between them. Now that she had her quarry in sight, she was in no hurry to make the final rush into the kill, she felt a sensuous pleasure in the approach, the excitement of the hunt.

Then, quite suddenly the girl stopped by a huge old oak

tree. It was the only oak in this part of the forest, a survivor from the days when all this area was open land. The other trees, spruce, pine, and larch, had been planted around the oak, but at a respectful distance, so that the old tree seemed to stand apart, like a sage surrounded by disciples. Maud began to speak, the soft, musical sounds of her voice floating on the air, and Ranee flattened herself, watching, listening, puzzled by this development. In her days of captivity, she had learned that when one voice spoke in this way, a second usually answered, and prompted by a cunning which grew sharper with each hour of freedom, she pricked her ears and ranged the surrounding growth with wary eyes, searching out its hidden dangers, alert for any other human movement. She found a certain relief in the momentary pause, in the chance to rest her heavy, swollen belly in the soft, damp earth.

When her caution was fully satisfied, she began slowly to slide forward, baring her great white canine teeth for the kill. The girl had remained in the same spot, talking still, her face a tiny, white patch against the dark immensity of the tree.

A mere ten yards separated them now, but as the tigress pressed her huge forepaws into the ground and raised herself, she checked yet again, halted this time by a strange noise. It was brief and explosive, like the sound she had sometimes heard coming from beneath the travelling-cage, and it seemed to reverberate through the forest like a living thing. And just as this sound faded away it was replaced by another, a long-drawn-out piercing roar of agony. Both sounds came from a long way away, but Ranee recognised the roar, she knew it to be the voice of Mohan. With a low, involuntary growl of apprehension, she backed off, her skin bristling, her head turned in the direction from which his cry had come.

She waited for the forest to settle back into silence and as the tension relaxed, turned her eyes once more towards the tree. But the girl was not there, she had gone! Ranee heard the sharp, brittle crackle of twigs, the heavy rustling of leaves and looking up saw that Maud had climbed into the lower branches and was moving higher. Opening her jaws in a great, brassy roar of fury, the tigress charged forward, and leaped upwards, reaching for her prey. She tried this three times, her claws extended to secure a grip on the lowest of the branches, but it was too much for her and abandoning the attempt, she began to circle the tree, roaring out her frustration, her powerful tail cutting invisible swathes in the heavy, humid air. Then, as though she had thought the thing through, she tried another solution.

Rearing up on her hind legs, she put her full weight against the tree, and embraced the trunk with her front legs, digging her sharp claws into the bark. The branches creaked uneasily as she clawed her way up to a point where she could pull herself on to one of the branches, but the weight inside her made it difficult and exhausting, she felt the pain shuddering in her limbs like the sting of a whip. At last, gathering her strength, she managed to haul herself up. Panting from the exertion, tongue lapping over the side of her mouth, she stretched herself along the branch and looked up. The girl had scrambled into a higher position but she was still tantalisingly close. Ranee could hear the quick, frightened breathing, sense the fear. The scent of the soft flesh tormented her nostrils, driving her to a renewed effort. She bared her teeth in a snarl and eased forward, towards the bole of the tree and the support which would enable her to stand on the branch and use the whole length of her body to reach upwards, but as she did so, the terrified girl sprang to life again. She screamed, and in the same moment she threw the heavy school satchel. It caught the startled tigress on the forehead, and fell to the ground.

More in surprise than anything else, Ranee reared up, spitting and hissing, and for an instant, the razor-sharp talons hovered within reach of Maud's legs, but the tigress could not retain her foothold and fell back heavily across the branch on which she was standing. The tree sighed as though it had lost patience and the branch, quivering and cracking under the sudden shock, sagged downwards as though on a hinge, and finally broke off. It dropped with a thud on to the soft earth taking the tigress with it.

Maddened with rage, Ranee seized the fallen satchel and tore at it with tooth and claw, scattering the pieces around the base of the tree. This small act of vengeance seemed to ease her frustration a little for afterwards she settled down in a screen of bushes a few yards away.

She turned her head towards the girl, as if to warn her that she had not given up the chase. To Maud, crouched in the treetop, making as little of herself as possible, the eyes of the tigress seemed to glitter like two fixed, unwavering stars; but she was not afraid any longer. After all, the tree had saved her at the critical moment, as she knew it would, and it would save her again if necessary, of that she had no doubt.

3

The rifle shot which had checked Ranee was heard by the men on patrol at the village, as was the animal scream of agony which followed, but both sounds were so faint and far away that no-one could be certain of their meaning. However, when the roar of the tigress crashed through the night a minute or so later, and was repeated, they were in no doubt. This was a tiger and it was on the prowl not more than a half-mile away. They thought of the little girl, Maud, who could not be found, and shivered with apprehension. Women hurried sleepless children inside slamming doors and windows in the face of the heat, the men on patrol kept closer together and checked their shot-guns, the unarmed men dragged up more logs and piled them on the bonfire.

They had searched the village, the nearby fields, and covered the roads to Whitford and the village of Cawby (where her school-teacher lived) along their entire length in the hunt for Maud Pickering, but without success. Only one man had believed it possible that a girl of eleven would slip past the patrols and venture into the forest at night—her brother, Kevin; even though the search-parties returned one by one with their negative reports, the others still clung to the not unreasonable view that she was hiding somewhere safe, that a child of that age would be too frightened to move around the forest in darkness, especially if she knew about the tigers. And how could she fail to know, with all this noise and activity going on?

Kevin, a forester like his father, was a big, muscular young man of twenty, a genial, easy-going character with little imagination and less ambition. The one person that he really loved was his sister. He was fascinated by her fragile fawn-like quality, her impudence, her determination and by the strange, impossible, old-fashioned way she spoke of ordinary, everyday things like trees. He was constantly astounded by the twists and turns of her mind, he found it incredible to think that she was his sister, sprung from the same stock. In his fumbling way, dimly, he perceived that Maud was a special sort of creature, not to be judged in the same way as others. She was his beauty, his darling, his diamond, and from the beginning he had spoiled and protected her. For the past hour he had been hunting for her with increasing desperation, covering the outhouses and the sheltered places where she might be hiding, and as each search proved fruitless, he became more and more certain that she must have gone into the forest. When he checked once more with his mother and learned that Maud had not been told of the tigers, he knew it to be beyond doubt.

He stood for a moment, blinking his eyes, his brow set in deep furrows as he tried to grapple with the problem, then turned and hurried back to the bonfire. He seized an

194

unlit torch from the pile nearby, ignited it, and seconds later, a shout rose from one of the patrols as they saw the dark figure running across the broad strip of pasture towards the forest.

Gosford heard the shouts and looked up from his conversation with Peter Street in time to see the glimmering torch move into the first fringe of trees. His reaction was immediate. 'Lend me that!' he said, and without waiting he snatched up Street's rifle and set off at a run across the pasture before the words of protest were out of the other man's mouth.

Once inside the belt of forest, Kevin slowed down and began to move forward cautiously, holding the torch high in front of him and calling his sister's name. He heard the undergrowth crackling and rustling behind him, and as he swung round, Gosford came up. He grasped Kevin's arm in anger, his chest heaving as he pumped the air into his lungs and the sweat, gleaming in the torchlight, streamed down his face.

'What the hell do you think you're doing!' he said at last, gasping out the words.

'She's in here, sir,' said Kevin quietly. 'My sister's in here somewhere.'

'Use your head, man! Is it likely that a child of her age would wander into this place at night?' He made a gesture towards the forbidding darkness beyond the tiny circle of light.

'Maud would, sir. She's different. She's not afraid, you see. She's not afraid of the dark nor the trees—I can't tell you anything she is afraid of.'

'But she knew about the tigers, she knew it would be dangerous to—'

'No, sir, she didn't know, don't you see?' interrupted Kevin. 'Nobody told her.'

Gosford shook his head in despair, suddenly aware of his own immense fatigue. 'This place goes on for miles. You could search all night and not find her. And it is dangerous, you know that, don't you? We're not playing a game back there.' And he added, with deliberate brutality: 'It won't help your sister or anyone else if those bloody tigers make a meal of you, will it? Will it?'

'I know one or two of her special perches, sir, her hide-outs. I thought I'd look there first. You go back, sir, I'll be fine, just fine.' He gave Gosford a gentle, stubborn, smile and turned to go forward.

'All right.' There was nothing else Gosford could do. 'We'll take a look together. At these special perches as you call them. If she's not there, we go back—and organise a full-scale search at first light—right?'

'If you say so, sir.'

They moved on, with Kevin slightly ahead, holding the torch. With every step Gosford scoured the forest to each side, looking for the tell-tale glitter of those cold eyes, but as they stumbled on he managed to relax a little. Tigers, he thought, with grim, perverse humour, tigers! What the hell will it be next?

4

The roaring of the tigress came to David Birk as a faint but distinctive echo and he estimated that she was probably some two miles away, towards Lyndholme. This gave him the time he needed to cut across the forest at its narrowest point until he reached the road, where ten minutes of brisk walking brought him to the land-rover. Buster, the dog, was stretched out in the back and he gave David an unusually warm welcome. David let him out to scamper in the forest for a few minutes while he relaxed with a pipe. The dog came back at David's whistle, and within fifteen minutes, they arrived at the village.

A group of men were standing talking together in the light of the bonfire: among them he recognised Hale, the Deputy Chief Constable and Peter Street. A line of men and women were waiting just beyond the group, looking silently towards the forest. They reminded David of miners and their wives waiting by the pithead at the scene of a mine disaster.

Street saw Birk's arrival and hurried to meet him. 'Mr Birk. That shot we heard, was that you?'

'Yes.' David climbed down, stretching his shoulders. He nodded towards the line of men and women. 'What's going on there?'

'Two men have gone in after a little girl. Gosford and her brother.'

'Gosford? The policeman?'

'Yes.'

'How long have they been gone?'

'About twenty minutes or so.'

'Armed?'

'A shot-gun.'

'Against a tigress? You might as well pelt her with pop-corn!'

'Ah, Mr Birk, I'm very glad you decided to join us after all.' David turned and found Hale at his elbow with two other man. As David's face hardened, Hale raised a placatory hand: 'No. Really, I wasn't being sarcastic. I've been doing a little checking, you see. I'm told that you are quite a hunter, something of an expert, in fact. May I introduce Mr St John Ronder, the Chief Constable and Sir Walter Buckeridge?' He turned to the two men. 'Gentlemen, this is the Mr Birk I was telling you about.'

The Chief Constable extended a brief hand, grunted with equal brevity and turned away. He had wanted to stay back in Scarby and leave things to Hale, but his wife had persuaded him otherwise. It annoyed her that her husband relied so much on his Deputy, she disliked Hale's habit of appearing suddenly at all the big, newsworthy occasions to collect whatever publicity happened to be going. 'He's only keeping the press out now, so that he can pop up at the right moment with a couple of dead tigers and claim the credit,' she had argued. Reluctantly, for he was a lazy man fundamentally, quite content to let Hale beaver around and do all the work, the Chief Constable had abandoned the following day's golf-match and his precious sleep to take charge of Operation Tiger, as Hale had dubbed it. And it had all turned out to be a waste of time, as he'd known it would be. Hale had organised everything, he had put himself in effective command, and in consequence the Chief Constable was bored and resentful.

Buckeridge on the other hand was all bright eagerness. A small, plumpish, balding man, with a tanned mahogany skin and button-bright brown eyes, he glowed with energy and health. Grasping David's hand in a grip which was deliberately firm, from man to man as it were, he exclaimed: 'Pleasure! Great pleasure. Come to lend a hand, eh? That makes two of us.' He patted the short-barrelled shot-gun under his right arm, and smiled broadly, disarmingly, showing firm, white teeth. 'Bit of luck this tiger lark, in a sort of a way, eh? I mean, don't often get this sort of chance, do you? I've got a bit of a grouse-shoot over beyond Scarby. Brought a few of the chaps over with me— thought this would liven 'em up, give 'em a change of pace.' He patted the gun again. 'Don't suppose the old girl would actually stop a tiger—but she'd make it bloody hard for the beast to sit down!'

The sentences rattled out like rallies on a kettledrum. God preserve us, thought David, and wondered how the people in the forest were feeling about this 'bit of luck', this 'tiger lark'. Yet there was something appealing, a sort of naïvety, about the man. Put him in 19th-century costume, and he could have passed for one of his ancestors. The world rolled on, the face of England changed daily, but somehow, somewhere, the Buckeridges not only survived but managed to keep, more or less, to their old patterns. David murmured a polite reply and turned to Hale. 'Who sent those men in there?'

'I wasn't here, so I can't be sure,' said Hale.

'We've got to get them out—and the girl, if she's there.'

'You're the expert, of course,' said Hale evenly. 'But I would have thought it policy to wait till it's light. No point in putting more people at risk is there?' His tone was quiet and reasonable, but the eyes glinted like blue glass.

David turned abruptly on his heel and went to the landrover. Once again, Buster looked at him expectantly but David motioned him to stay. 'Wait, old boy,' he said. 'Your turn will come.' He took out the rifle and the flashlight, checked that the bullets were in the pocket of his bushjacket, and started towards the forest. Buckeridge hurried after him, and grasped his arm. 'Look, if you're going in after them, I'd like to come with you.'

'No,' said David, but he was touched by the gesture, and added, with as much tact as he could muster. 'They're short of experienced men here. The tigress might move this way—you'll be needed.' He didn't tell him that he had no wish to be shot accidentally by an enthusiastic amateur.

Disappointment showed on the shining, schoolboy face for a moment and then Buckeridge nodded in assent. 'Right. I get the idea. Right. Good luck, old man.'

At the perimeter of the forest David paused to load the Winchester, and as he did so, he heard the tigress speak again.

5

Ranee knew that the men were coming, heard one of them calling, long before she saw them. She backed into the undergrowth, seeking cover from which she could observe this new development yet still maintain her watch on the tree. There had been no movement from the girl, no sound, but the tigress could see her, curled tantalisingly in the upper branches, and she did not intend to be deprived of her kill.

Soon she made out a flicker of light moving towards her.

It was no more than a spark at first, there one moment and gone the next, like a will-o'-the-wisp, but gradually it assumed firmer, bigger shape and in the circle of yellow light she saw the two men. The man in front shouted again, a long, echoing call.

'Maud! Maud! Where are you? Maud!'

And suddenly there was a movement in the tree and the girl called back: 'Kevin! Kevin! I'm here! In the oak, in the oak!'

'Maud! We're coming—we're coming! Hold on!'

The men began to run, but she called again. 'Kevin! Watch out! Watch out! It's here—it's somewhere near here!' They stopped for a moment, then moved forward again in a slow, cautious walk. Ranee watched as they passed within ten yards of her cover, following them with her eyes until they reached the tree. She found the harsh light of the torch painful, she could not bring herself to look at it directly, but the ache of her hunger was worse. Inch by careful inch she raised herself from the ground, flexing her powerful muscles, and as the girl started to move down the tree, she braced herself, and sucking up all her fury and hatred, released it in an immense, blaring, terrifying roar. In the same moment she launched herself, swift as a bolt, into the attack.

Both men were on the alert, but neither was prepared for an assault so sudden and shattering, delivered with such ferocity and speed. A flash of fierce white teeth, the hot, pungent animal smell of the flashing body, and she was on them.

Ranee aimed herself at Kevin, coming at him from the side, but as she did so Gosford swung round and fired blindly at the springing animal. The shot ploughed along the thick fur, doing no more than furrow and burn the skin, yet the shock and the rocketing explosion were just sufficient to cause the tigress slightly to veer in her attack, so that she struck him at an angle. The heavy paws clawed at his head and chest; but she failed to lock her great canines as she had intended; man and beast crashed against the tree in a whirling mass of limb and paw. Snarling and spitting in fury, Ranee turned on the fallen Kevin to make her kill; he was barely conscious, the blood was already gushing out from a wound in his shoulder, but he still had hold of the torch and in desperation he thrust it into the looming face. She screamed and backed off, turning her head away from the naked flame.

Kevin pulled himself up and hurled the torch, but his strength was gone and it fell into the undergrowth only three or four yards away. Ranee retreated, but then held her ground, snarling in pain and anger.

Gosford took aim and fired again, but the only result was a dull click. Grasping the barrel, he swung the rifle at the tigress as she came forward once more. She took the heavy butt in the mouth, snapped her jaws like a steel trap, and wrenched it from his grasp. She shook the rifle in anger, as a cat would shake a mouse, and tossed it aside, but it gave Gosford the few seconds he needed to seize the torch and back up against the tree. The tigress moved in closer, but she was wary of that searing flame, and could only bring herself to make small, tentative darts at the man; after a while she abandoned this painful tactic, and took up a station out of range of the torch, where she paced up and down, back and forth, as she had once paced her cage. It was as if she knew that the flame was burning lower and beginning to flicker, that she had only to wait.

David Birk saw the tigress indistinctly in the fading light of the torch and he fired three times in rapid succession, more to scare her than with any hope of scoring a hit. Ranee gave a startled look in the direction from which the sounds had come, hesitated as though contemplating a new attack, and then, as David fired again and the bullet sang past her ear, she turned and bounded away. Gosford waited, listening, as the crashing in the brittle undergrowth grew fainter and finally faded, then he closed his eyes and dropped his head back against the tree. David

201

reached him two minutes later and he was still in the same position, the torch in his hand no more than a red, smouldering glow.

As Gosford opened his eyes, a small voice spoke from above.

'I think it's gone now. Can I come down?'

CHAPTER ELEVEN

1

As though to underline the sense of release, a light wind began to blow in from the east, piercing the screen of humidity and bringing a blessed freshness to the night. It fanned the faces of the three men and of the girl, it blew into the forest, rustling the tree-tops, gently stirring the bushes.

Near Maud's friend, the ancient oak, it found a patch of undergrowth which bore a warm, brown scar, no bigger than a handkerchief, made by the fallen torch. As David carried the unconscious and badly-wounded Kevin out of the forest, followed by Gosford and the little girl, the wind caressed the burned patch until it glowed bright red; a tiny flame flickered and faded and flickered again, then gathering strength it stood upright like a yellow and crimson crocus.

2

Ranee stopped to rest about a half-mile from the oak, and when she had recovered her strength, she began to circle back towards the same spot. She could not forget the scent of the girl, the promise of that white flesh and this time she was determined not to be robbed of her prey. She was troubled by thirst now, in addition to increasing hunger, and she knew also that time was short, the first, hesitant hints of daylight were beginning to filter through the canopy of trees; but as she drew nearer, she saw the gleam of fire near the oak, and remembering the painful thrust of the torch, she uttered a low, moaning growl of complaint and crouched down. As she watched, the flame seemed to lift and grow, and to be joined by others, until there were a dozen, leaping tongues of fire, spreading outwards, crackling as though in pleasure. In the few moments that she lay there the flames seemed to gather strength and height and to move towards her at an incredible speed. This was an enemy she could not overcome, and as the fear pricked her skin, she turned again and set off at a loping run, not pausing until she left the trees behind and emerged on to the moor, near the hollow where she had rested with Mohan the previous afternoon.

She quenched her thirst and cooled herself in the beck but this only seemed to put a sharper edge to her ravenous hunger, and she set off again, moving away from the forest, climbing upwards towards the dark escarpments that marked the high moor. It was not only the need for food that drove her on; other pains were stirring in her body and she knew that she was near her time. Instinctively she was seeking a safe and secret place where she could bear her cubs and protect them from the dangers of this place, from the searing flames, from the humans, from those cold, iron boxes in which they caged her kind.

She covered three miles, growing more desperate as time passed, for the light was edging in across the horizon and despite the cover of the heather and bracken, she felt more and more vulnerable. At length she reached a rocky outcrop, a massive flat-topped slab of granite known locally as Caesar's Table, which lay beside a rough, overgrown track and was surrounded by heaped stones. Ranee clambered to the top of these boulders and bracing herself, sprang on to the table of granite. It had a slightly hollow formation, and she found that by pressing herself flat, she was hidden from view by the sloping sides. She settled herself into the hollow, giving herself up momentarily to the sagging weariness which seemed to be taking possession of her body.

She lay there for some time, half-asleep, soaking up the firm coolness of the stone, the wind lightly rippling through her fur, and then suddenly, her quick ear caught a low, harsh, rhythmic sound, a humming noise which grew slowly more distinct. She rose on her perch and in the distance, coming towards her she saw a series of tiny black figures, like a file of shadowy, stiff-limbed animals.

She was, in fact, looking down upon Bernie and his friends, now on their way back to Whitford after spending two fruitless hours camped outside David Birk's house. They had eased their frustration by leaving a calling-card, a small memento of their visit, in the shape of a broken dry-stone wall, shattered windows, lawns and flower-beds cut up by the churning wheels of motor-cycles. They were tired, but more or less happy.

Progress was slow because of the nature of the track and they rode in single file at low speed, with Wayne leading, and Bernie bringing up the rear. Pearl had somehow lost interest in him. During the course of the night she had taken him out on the moor to console him for the absence of Libby, but she had found him clumsy and uninspiring and abandoned him in favour of Rick.

Ranee, crouched on her vantage point, watched with unwavering eyes as the procession came nearer; she could now hear the occasional shout and distinguish the indi-vidual humans astride the moving machines. The hunger beat at her flanks with renewed desperation, the saliva rose in her mouth and dripped from her half-open jaws.

The track rose sharply towards the granite outcrop, and then swung sharply round Caesar's Table, before it de-scended with equal sharpness to the level of the moor, and when the riders reached this point they were forced to tread ground as they urged the heavy machines up the steep rise and around the bend.

No-one was aware of Ranee waiting on the rock above. Pearl, a bright, red scarf trailing behind her, shouted something to Rick, with whom she was riding pillion, and laughed. The laugh was drowned in a great roar of fury and challenge as the tigress stood for a moment, poised like a silhouette against the light eastern sky, and then launched herself towards the red scarf. The boy and the girl were sent crashing from the machine, and as they rolled over, the tigress straddled them, spitting and snarling, striking out with her huge forepaws, baring her teeth for the kill.

The machines behind crashed into each other, toppling their riders; they picked themselves up, screaming in naked terror, and fled back down the rise, to dive for the cover of the moor. Those in front accelerated away as best they could, and they too, made for the shelter of the heather and bracken. The tigress made no attempt to follow them. Tail swishing, roaring her defiance, she stood amidst the chaos of spinning wheels and spluttering engines, guarding her prey; she did not even move towards Rhoda, who lay not more than ten yards away, alternately screaming with the pain of a broken leg and calling for help.

It was Wayne who found the courage to leave his cover and move back to help the injured girl. With small, cautious steps, his terrified eyes never leaving the tigress, he edged towards Rhoda. The tigress growled as he drew nearer, but she still made no move; straddling the dead body of one victim, and with one forepaw pinning down the other, she seemed to be challenging him to try and rob her of the kill. Eventually he reached the sobbing, hysterical Rhoda, helped her upright, and carried her back the way he had come, expecting any moment to hear the animal close in on him.

After this they lay on the moor for a long time, too shocked and frightened to move. One boy, ashen-faced and wild-eyed, gibbered ceaselessly to himself, as though he had lost his reason. Another opened his lips to whisper to his companion and found that no speech would come, no sound.

A half-hour passed before Wayne gathered the strength to show himself again. When he did so, he saw that the tigress had gone. Rick's body had been dragged into the shadow of the rock, but of Pearl there was no sign.

3

The reports from the watch-towers were ominous. The wind had stiffened and the fire was spreading out from the centre of the forest at frightening speed. The flames had already leaped the road and were now at work on the second lung of the forest; the patient planting and nurturing of fifty years was going down before their relentless advance. The deer and some smaller animals were already fleeing before the blaze, seeking safety on the moors to the north, but these areas, baked dry by the long heat-wave, provided a doubtful refuge. If the fire could not be contained, mile upon mile of heathland and moor would burn, even the more fertile dales could not be ruled out of the reckoning.

Every possible man and appliance was called up for action; volunteers, many of them holiday-makers came in from Whitford, Scarby and nearby villages. Armed men were attached to each squad, for it was thought that the tigress was still in the forest and that she might come bursting out of the trees at any moment, but for most of the men she now represented the lesser danger, their minds were concentrated on this more familiar but more destructive enemy.

Within two hours the fire had broken through to the moor. Three men had lost their lives, six others were severely injured. Army reinforcements were called up from the base at Osterwicke, twenty miles away, all heavy moving equipment in the district was requisitioned to build new fire breaks. The thick, black smoke could be seen from Scarby and other towns along the coast.

And then, as though satisfied that the fire had taken a firm grip of the northern moors, the wind veered, and began to drive the flames south, towards the lower moors above Whitford. In the southern lung of the forest the destruction was almost complete. The fire checked for a while when it reached the marshy ground where Mohan was lying; it circled the area warily, spitting and hissing its frustration but slowly the flames pressed inwards, closing the circle. In the bright, flickering light the tiger's orange and black coat gleamed like satin.

4

In many ways, Hale was at his best at a time like this. The crisis called for a military-style operation with military-style discipline and a firm, central command, and he responded to the need. All his resentments seemed to be forgotten as bright-eyed, alert, he disposed his forces, issuing direct, clear orders, countering each bizarre twist in the situation with decisive action. It was as though he had been saving his quality for just such a moment.

He toured the key points in a utility truck, driving on his tired men, but in such a way that they reacted with renewed effort, for they felt a subtle change in his attitude. They sensed that for once he was identifying with them as human beings, not just as names and numbers on a duty roster, and their instinct was right. He was truly proud of their response, of their courage, of their manliness, even of their sweat, and it showed in the way he handled them.

Watching him, Gosford thought he had never seen the man so happy. Yet happy, he decided, correcting himself, was not the word. It was something more, a kind of exaltation. And Gosford was reminded yet again, and sadly, of the officer he had known in Korea; a man like Hale, bitter, cynical, resentful, who seemed to assume the proportions of a full human being only in the tensions of battle. Strange how some men seemed to need war, the scent of fire in their nostrils...

Hale's attitude to Gosford reflected this change. He assigned Gosford to a sort of roving commission, instructing him to visit the key points and to take whatever emergency measures were necessary on the spot and on his own initiative. For a while Gosford thought that this was Hale's indirect, stiff-necked way of wiping clean the slate. He soon learned otherwise.

A small Command Centre had been set up in the village hall at Lyndholme and during a short lull in the frenzy of activity, Wayne was brought in. As he entered, waxen-faced and shaking, Gosford saw the shadow in Hale's eyes, felt him stiffen with the old coldness. He stood beside Gosford at the table tapping a hand against his thigh, as in a voice a little above a whisper, the boy described the encounter with the tigress at Caesar's Table.

'Speak up, lad, speak up!' he said sharply as Wayne, overwhelmed by the thought of what he had seen, lapsed into a mumble.

Gosford could see that there was little point in prolonging the interview; the boy was in a state of severe shock, and, in any event, there was little they could do now. 'All right, Wayne,' he said. 'We'll send somebody up there. Have you seen a doctor?' Wayne shook his head. 'Then that's what you'd better do next. Get back to Whitford and ask your doctor for something to help you sleep. We'll be in touch.'

'Wait!' said Hale, as Wayne rose to go. 'What were you doing up on the high moor at that hour in the morning?'

'It was a hot night, sir. We went out for a bit of a scramble like.'

'Hell's Angels, are you?'

'No, sir. Just a sort of club—you know.'

'No, I don't know. What's that supposed to represent?' He tapped Wayne's chest with his index finger, indicating an emblem on the black leather jacket. The boy looked down awkwardly as though he had forgotten what he was wearing.

'Oh. It's nothing, like. Supposed to be a panther's head.'

'Is that what you call yourselves—panthers?'

'No. Nothing like that, sir. It was on the jacket when I bought it.'

'Hmph.' Hale smiled grimly, and with a viciousness which shocked even Gosford he added: 'Better change it now, hadn't you? Wrong animal.' And as the door closed behind Wayne he chuckled softly, cynically.

Gosford tried to keep his voice steady. 'What are we going to do, sir?'

'About what?'

'The other tiger. If it's broken out of the forest and got as far as Caesar's Table—' He left the rest unsaid.

'Where's this fellow Birk?'

'Working with one of the fire-fighting teams.'

'Pull him out. He's wasted there. He'll be better employed getting after this tiger. He's bagged one—he might as well make it a pair while he's at it.' He made it sound like a pigeon-shoot and Gosford, remembering those long, forever moments in the forest when he had looked into the face of the tigress, closed his eyes and shuddered inwardly.

Hale seemed not to notice or if he did, he ignored it. 'Yes. Find Birk, ask him to go up to this Caesar's Table and see if he can pick up any sort of trail. You might go with him, as a matter of fact. I've got reinforcements coming in from three neighbouring counties, we'll be able to manage here. You can pull out two of our trained riflemen and take them with you. And if you should need an extra gun, I'm sure Wally Buckeridge will be happy to join in.'

He turned to leave, but at the door he paused. Gosford saw that strange shadow flicker across his eyes again, and suddenly knew what was coming.

'Incidentally, Chief-Inspector,' said Hale, 'I wouldn't want you to run away with the notion that what happened yesterday is dead and buried. My hands are rather full at the moment and I need all the men I can muster. But I haven't forgotten that you wilfully went against my orders. It's a matter of record, and in due course I shall come back to it.'

'As you say, sir,' Gosford said wearily.

Hale looked at him quickly as though he had caught a note of insolence in the tone, then he nodded curtly and went out.

5

It was something like war-time. On their way up to Caesar's Table, David Birk and Gosford passed columns of soldiers and civilians falling back before the fire as from an enemy. Huge earth-moving machines were trundling into position, and the line of a second fire-break was being drawn across the moor. In the near distance, the sky was heavy with drifting black smoke and below this the golden gleam of the flames as they danced with delicate menace across the moor. At the turn-off, where the track wound upwards to the high moor, they met a convoy of three families coming away from their threatened homes; children sitting on carts stacked high with household possessions, plodding horses and cattle, the men and women walking in silence, with the heavy, sad-eyed look of refugees. Further up the track they met an old man with his dog, driving a flock of Swaledale sheep down to what he hoped would be safer pastures.

He paused to ask the progress of the fire and when Gosford told him, he shook his head. 'It had to come,' he said, 'had to.'

'How's that?' asked Gosford.

'They keep trying to take the moor. I seen it over and over. But it won't be took.'

'Who?'

'Who? Them! Them!' He waved a thick, brown hand as if the statement needed no further expansion. 'The moor won't be took. She bides her time and then she turns. I seen it over and over.' He moved on, muttering to himself, shaking his head.

Wayne and his friends had taken Rick's body into Lyndholme but his motor-cycle was still lying on its side in the shadow of the rock. Clinging to it, fluttering like a torn flag in the breeze, was a length of bright red scarf. Along the track patches of oil gleamed like small rainbows, and near the fallen motor-cycle there was the darker glow of a pool of blood from which an irregular line of spots dribbled away into the dust to disappear into the heather. There were signs of a body having been half-dragged, half-carried along this same line, and the clear impressions of the animal's paws.

Gosford looked round at the bleak scene, the motor-cycle with its pathetic red pennant, the pool of blood, and shook his head. 'The Great Davino! I hope there is a life after death, I hope I meet up with him sometime! Jesus! Oh, Jesus!'

'I'll tell you something,' said David. 'I know how he felt.'

'That's a great consolation. It helps a lot,' said Gosford bitterly.

'But I do know,' said David. 'He had to bust out. He wasn't releasing the tigers, he was releasing himself. Haven't you ever felt that way?'

'Not lately.'

'No? What about the Deputy Chief Constable?'

Gosford looked at him in astonishment. 'Hale? What about him?'

'I saw him crack the whip—I saw you all jump. Don't you ever feel like busting out of the cage?'

'He's a good officer,' said Gosford weakly.

'Balls! I've seen a dozen like him. Paranoia—he reeks of it. He's a bloody sight more dangerous than a dozen tigers!' Gosford remained silent, and after a pause, David continued: 'Still, what does it matter? We're all half-crazy.

Do you know what I'd do if I had my way? I'd blow up all the cages in the world except one.'

'I'll buy it,' Gosford said. 'What would you do with the one left over?'

'Put a couple of men in it, put them on show, teach them to jump through hoops—and see how they liked it!' He went back to the land-rover and released the dog. 'Come on, Buster,' he said, 'let's see what we can find.'

The dog ran along the track, sniffed at the trail of blood two or three times, and plunged into the heather. David checked his rifle, loaded it, and slipped up the safety-catch. He noticed that Gosford was watching him closely. 'Anything wrong?' he asked.

'No,' said Gosford, 'no. I was just thinking—I know nothing about you—next to nothing.'

'What do you need to know?'

'Nothing. None of my business—'

'But?'

'I'd guess—it would only be a guess—that you're some sort of policeman. Or you were. Not the ordinary, common or garden kind like me—something special.'

'Who says you're ordinary?'

'I do,' said Gosford. 'Seriously. That's not bullshit. I really do know my limitations. I'm no wonder-boy. I've got about as high as I will ever get in the force. I'm married, I like Frank Sinatra, bacon and eggs, watching television, arguing about football. I worry about the future, I don't trust politicians, I'm going bald. Oh, I'm ordinary, believe me.'

'Keep it that way,' said David. 'There are worse things.'

'We were talking about you. You're dodging the question.'

'I'm not ordinary, I'll admit that. In my trade, there's no such word. You're either useful—or useless.'

'And you're useful?'

'Let me put it this way, Mr Ordinary,' said David. 'The firm I work for used to be big, important. It isn't any more, but we refuse to believe it. We carry on as if we still owned half the world—an old pussy-cat pretending to be a lion. That's why they keep me on—why they want me to go back. So that we can go on pretending we're as big as the other fellow. What you do in a day is worth more than anything I do in a year.'

'If you feel that way—'

'Why don't I bust out of the cage? A good question. I came up here to think about it—and I still can't decide. I'm a bit of an anachronism too, you see, part of the post-Imperial hangover. Like that tigress—a member of a doomed species, I'm not really equipped for life in the last half of the twentieth century. And frankly, the more I see of it, the less I feel inclined to care.'

6

The dog began a furious barking about 200 yards away, to the north of the track.

'He's found something,' said David. 'The tigress could be around here somewhere, lying up for the day. She won't go too far away—she'll want to come back towards sunset in the hope of finding the other body.'

'Not unless they can check that fire!' said Gosford, looking towards the pillars of smoke in the distance. 'They'll have to get their fingers out. It's moving too bloody fast for my liking.'

'You wait in the land-rover. Keep your eyes skinned. I'll go and see what the dog has turned up,' said David.

'No,' said Gosford, 'I'm coming with you.'

'I told you back there when you offered me those police marksmen that I always work alone.'

'Actually,' said Gosford, 'it's not the tigress. It's you. I'm beginning to like your company.'

David laughed and tapped the short-barrelled shot-gun that Gosford was holding. 'All right. But be careful with that blasted pop-gun. A lot of good hunters have been lost that way.'

He took his pack from the land-rover and led the way towards Buster who was still sending up agitated signals. The trail was easy to follow, for the growth had been crushed into a path a foot or more wide, but David moved along it cautiously, his eyes scanning the ground on either side, and he paused at intervals, slightly lifting his head, as though he had caught a scent or heard a tell-tale sound. The dog had relapsed into a low plaintive whine and they found him crouched on the edge of a small hollow where the heather and bracken gave way to a covering of Mat-grass.

Scraps of clothing were scattered in the hollow, and the flattened grass was sticky with blood. Gosford caught the glint of metal half-hidden in the grass and stooping down, picked up a thin, silver necklet from which hung a flat pendant in the shape of the letter P. Nearby he found a cheap wristwatch, the hands still moving. And these two articles, together with some bone, intestine, and torn pieces of flesh, were all that remained of a girl, a silly rather feckless but good-natured seventeen-year-old human being named Pearl Longman. Gosford slipped the necklet and the watch into his pocket and turned away: his stomach was past complaint, he was beyond shock.

'Still! Keep still!' hissed David suddenly, and gripped Gosford's arm.

As he spoke, the dog stiffened suddenly, pressed his head to the ground, and fell silent, watching his master. The bracken around the hollow quivered and parted, and slowly the face of the tigress appeared, so near that Gosford could see the irregular white patches above the clear, saffron-coloured eyes, the broken black stripes overlaying the white cheeks, the great sabre-like canines.

Neither man nor tigress moved. Rigid as marble, they faced each other; even the moor around them seemed to fall silent. Gosford could feel David's grip tightening on his arm, the strong fingers pressing painfully into the flesh.

A minute passed, taking more than its due time, and then with a sort of contemptuous, sinuous grace, the tigress rose to her full height, gave them a final, chilling stare, then turned in one flashing, graceful movement and bounded away.

It took David a single stride to reach the rim of the hollow. He caught one brief glimpse of the tigress as she paused and looked back, and he fired twice. She bounded on, and a moment later, was lost in the cover of the moor.

Gosford came and stood beside him. 'Why didn't she attack, for God's sake? We would have no chance, no chance at all!'

'I don't know!' said David, and the bitterness in his tone surprised the other man. 'Tigers aren't civilised like us. They rarely kill just for the hell of it. They like to have a good reason!' He took a deep breath and continued more reasonably: 'I don't know. Nobody can predict what a tiger will do. The jungle is full of the bones of men who thought otherwise!' He paused again. 'I'm sorry. My damned fault. Led you into it. Should have known better. If I'd been alone it wouldn't have happened.' He glanced at Gosford and added quickly: 'No. I didn't mean that. It could have happened anyway. As I said, with a tiger you never can tell.'

'Did you hit her?'

'No. I missed. Caught just a flash, and then she was gone. In a way, I'm not sorry.'

'What are you talking about?' Gosford stared at him in amazement.

'She's with cub. And very near her time.'

'What the hell difference does that make!' asked Gosford angrily. 'For Christ's sake, man, you saw what she did back there to that girl! She's a man-eater, a killer! She has to be stopped!'

'All right,' said David, 'she's a man-eater. That's more our fault than hers, but never mind. All right—she has to be stopped. But listen—she's eight, maybe nine years old.

She's already spent half her allotted span of life in jail, in a kind of jail—for nothing, for no crime at all. She's known one day of freedom in her entire life, one free, natural day, that's all.'

'What do you want me to do—weep?'

'No. Though perhaps you should—we all should. No. But don't you reckon we owe her something?'

'Like what?'

'Like just a little more time?'

7

Ranee dragged herself to the top of the rise and looked down. In the distance, pillars of smoke dominated the sky, like a line of dark, cantering horses, but she was more concerned with the farm buildings which lay just below. She watched for as long as she dared, for she knew there was little time, and then began to move cautiously down towards the little farm. There was no sign of any humans; the only movement came from the doves fluttering around the roof, and from the chickens clucking and pecking in the rough grass at the rear.

She reached the yard and paused, the pain rippling urgently in her belly. The door of a tall outbuilding was half-open, the shadowed interior looked cool and inviting. She padded across and went inside, relieved to be out of the sun, but still uncertain. All her instincts warned her that she must find a place where her cubs could be secure, where she could defend and protect them. She noticed a long platform above the door stacked with bales of hay and with a ladder leading up to it. The sweet scent of the hay, the silence, pleased her, she felt that up there, above the ground she would be safe.

Laboriously she hauled herself up the ladder, rung by rung until she reached the loft. Shafts of sunlight were spilling in through an open hatch which overlooked the yard. She looked out for a moment, and then, throbbing with exhaustion, she went into the far corner, in the shadows, behind the bales of hay, and lay down.

She knew the signs, she knew what to do. This would be the third litter she had borne, and despite her tiredness and the sharpening pains, she felt a sense of well-being, an anticipation. She remembered the soft warmth of the other cubs, the feel of her tongue on their coats, their excited pressure against her body as they sucked her milk. She stretched herself at full length, her eyes half-closed, pressing down as pain built to a crescendo and the movement in her stomach began . . .

An hour later, weak and exhausted, she began to lick herself clean, and when this was done, she turned her attention to the three tiny balls of damp fur which lay squirming against the curve of her stomach. She picked them up in her mouth, one by one, and set them down before her. Two males and one female. She examined them carefully, probing their bodies with her tongue, touching them with a gentle, tentative paw, filled with an immense, fierce pride; then, like a stern mother she washed them with her tongue, ignoring their feeble protests. After a while, they curled up against her and settled down to sleep. Satisfied that they were safe, content to feel the gentle rhythm of their breathing, she closed her eyes and allowed herself to rest at last.

Sometime later, in her sleep, she heard footfalls in the yard outside, and as she lifted her head and opened her eyes, the loud barking of a dog. She was on her feet instantly. She scuffled some hay around the cubs and moved cautiously to the hatch. Gosford and Birk were standing in the yard, and as the tigress appeared Gosford looked up and shouted a warning. In the same moment, Ranee, furious at their intrusion, desperate for the safety of her cubs, launched herself at him.

Gosford had no time to react. There was a moment of darkness as the huge body loomed above, and then she was on him. They crashed to the ground together, and she pinned him there, tearing at his flesh with tooth and claw. The dog ran in, snapping and snarling but she flung him aside with one, swift contemptuous flick of her forepaw.

As she turned to face the other man, the yard exploded with sound and she screamed in agony as the bullet crunched through the bone between the eyes. She fell back against Gosford, and then, incredibly, staggered to her feet and faced David again. Tensing her body, dredging up all her strength, she gave vent to a last blaring roar, half challege, half despair. She had nothing else to give. The sound echoed and faded, the clear eyes seemed to mist over and she fell back once more and lay still.

David found a tarpaulin sheet and covered Gosford's body, pulling it gently over the mutilated face, in which only the eyes seemed to be untouched. The dog limped up to him whimpering, a deep gash on his right side, and David dressed the wound as best he could.

Later, as he came back into the yard with the cubs inside his shirt, a utility truck drove into the yard and braked sharply. The young policeman at the wheel jumped out and shouted at David: 'What are you doing here? This place is supposed to have been evacuated—lucky for you I decided to check! The fire is only—' He stopped suddenly and his jaw dropped as he saw the body of the tigress. 'Christ,' he murmured, 'Christ!' And pointing to the tarpaulin, 'What's that?'

David lifted the edge of the tarpaulin, and the policeman looked away quickly. 'Who is it?' he whispered.

'A man named Gosford,' said David, and it was as though he was speaking to himself. 'Married, liked Frank Sinatra, television and football. Worried about the future, didn't like politicians. Just an ordinary man.'

The young man gave him a puzzled look, and said gently: 'We'd better put him aboard and get out of here. There isn't much time.'

'There never is,' said David.

The fire raged for three more days before it was checked. It devastated a million acres of forest and moor; at its height, more than three thousand men—soldiers, policemen, firemen, civilian volunteers—were engaged in the fire-fighting. Two special planes, each capable of dropping one thousand gallons of water at a time, were loaned by the French government; in addition, ten helicopters were used to drop water bombs, backed up by three hundred fire-fighting appliances and batteries of foam-spraying cannon. Over one thousand people were evacuated from villages and isolated homesteads, the loss of animal and bird life was enormous.

Ignoring the Official Secrets Act, the flames invaded a secret Government Research Station, set in an isolated fold of the high moor, and an emergency evacuation was organised in some haste. Trucks loaded with papers, equipment and hundreds of black cylinders, all of them under heavy military guard, rumbled away to the West, towards a destination known only to the army colonel in command and the Director of the Station. One hour after the departure of the convoy, the fire reached the main laboratories and offices and gutted them completely. The front-line fire-fighters, building new breaks about a quarter of a mile distant were disturbed to hear strange screams and cries coming from the compound, but there was nothing they could do. Later, when the fire was quelled, it was rumoured that the charred remains of dozens of animals, large and small, had been found among burned-out cages in the ruined buildings.

At the end of the three days, the main fires were under control, but on some areas of the moor, the fire had caught to a depth of two or three feet and was expected to burn for months.

The final death toll was eleven—five firemen, four

policemen, one soldier and one forester, and more than one hundred people were injured. The Chief Constable was awarded a knighthood in recognition of his leadership, and his deputy was made a Commander of the British Empire. Chief-Inspector Gosford was posthumously awarded the George Cross.

When the police were free at last to concentrate on their normal duties, their investigations into some other matters provided James Topping, who had left the *Whitford Gazette* to work as a free-lance correspondent, with much useful and interesting copy. A schoolmaster, his wife and a local business man were charged with conspiring to procure children to commit acts of gross indecency and with themselves committing acts of gross indecency.

The Fraud Squad, following up notes found in Gosford's desk uncovered a local government scandal which concerned some leading citizens of Whitford, including the late Tom Pickford, but which soon turned out to be of national proportions, involving a prominent London architect and a payroll which included two M.P.s and several County Councillors.

And, like ripples on the surface of a pond which continue to show and expand after the stone which caused them has sunk to the bottom, there were other developments which were to affect the private and professional lives of many people in Whitford and the surrounding country for many months, even years, ahead.

The tigers and the great fire became a staple item of Whitford conversation; but there were some among the older men who spoke only of these things among themselves, and then in guarded tones. To them, the moor and the forests were filled with unknown and unknowable mysteries, with roots which went back to other times and other gods. The stone shrines, the weird rock formations, the long burial mounds of the ancient dead, were more than relics, they were both a presence and a promise. They wondered, in their hearts, if the old gods had returned in the bodies of the tigers to claim the land again. After all, hadn't they appeared from nowhere, conjured up out of that extraordinary summer's scorching heat and wasn't it possible that they had transformed themselves into fire? It wasn't difficult, remembering those soaring flames, to see in them the form and outline of tigers, thousands upon thousands of them, leaping and roaring, scorching the earth with their fierce, hot breath.

And then again, wasn't it true that the strange silent man who lived alone on the high moor, had left the district immediately after the fire, taking with him, so it was said, three tiger cubs?